BLEEDING BLUE

A BOSTON CRIME THRILLER

BRIAN SHEA

Severn River
PUBLISHING

Severn River Publishing
www.SevernRiverPublishing.com

This is a work of fiction. Names, characters, businesses, places, events and incidents are either the products of the author's imagination or used in a fictitious manner. Any resemblance to actual persons, living or dead, or actual events is purely coincidental.

ISBN: 978-1-951249-74-8 (Paperback)
ISBN: 978-1-951249-76-2 (Hardback)

ALSO BY BRIAN SHEA

The Nick Lawrence Series

Kill List

Pursuit of Justice

Burning Truth

Targeted Violence

Murder 8

The Boston Crime Thriller Series

Murder Board

Bleeding Blue

The Penitent One

Never miss a new release! Sign up to receive exclusive updates from author Brian Shea.

BrianChristopherShea.com/Boston

Sign up and receive a free copy of
Unkillable: A Nick Lawrence Short Story

Mom, this one's for you.
When you read it, you'll know why.
Thank you for choosing me to be your son. And thank you for the endless love and support.

1

For some, hardships are but bumps in the road. And for others, struggle comes with such frequency, a person knows nothing else. Muriel Burke would be categorized as the latter.

She worked two jobs for the better part of her life. Her family had immigrated to the United States sixty-two years ago, while her mother was pregnant with her, so she would be born a citizen. Her parents sought to give her a better life. To gift her with the American dream. What she'd learned over a lifetime of toil is that dream, while grand in theory, did not always prove fruitful. Her mother died due to complications in childbirth, and though Muriel's father did his best not to blame her for the tragedy, his battle with resentment was a daily one. More times than not, it won over his resolve.

Fortune never found the Burke family. Her father worked seven days a week on the Boston harbor docks, and Muriel found herself dropping out of school by age twelve to help earn money. Over the past fifty years, she'd held practically every job imaginable for an uneducated girl who grew up in the Upham's Corner section of Dorchester. She currently divided her time between Kang's Laundromat, where she folded clothes eight hours per day starting at five a.m., and Tyson's Market.

Muriel ate her lunch every day on a bench outside the Dorchester North Burying Ground, a historical city landmark built in 1634. The boneyard was home to many interred historical figures, but most interesting to Muriel was William Stoughton, the presiding judge over the Salem Witch Trials. When she'd been young, it was one of the few stories her father had told her. She had a pleasant memory of sipping tea and listening to her father, a man of few words, recount the tale of that most preposterous of trials. She never quite understood his fascination with it but reveled in the fact he'd been willing to share anything with her.

Muriel didn't have the money to afford a proper funeral and burial service when her father died twenty-seven years ago. She received state aid to have him cremated, and now the ashes sat in a cheap urn on the mantel in her small apartment next to a weathered photo of them standing next to an unremarkable apple tree on an unremarkable day. She never married. Never moved forward. Her only real connection to the world was found in the memory of her dead father. She always envisioned earning enough money so that he could be buried in a proper grave, one that she could visit and place fresh flowers at the foot of the headstone. In lieu of that, Muriel pretended her father was buried within the historic grounds of the cemetery she passed every day. Many years ago, she had taken a bit of his ashes with her during her afternoon commute and scattered the dusty remains through the black wrought iron bars near the large oak on Columbia Road. So, in truth, his remains were now buried among the dead lying within the graveyard's boundaries.

She spent every lunch eating a ham and cheese sandwich on white bread dressed in a thin coat of mayo, allowing herself thirty minutes to sit and eat. Muriel would nestle her narrow frame onto the concrete lip near the gated entrance, her favorite spot that caught the shade of an overhanging tree and brought the welcome refresher of the cool concrete. As awkward as her makeshift bench was, it served to give her legs a much-needed break. Afterward, she would commute to her second job at Tyson's Market, a small corner store located off Everett Avenue. She stocked, organized, and cleaned the store. Eight hours' pay at half the current minimum wage. Muriel never complained.

Muriel Burke was closing in on her last hour of work. The store closed at nine, but she stayed until ten to straighten up. She'd recently replaced the insoles in her shoes with one of those fancy gel types, but her sixty-two-year-old legs and back still ached. The pain served as a reminder that her nearly sixteen hours of standing were coming to an end. She looked at the clock above the cooler she was restocking. Its red digital light flickered 8:56 p.m. Four minutes and the store would be locked to the outside world.

Muriel rarely communicated with people and avoided human contact at all possible cost. A speech impediment that had gone uncorrected caused her great anxiety when talking with others, which had developed into a full-fledged phobia after her father's passing. She kept to herself, long since giving up delusions she would find a boyfriend, or even a friend. She hadn't said one word to the young man working the register tonight. He was new, only started a few weeks ago. She only knew his name because of his nametag. Tucker. She hadn't yet formed an opinion of him.

Muriel tore at the plastic covering shrink-wrapped over the case of Monster Energy drinks, peeling it back and exposing the tops of the tall cans. She opened the fridge door and began loading the cans into their place. The cold air seeped out into the humidity of the store, creating a misty plume that coated her skin. She was grateful for the refreshing blast beating back the summer's heat and drying some of the sweat pooled around her neck.

She shut the door. The magnetized rubber stripping sealed the cold air back inside, leaving Muriel in the humidity. Sweat immediately began to seep from her skin as she bent to retrieve more cans. The chime rang out from the front door. The ding was hit or miss, working less than fifty percent of the time. The owner had made a comment about getting it replaced but never had. Much needed fixing around the store, and one would figure at her meager wages, he could use the surplus saved to invest in some repairs, but Muriel knew better. Even though this store belonged to Mr. Costa, extra expenses needed to be paid to operate such a business within the area of the city run by Conner Walsh.

Muriel had overheard Mr. Costa on one occasion complain about the extortion. It had been a very brief conversation with one of Walsh's employees, and she spent the better part of the following hour scrubbing the blood from the floor. She distinctly remembered the gash left above the kind-hearted store owner's right eye. Mr. Costa never spoke of the incident and neither did she. He also never again argued about the weekly extortion. Muriel Burke had a keen eye and an even keener memory. She'd seen Mr. Costa's assailant numerous times after the assault but never spoke about it. And never would.

Muriel peered from around the chip aisle and eyed the last-minute customer who had just entered. The man wore a dark baseball cap, plain with no lettering. The visor was cinched down on the man's head to the sunglasses. *Odd. Who wore sunglasses at night?* She noticed the man had a blue bandana around his neck. He walked, head down, until he stopped in front of the register. The man's movements were almost robotic. He spun to face Tucker. As he did so, his left hand pulled the bandana up to his face, shrouding it from view. In his right, he held a black pistol.

Muriel almost shrieked but controlled her panic. She'd been in the store on three separate occasions when it was robbed. During the first, she'd actually wet herself. But by the third time, she learned these crooks were there for money, booze, or cigarettes. Sometimes all three. She just had to wait out the few minutes of chaos until it was over. On all three occasions she'd seen the robber but lied and told the cops she hadn't. She had told Conner Walsh's men, who came in after the cops, the truth. She knew not to lie to them. Muriel never saw any of the robbers again, in the store or elsewhere around town. She may not have been educated properly, but she was a quiet observer of the world around her and knew very well what had befallen the men who took from a store under Walsh's protection. She was rewarded with an envelope containing one hundred dollars each time she assisted. And she understood its meaning as well.

"Give me the money!" the gunman commanded. His voice, somewhat muffled by the bandana, was clear enough to leave no doubt about the seriousness of his command.

The gun looked real too. The second time she'd witnessed the store being robbed, she could see the orange tip of the BB gun. This time there was no such tip. The man holding it was more menacing than the others. An engorged vein along his neck rippled and Muriel found herself staring at a tattoo on the right side of the man's neckline. From what she could see in her crouched position, it looked like the letters CB. She instantly committed the image to memory with the hope of another hundred-dollar payout.

Muriel watched as Tucker fumbled with the register. This was obviously the first time a gun had been pointed in the boy's face.

"Open it or you're dead!"

started out bad. "Life is like a choose-your-own-adventure book."

"A choose-your-own-adventure book?"

Kelly realized the series of popular books from his childhood was no longer marketed to today's youth. "They were these fantastic stories where at the end of each section you were given a choice. And depending on what choice you made, the book would have a different outcome."

"Cool."

"Cool is right." Kelly made a mental note to look for some of his old books in his mom's attic. "So, I've always seen life in the same way. People are given choices. Each one will lead to other choices and have a different consequence. If you make too many bad ones, the end result of your life can be pretty grim. And therefore, you may be considered a bad person by others."

"How will I know which choices are right and which are wrong?"

"Sometimes you will just know. You'll get this little feeling. Something you may not be able to place, but your body will react. Basically, your caveman brain will alert you. Like when the hairs on the back of your neck stand on end when you're scared. It's like your body's warning signal. When you get that tingle, make sure you listen to it. That's your brain telling you something's wrong. Too many people ignore it."

"What if I don't get that feeling? What if I make the wrong choice?"

"It's okay. Those are called mistakes. Everybody makes them."

"Even you?" Embry looked up at him with unabashed awe.

"Yes, Miss Squiggles. Even me."

Embry seemed to absorb the impact of the statement. Kelly knew she was still in the developmental stage where he, as her father, took on an almost superhero-like persona. He also knew it wouldn't last forever. Kelly thought it was important for his daughter to see him more plainly, as a fallible human being doing the best he could.

"What happens if I make too many wrong choices? Will I end up a bad guy?"

"No."

"How do you know?"

"Because I would never let that happen."

"But you're not always around, especially since you and Mom got divorced."

And there it was, a well-placed psychological gut punch. His daughter had begun to expertly deploy these on a more frequent basis. Each one stung. Each one a painful reminder of his failed marriage. "I know. Life's not perfect. But hopefully, your mom and I will fill you with enough street smarts to help you make the right choice even if we're not there."

"Okay—then promise me."

Kelly swished an X across his chest and leaned down to kiss his daughter's forehead. "Cross my heart."

Embry's arms swallowed him up. He hoped her legendary hugs would never run out of stock. Unbeknownst to her, they were the battery power fueling his daily life.

While holding his daughter, Kelly felt his phone vibrate in his pocket. Breaking contact, he sighed and pulled it out. Sergeant Sutherland was calling.

"Hey, boss."

Embry looked up at him. He registered the immediate disappointment on her face as he sat up.

"We got a body down at the corner store at Stoughton and Everett in Upham's Corner."

Upham's Corner was a section of North Dorchester not too far from where Kelly lived. The relatively small geographic landscape of the Boston Dorchester neighborhood was subdi-

3

The corner brick exterior of Tyson's Market was painted in the red and blue wash of light from the police cruisers blocking off the adjoining streets. Perimeter tape had already been rolled out and pockets of people had begun to gather, craning for an opportunity to see the carnage. Kelly pulled his Impala up to the line and stepped out.

Before addressing the patrolman working the scene entry log, Kelly looked around, taking in the crowd. Depending on the nature of the crime, many criminals returned to the scene as a bystander. Sometimes it came from an innate curiosity. Other times, the need to stay connected to the act of violence, a way of holding onto the moment just a little bit longer. And for some, it was a sickness. Firebugs, or arsonists, derived a euphoric high, almost sexual in nature, from watching things burn. Nobody among the group registered on Kelly's radar, but that could change.

He then surveyed the buildings nearest the small convenience store. Across the street was a state-subsidized apartment building for the elderly. A few triple-deckers littered the adjacent Everett Street, but most of the windows were boarded up on the unit closest to the market. Kelly didn't see any external video cameras, but with security devices like Ring it didn't necessarily mean they weren't there. Patrol would canvass the area and document potential surveillance.

Kelly grabbed his crime scene bag from the trunk and walked over to Hugh Thomas, who was standing in the center of the sidewalk behind the bright yellow police tape. Thomas had been a member of Boston PD for over two decades and was one of Kelly's first field training officers. A good cop with a solid work ethic and a man Kelly respected.

"Hey, Hugh. How goes it?"

"Michael Kelly! Here among the working stiffs. And what brings you out on such a beautiful night?"

Kelly slipped under the tape, and Thomas handed him the log to sign into the scene. Kelly also noted the time in his own notepad. "I decided I'd come slum it with you guys for a little while."

Thomas laughed.

"What am I walking into in there?"

"Dead clerk. One in the head. He's behind the counter."

"Robbery?"

"Looks like it. Got a witness. An older woman. She stocks and cleans the store. That's about all she's said so far. Other than that, she's not saying much. Pretty shook."

"I thought you could get anyone to talk."

Thomas smiled. "Me too. But my charm's had no effect. Maybe you'll have more luck."

"Where's she at?"

Thomas pointed at a stout woman standing in front of a patrolman Kelly didn't recognize.

"Good seeing you. Say hello to Haley for me."

Kelly stepped by his old mentor and friend, taking his digital camera from his bag. He snapped a couple photos of the mini market's exterior. The door was propped open with a wooden wedge. Kelly stood at the threshold, the toe of his shoe pressed against the metal lip at the base of the door's frame, and snapped several photos at multiple angles.

Laying the small charcoal gray duffle on the concrete sidewalk, Kelly unzipped and rifled through it to find the box containing the Tyvek booties. Slipping the powder blue cloth material over his shoes and stuffing his pants inside the elastic banding, he then retrieved four latex gloves. Double gloving each hand, Kelly stood. He could already feel the sweat moistening the interior of the nonpermeable material.

There were a few bloody shoeprints on the linoleum floor, and Kelly squatted low to examine them. From the treads, he guessed them to be boot prints. Most likely from the officers responding to the scene. He'd confirm before dismissing them.

The sensor located on the interior of the doorframe dinged, announcing his entrance as he stepped inside. The external commotion faded away, and Kelly was left with only the loud hum of the air conditioning unit, which was working extra hard with the open door. Kelly did not go directly to the clerk's body. He wanted to see the scene from a variety of angles before becoming engrossed in the details of the body.

Kelly stepped to the right, taking care to avoid the rust-colored footprints. He navigated around an aisle containing a sparse selection of cleaning products. As he rounded the corner, he saw a stack of sodas on the floor near the back wall of refrigerators. Kelly took a photo and approached.

Standing by the half-stocked pile of Monster Energy drinks, Kelly turned and faced the front door. He shifted his gaze to the counter, then positioned himself as though he were going to resume stocking the refrigerator, taking a knee beside the box of cans. From his new perspective, he again looked at the front entrance area. He had a relatively clear vantage point. *She must've seen everything*, he thought.

The door chiming caused Kelly to rise. His partner, Jimmy Mainelli, stood at the threshold. He was a short man with a thick waistline, and wore a button-down short-sleeve shirt with a brown tie. Mainelli took a strange pride in his appearance and called it his "Sipowicz look," a homage to the iconic detective from television's *NYPD Blue*. His midriff paunch was starting to resemble the fictional detective in that regard as well. Mainelli blamed that on his wife's cooking.

Mainelli wiped the sweat from his brow. "Got here as fast as I could. What'd I miss?"

"Just getting started."

"I see the uniforms danced in the paint a bit."

"Looks that way. Unless the doer was dumb enough to walk around the counter and stand in the blood."

Mainelli looked over toward the counter area. "You already take some photos of the body?"

"Not yet. I was working my way around from here. Looks like the stocker was probably over here when it happened. She would've had a pretty clear line of sight to the shooter."

Kelly walked past the chip aisle and approached the counter's entrance. The three-foot wood door was already unlatched and open, most likely done by the responding patrol officers during their efforts to evaluate the downed clerk. Didn't look like much evaluation was needed. The dime-sized hole in the clerk's forehead just left of center and a fraction of an inch above the eyebrow told the tale.

"Do you know who's coming in from Crime Scene?"

Kelly squatted down, balancing his body by resting his forearms against his knees. He positioned himself in a wide straddle, avoiding the pool of dark blood that had begun to overpriced rent. But for him, it was a potential treasure trove of opportunity.

He set out in the opposite direction of the couple. Moving along the sidewalk, he slowly drifted toward the curb line and near the stacked column of cars packed in bumper to bumper. Only a fire hydrant broke the chain of vehicles.

The ache in his stomach was now accompanied by a pulsing headache, the two working in concert to torment him. He did his best to put the discomfort out of his mind, but his intolerance for pain was one of the reasons he was in his current predicament. Looking around for any watchful eyes, he slowed near the passenger side door of a maroon Kia.

He tried the door, but it remained closed. Locked. No need to break the window and draw unwanted attention. He moved on down the line. Even in a city the size of Boston and in a neighborhood as rough as Dorchester, people still left cars and homes unlocked. It was either done out of an unnatural sense of safety or forgetfulness. Regardless of the reason, it made for easy pickings and had aided in his survival since he turned to the streets. In colder months, unlocked cars typically became his shelter from the harsh New England winters.

Six cars down, he felt the handle give way to the sweet release. The faded blue older-model Honda Accord wasn't clean by any stretch of the imagination. He pulled the door open, scanning the interior. From the looks of it, the owner used the floorboards as his personal trashcan. Stacks of empty coffee cups and fast food wrappers were littered in heaps. The air emanating from inside was stale, a mishmash of cigarette ash and fry grease. But to the filthy man, the odor was barely noticeable. He didn't care about the mess on a personal level, but the physical state of the car lowered his expectation of finding what he was looking for.

Giving one last nervous look around and not seeing

anybody, he slipped inside, closing the door behind him. The muted yellow of a nearby streetlight penetrated the windshield, giving him just enough visibility. Sitting on the stained cloth upholstery of the driver's seat and working quickly, he began riffling through the center console. He found a packet of gum with one piece remaining. He pushed on the plastic, punching it through the thin blister back. He popped the hard-shelled white rectangle into his mouth, the intense minty flavor replacing the bitterness of the bile's residue.

Chewing noisily, he continued his search. Wedged between the seat and the loose center console, he saw the soft green of cash. It was partially buried, covered by a cigarette butt and dried-out french fry. Forcing his hand into the tight space, he wriggled his fingers down, his sweat acting as a natural lubricant. Scissoring the money between his index and middle fingers, he worked to extract the cash from its trash-covered burial ground.

Success! He unfolded the bill and smiled down at the stoic face of Alexander Hamilton. With the money in hand, his pain was suddenly replaced by a new desire, one that had overpowered everything in his life since the first time he jammed the spike into his vein. From that moment forward, everything focused on getting a fix.

After the find, he spent a few more minutes digging around the car, testing his luck. Nothing but a near-empty Parliament box containing three cigarettes and a Bic lighter. Pocketing his treasures in the front of his jeans, he peeked out the window and looked down the street. Deciding it was safe, he exited and closed the door behind him. He didn't worry about leaving prints. Cops didn't spend the time or effort to process a car break on an unlocked motor vehicle, especially in a city filled with more important crimes to worry about.

Walking away from the Honda, he felt the ten burning a

hole in the front pocket of his pants as it pulled him toward his next destination. Bilbo Baggins had nothing on him when it came to the desire driving him. There were times when he actually thought he heard the needle in his pocket calling to him.

It was late and most businesses were closed for the night. But the ones he sought kept much different hours. Rounding the corner, he walked to the fourth building and bounded up the concrete steps. The entrance to the first floor of the triple decker was propped open with a folded copy of last week's *Herald*. He'd sent the text while on the walk, asking if he could get five for ten. A good price for dope. Friend rate. The answer was simple and direct, leaving no room for further bargaining. Three for ten. It wasn't great, but better than nothing. He'd been charged more in the past. The fact he was now able to haggle the cost down meant his status as a frequent client had improved, but he hadn't reached friend-rate status. For the man who'd effectively severed every personal relationship, friend or otherwise, he was saddened by the realization his closest contact came in the way of a low-level heroin dealer named Zorro.

Zorro preferred people called him Z. But nicknames were like birthmarks, and it took lots of work to make them disappear. Zorro got his a few years back. He was in a stash house packaging up product when the narcs hit the door on a raid. In a panic, he dived face first through a plate glass window in his failed escape attempt. Not only was he immediately caught by the police officers staged along the perimeter, he was permanently scarred from the jagged shards lacerating the left side of his face. When the doctors finished stitching him back together, he was left with a misshapen zigzag reminiscent of the famous Spanish swordsman's signature mark. And thus, Zorro was born.

Standing outside, he wondered what Zorro called him since

they never really spoke to each other. Their communications came in brief text messages like the one used tonight to arrange the deal. He doubted the scarred man paid him any afterthought.

Three bags should get him right, at least until morning. That's all he needed. Get his head straight, push back his sickness, and then he'd figure out his situation. Same shit repeated on an endless loop—get sick, get money, get high. Someday he'd break the cycle. Either that or he'd end up dead. It was a coin toss as to which would come first.

He sent the follow-up text message. *Here.*

Slipping inside, he waited. Normally when he'd send a message looking for a score, Zorro would direct him to a meet location. Only on a few occasions had he been told to come to his residence, either when Z was tired or busy with a girl. He'd made the mistake of going to Z's third-floor apartment during his first visit and was charged extra for that mistake. It was one he'd never made again. The main entrance, bottom of the first-floor stairwell, was where he usually waited. That way cops could never do a direct buy in Zorro's apartment and therefore never get a search warrant to raid the place.

Standing in the quiet, he waited for the sound of the door opening and footsteps. His body prickled and a chill caused goosebumps to rise. In the oppressive heat, he was suddenly cold. It was bad tonight. He couldn't remember a time when the hurt was so terrible. Dope sick equaled catching a debilitating strain of the flu. Rubbing the outside of his dirt-covered jeans, he felt the outline of the needle in his pocket. The thin cylinder gave him solace his pain would soon pass.

He slid the last of the cigarettes out of the box he'd boosted from the blue Accord. There was only the one left. He'd smoked the other two on the walk over. He lit it and took a long drag, the cigarette shaking in his trembling fingers. *I need to get right. Once*

I'm straight, maybe I'll try rehab again. They won't take me clean anyway. Need to piss dirty if you want a bed at the clinic. Really a vicious cycle. But as soon as he had drugs, the last thing he wanted to do was go to a clinic.

Junkie dreamboat, he called it. The drug-shackled victims of its cursed loop always told themselves they'd get clean. He allowed his mind to indulge in such a fantasy, believing his own lie. He'd told himself this was the last time, knowing full well he would find himself fiending a few hours later.

A door opened and closed from somewhere up above. The sound of footsteps followed, clunking loudly on the old hardwood. His heartrate increased, the palpitations causing him to twitch. The chill dissipated and was replaced by warmth as sweat once again began to flow from his pores. As the footsteps grew louder, he teetered on the edge of giddiness. The emotional rollercoaster of his addiction was almost at its ritualistic end. Until the cycle started back up once again.

Zorro came into view as he rounded the landing and descended the final few steps.

"What's good, Z?"

A sneer and look of annoyance were evident on the man's face as he shrugged his indifference to the small talk. Shirtless with a light sheen of sweat on his mocha skin, Zorro had obviously been with a girl, and the ten-dollar interruption was not wholly welcomed. No smile. No handshake. This meeting had none of the cordiality of a real business interaction. Z held out an empty hand, waiting with a look of disgust. Greeting him the way most drug dealers did, with complete and utter disdain.

"Cough it up."

Pulling the crumpled bill from his pocket, he eagerly placed the money in the outstretched hand.

Zorro tossed him the bags. The thin slips of folded wax paper landed on the ground near his shoes, as if Z was too disgusted to place them in his hands. He bent over to retrieve the purchased merchandise as Z bounded up the stairs. The whole transaction took place in under thirty seconds.

He thought about booting up right there in the hallway, but if Zorro caught him doing it, he'd lose his mind. No using where the deal took place, especially if that place was the dealer's home.

Stuffing the three bags into the pocket where the money had just been, he pulled open the door and left. Walking at a quick pace, he headed off in the opposite direction.

He wasn't too far from the unlocked car and debated doubling back, returning to it and shooting up there. If it were winter, he definitely would have taken advantage of the privacy offered by the Honda. Most likely he would have slept in it overnight. Unlocked cars made excellent beds and were safer than most shelters. But tonight, it wouldn't be needed. Just a few minutes of privacy and all would be good again.

Continuing at a quick clip, he walked a block before cutting in behind a closed bakery. Sitting on the back stoop, he pulled out his needle, plastic bottle cap, tie-off, and lighter. Setting the items on the concrete, he stretched his leg out in front of him, making access to his pocket easier as he worked to retrieve the thin bags of dope.

Headlights flooded the back lot. He released his grip on the drugs, leaving them inside his pants. Tucking his kit under his thigh, he raised his other hand and shielded his eyes from the light.

Shifting away from the approaching vehicle, he prepared to grab his stuff and go. Turning, he quickly saw the problem in his logic.

Two men were coming up fast on him. Both had guns in hand.

The bigger man with a cleanly shaven bald head shouted, "Hands! Let me see 'em now. Slow and easy."

Overwhelmed and panic-stricken, he released the needle under his thigh and slowly began raising his hands.

The bald man stopped and stood a few feet away, the headlight from the car bouncing off the shiny surface of his smooth scalp. The other man, thinner and slightly shorter than his loud counterpart, moved closer and grabbed him by the wrist. He was jerked up from the concrete stoop, and then a jerk and twist of his arm spun him around, causing his chest to crash into the wall beside the closed business. The rough brick façade snagged his thin, sweat-soaked T-shirt. The pressure on him kept his upper body suctioned to the wall as his hands were wrenched behind his back.

"Hey, pal, don't even think about moving." The man's breath in his ear was hotter than the oppressive air around it. "Where is it? It better not be up your ass. I'm really not in the mood to be digging out your nasty crack."

"I don't know what you're talking about."

"We know where you just came from. Tell me where it is, and this goes a lot easier. And I don't want to get poked by one of your dirty needles. Is that one there the only one you've got?"

He nodded and sighed.

"Easy or hard. You decide, but my partner over there hates to wait. And between you and me, he prefers the hard way."

"Front pocket."

"Which one and how much."

"Right side. It's only three bags."

The man grabbed the outside of the pocket, pinching and manipulating the contents inside in tactile confirmation.

He felt the metal of the handcuffs bang against his skin, starting at his right wrist and then locking on the left.

The cop kept him pressed against the wall with a forearm

firmly centered on his back. Then, sliding on a pair of latex gloves, he shoved the gloved hand into the pocket. Holding up the thin bags, he called over to his partner, "Only three bags."

The cop gripped him tightly by the shoulder and spun him around. This guy had obviously missed the sensitivity training, he thought in amusement. Facing the plain clothes officer, he felt defeated. A wave of exhaustion swept over him and he wanted nothing more than to curl into a ball and sleep. He was mentally kicking himself for not shooting the dope back in Z's hallway. At least he would've been high during this shakedown. And for him, being high helped him cope with most of life's challenges.

The cop's badge hung from a chain around his neck, dangling in front of his chest. His shirt was unbuttoned, exposing a sweat-stained wife beater. Dark curls of hair protruded from the undershirt's low-hanging U. If he'd had a mustache, the motif would have been complete, and he could have served as a stunt double for Selleck's *Magnum, P.I.* character.

"Got some ID on you?"

He started to shake his head when he heard the car door open and close. A man walked up, partially blocking the beam from the headlights. "He doesn't need one."

The Selleck imposter turned to the approaching man. "You know this guy?"

"I do," Lincoln White said, walking closer. "How you been, Brayden?"

Brayden dropped his head. Selleck let go of him, and he wanted nothing more than to slink down the wall and disappear into the nearby sewer drain. "Hey, Linc. Been a while."

Selleck looked back and forth between the two, furrowing his brow in confusion. "Is he one of yours?"

"No. He's Michael Kelly's kid brother."

He thumbed in Brayden's direction. "You've got to be shittin' me. You're telling me this skell is Saint Michael's brother?" He continued as if Brayden weren't standing within a foot of him. "Man, and I thought my family had some train wreck losers."

White took out his cell phone. "Do you want to tell him, or should I?"

Brayden felt a new wave of sickness wash over him. Not from the dope; this time his nausea was stress-induced. As much as he hated to admit it, seeing the look of disappointment in his brother's eyes was always devastating. Mike had bailed him out of trouble too many times to count over the years. And the toll it had taken on their relationship was daunting.

Brayden groaned. "Neither."

"Hey, Brooks, give me a second with him, would you?" As the Selleck look-alike turned to walk away, White stopped him with a slight tug of the elbow. "Let me see what you got off him."

Brooks opened his gloved hand to reveal the three thin bags of heroin. The waxy paper was stamped with a red Z.

"Why don't you leave that with me?"

Brooks didn't object, handing over the packets before walking over to his bald partner.

White narrowed his eyes and stepped closer. "What's wrong with you? Do you want me to bring you in on a couple bags of dope?"

"No. I'd prefer you didn't."

"Then what? You don't want me to call your brother. You don't want to go to jail. By the looks of you, I'd venture to guess you're probably more afraid of the sickness than the cell."

Brayden was sweating profusely now, like somebody just ran by and hit him with a water balloon. He fought the urge to vomit again. Releasing his guts in front of White, or on him, would be the ultimate in a string of recent lows.

"Brayden, you know how this works. Your brother was in

this unit for a few years. And you've been in the drug game longer than that. Give me something to work with so you and I can pretend this night never happened."

"I ain't no snitch." He straightened his posture as best he could, pressing against the wall for additional support.

"Funny thing about that. Everybody is. Some of the most powerful people in the game work for us or the feds. It's a give and take. Little pissants like yourself always think there's a code of honor in the drug world. Couldn't be further from the truth. If the need is there, people make a deal. And looking at you now, I can see you need more than anything to get yourself right." He dangled the bags in front of Brayden's face.

"What—you're just gonna let me have my drugs back?"

"Like I said, there's a lot of wiggle room as to how I handle things. Me and my unit get some leeway in how things work because we get results. We see the big picture and are working toward the greater good."

Brayden eyed the bags, entranced. "I tell you something and you let me walk—with my dope?"

"Simple, right?"

"What do you want to know?"

White cocked his head. "I've got another option for you. A better one for both of us. It'll help your situation and keep you from having to call in favors from your brother when you screw up again." He broke into a wide grin. "And trust me on that, you will screw up again."

"What is it—this option you're giving me?"

"Work for me. Do some buys into some guys. Get me into some people. Easy work, really. Each buy gives you eighty bucks in your pocket. Think about it. You do a few buys in a day and you'll have some decent walking-around money. You won't have to go breaking into cars."

Brayden's pale cheeks reddened. It was bad enough they

caught him buying dope, but apparently, they'd watched him break into a car to get the money for the purchase, adding insult to injury. He was angry at himself for being so blind. There was a time when he could spot a cop a mile away. He was slipping and he only had the dope to blame.

"If Michael ever found out I was making buys for the narc task force, he'd kill me himself."

"He won't know. Because nobody's going to tell him. And if you get picked up by somebody on patrol, all you need to do is drop my name. I'll vet you and you'll be on your way. That is unless you screw me over." White leaned in close, his cologne a musky leathery smell. "Then, I'll make sure your problems come back tenfold. And this little meeting of ours will seem like a bright spot in your life in comparison."

Brayden didn't cower at the threat, although he wanted to. He knew the man well enough to know it was more of a promise. Lincoln White had a well-earned reputation on the street as a cop not to cross. And Brayden had no intention of getting on his bad side.

White stepped back, fiddling with the bags in his hand.

"Okay. I'll play ball."

They exchanged cell phone numbers. As he turned to walk away, White stuffed the three bags back into Brayden's front pocket. "Get yourself straight. I'm going to need you very soon."

"Don't you need some information from me?"

"Not now. We've got much bigger dealers in our sights than your friend Zorro. And you're going to help me get them."

Brayden watched as the man casually walked back toward his car. The lights, no longer blocked by White's frame, resumed their blinding brilliance, causing him to dip his head. As he tipped his head to shield his eyes with the brim of his ball cap, sweat continued to drip down his face.

"Cut him loose. We've got bigger fish to fry." White didn't break stride and got into his car.

Brooks walked over and spun him to face the wall. No words were said. The only sound was the metal click and ratchet of the cuffs' release. Freed from the restraints, Brayden turned. Selleck's stunt double and his bald partner disappeared around the corner as the unmarked cruiser backed out of the lot.

Brayden waited only a moment or two before resuming his seat next to his kit. Removing the contents from his pocket, he prepared for the rush of his fix. Spitting into a bottle cap he carried for such occasions, he mixed in the brown powder and used all three bags to stir the slurry with the tip of the needle. Heating the bottom of the cap, he brought the contents to a slow bubble. Drawing the murky off-yellow liquid into the needle, he eyed his best vein.

Within seconds, he was transported from sickness to euphoria, the hot liquid transporting him away from his troubles.

For now, he enjoyed the drug-induced bliss. He slumped back against the wall, knowing he'd just made a deal with the devil.

5

Bobby watched the man stir his amber liquid. The Tootsie Pop clinked against the tumbler. Nobody spoke. Each member silently waited for their leader to open the conversation. The meeting, earlier than most would have liked, was scheduled to discuss last night's shooting.

Conner Walsh removed the dark red lollipop from the glass and stuck it in the corner of his mouth. The candied ball forced the man's gaunt cheek to bulge. He lifted the glass and drained the two fingers of Tullamore Dew triple distilled Irish whiskey, the only drink Bobby had ever seen the man consume. Even at eight in the morning, the sight of the Savin Hill Gang's founding member drinking it was no shock.

Setting the glass on the bar, he turned slowly on the stool to face the most trusted members of his crew. Bobby stood a few feet away and leaned against a wooden pillar.

Walsh pulled the pop out of his mouth and rested it inside the empty glass. "We've got a problem. As you know, somebody dared to rob one of our stores last night. You've had a night to dig into your network of sources. I'm expecting one of you to have an answer to the question I'm going to ask."

Several men stirred around the room. Bobby watched them, searching their faces. Only one seemed unfazed by Walsh's words. William Fitzpatrick, or Fitzy as he was known, stood still with an air of confidence the others, including Bobby, didn't possess.

Walsh exhaled slowly. "Who was dumb enough to not only hit one of our stores, but kill somebody under our protection?"

A few of the men looked down and away from the sixty-four-year-old mob boss. At an age when most would be working on their golf swing at some Florida retirement village, Conner Walsh still maintained the ability to strike fear into men half his age.

Fitzpatrick cleared his throat. "I got something from a reliable source."

Walsh directed his attention to the man. "And what did this reliable source tell you?"

"The shooter had a tattoo on his neck. Two letters. C and B."

Walsh's hand began to fidget, and he retrieved his lollipop. A man with few tells, this twitching of his index and middle fingers was the most noticeable. Since his boss had quit smoking a year ago after a cancer scare, Bobby had noticed the twitching. The candy had replaced Conner's chain smoking.

"You're telling me some corner hustling little gang is trying to make a move on my territory?"

Fitzy had been with the gang for only a couple years, but he'd earned Walsh's trust. One of the ways he achieved it was to never apply the why to the what. Fitzpatrick just gave the information and left the interpretation of said facts to the senior man. "I'm not sure why they did it."

"Doesn't matter why. Doesn't matter if they didn't know who runs protection for the market." Walsh bit into the hard candy coating with a loud crunch, spitting bits as he continued. "The fact is they did!"

Walsh stood up and began pacing the bar floor. His fair complexion reddened. He ran his hands through his salt-and-pepper hair, now more salt than pepper, as he eyed the men.

Fitzy then uncharacteristically spoke out of turn. "I say we hit hard. Send a message."

Danny O'Toole, Walsh's oldest friend and the longest living member of the gang besides Walsh, offered, "That's a great way to get the police breathing down our necks. We've got to approach this thing more diplomatic-like."

Walsh's glare ping-ponged between the two debaters. "Fitzy, you want to start a war? Is that right?"

"I didn't say war. I just said we hit 'em back hard. Let those skells know who runs the Dot."

"Please tell me how we hit them back without turning the neighborhood into a freakin' shooting gallery."

Fitzy shrugged. "We find the kid who shot up the store and put his body on display."

O'Toole rubbed at the roll of fat along his thick neckline. "Let's handle it like we did with the Rakowski family a few years back. Get the heads in a room and come to a meeting of the minds. An agreement of sorts."

"You want to parlay a truce with a bunch of savage street thugs?" Fitzy fired back.

O'Toole didn't address Fitzpatrick, directing his answer to Walsh. "Conner, wasn't like we started out on top. Maybe these youngsters can be reasoned with."

Walsh walked back to the bar and eyed Cormac, the bartender, who immediately refilled his glass. Taking it in hand, he turned back to O'Toole. "Could you set a meet?"

"You're not seriously entertaining the idea of a truce, are you?" Fitzpatrick stood his ground.

"Last I checked, this was my gang to run as I see fit. If you got a problem with that, I can make a new arrangement for you."

Fitzy stepped back. "Not what I meant. Just looking out for us is all. Didn't want some low-level pukes thinking they can take what you earned."

Bobby watched as Walsh evaluated the man and his attempted usurping of authority.

"This is something that needs to be addressed immediately. Set the meet. If they can't bring me the shooter, then we'll look at Fitzy's idea of a solution. One thing's for certain, nobody's taking what I earned."

6

Kelly liked his office in the early morning hours when most of the members of his unit weren't there. Either they were still making their commute in through the clogged arteries feeding into the heart of Massachusetts or on their desperate hunt for the morning cup of coffee. Quiet was not the norm, and he wholly embraced it.

Murder always woke him early. It felt wrong to sleep in when every critical second that ticked by meant potentially lost leads. He shook off the fatigue shrouding him. It had been a late night. They hadn't finished processing the scene until one a.m. Mainelli had left, but Kelly returned to the office to type up his initial case report before calling it quits for the night. He had considered giving in and taking up the couch in the break room. The couch was worn thin in spots from the many years it had served the unit as a makeshift cot. He'd used it numerous times in the months since he'd been assigned to Homicide. But with Embry home, he wanted to see her before beginning his second leg of what would undoubtedly be a very long day, even if she didn't see or know he was there. Being in her presence helped him hit the mental reset button, giving him perspective. And as predicted, he was out of the house before she woke.

His mother was now familiar with the drill. On nights he was called in after hours, she'd wake early and check for the note, always left by a fresh pot of coffee. It was a system his daughter was also becoming far too familiar with. Ever since the divorce, the teamwork lost from his dissolved marital partnership now fell upon his mother.

Notes and photographs were strewn across his desk, and he set about organizing them into logical order. As he did, a pang of guilt, a dull, achy reminder of his failings, swept over him. Perspective.

Mainelli had messaged him a few moments ago to tell him he'd be running late, as usual. Something about his son vomiting on his way out the door and his battle with finding suitable childcare for the day. Life didn't seem to care much for the dead, always pushing along in its usual fashion.

The computer screen bathed him in a milky white light. Sipping from his second cup of the morning, he rubbed his eyes and began rereading last night's report. One line stood out and nagged at him.

No shell casing located on scene.

It was plausible to think the murder weapon had been a revolver, but if it hadn't and a semi-auto had been fired, the shell casing would have been ejected from the gun. He, Mainelli, and Charles had gone over every inch of the store looking for the spent brass. They'd checked the floors, racks, and boxes. After the scene was photographed and processed, they recreated it, with Mainelli standing where the shooter most likely would've been at the time the shot was fired. The three seasoned investigators postulated where the projectile would have landed and hunted high and low. Nothing. Zilch. Nada.

Once the ballistics came back on the slug retrieved from the wall behind where the clerk had been standing, he'd know more. He picked up the phone and dialed Ray Charles's extension. It went to voicemail and Kelly hung up.

Kelly accessed the department-wide report database, a digital file cabinet connecting all the districts. In years past, he would've lost valuable time to the search, driving to respective district offices and physically pulling the records. But now it was a matter of simple keystrokes, and any case files entered or in progress would be at his disposal. The designers made the system user-friendly, enabling investigators to narrow searches using key terms. Another function, one Kelly found extremely useful, gave him the ability to analyze crime data by geographic location. The bosses used this mapping feature for their stat meetings, but Kelly used it to visually look for patterns.

His search focused on armed robberies within the last month where a firearm was used or displayed. Before he could take a sip of his coffee, the search engine finished compiling the related cases. Red dots popped up across the two-dimensional digital map of the city, each dot representing a specific case. He could click on any of the icons and the system would redirect him to the case file.

Kelly zoomed in on the location of last night's robbery murder. Using the mouse to highlight a ten-block radial area from Tyson's Market, he watched the red dots reduce to seven. Seven cases of armed robbery occurred in the last thirty days.

Accessing each file, he saw no shots were fired during the commission of any of the other robberies. In three of them, a firearm wasn't displayed, only implied. Two of the cases where a weapon was displayed resulted in arrest. He accessed the Department of Corrections portal and saw both were still in lockup. The last one had a video clip attachment. Kelly clicked the icon and watched as the black-and-white video played out on the screen.

The robber, a tall, lanky man, entered the store quickly. He was gloved and masked, but the video quality was poor and showed little in the way of physical details. Kelly studied the man's movements. They were erratic. Amateurish. He waved the gun around wildly, pointing it in multiple directions. He grabbed a donation jar off the counter and flung it at the clerk. The clerk opened the register, and the masked gunman extended his torso over the counter and shoved the man back. He grabbed the money and retreated, shoving the clumps of cash into his pocket. Loose bills trailed the man out the door. It was over in less than twenty seconds. Kelly had no video to compare his case to the one he had just witnessed, but what he saw didn't match the case facts he had established. The man on the screen was most likely a junkie looking for quick cash.

He closed the digital file, deeming it unrelated. He'd wait to see if any additional evidence, DNA or otherwise, linked the cases. But as of right now, his case looked to be unique.

Kelly grabbed his notebook and prepared to head down to the forensic lab as Mainelli walked in. His partner looked haggard. The button-down shirt was wrinkled and partially untucked. His eyes were bloodshot. If Kelly hadn't known the man better, he would've thought he'd just waltzed in after an all-night bender.

"You look like you slept in your car."

"Well, aren't you a bucket of sunshine." Mainelli plopped into his seat and sighed. "I swear, some days I'd rather not go home. It's like a war zone in my house. Screaming kids and projectile vomiting are not the way to start your day."

"Builds character."

"Whatever you say. It's going to lead me to an early grave."

"I thought you Italians were all tough as nails. I saw *The Godfather*."

Mainelli chuckled and took a long pull from his cup of coffee.

"Don't get comfortable. We're going to take a walk down to see Ray."

"I just got in. Can you give a guy a minute?"

"Just did." Kelly stood and gave his partner a wink. "Early bird gets the worm."

Mainelli grumbled, pushed himself up, and eyed the files atop Kelly's desk. "I see you've been busy this morning. Got anything figured out amidst your pile of notes?"

"Checked some local armed robberies in the area. Nothing in the case files seems to match our shooter from last night. I'm hoping Ray burned the midnight oil and found us our needle in the haystack."

The two walked through the Homicide Unit's secure doors and into the hallway. BPD's crime scene technician, Raymond Charles, exited the elevator pushing a cart stacked high with boxes.

"You got your walking papers?"

Ray looked up at Kelly and pushed his cart aside. Even though headquarters was kept at an even temperature, the senior crime scene tech was sweating profusely. "You forgot? It's moving day for us down in the lab."

"Oh crap, that's right."

"Yup. No more mushroom life for us in forensics."

"Mushroom life?" asked Mainelli.

"Ya know—kept in the dark and fed shit all day." Charles smiled broadly. "Forensics is no longer going to be in the base-ment. We're going to be neighbors."

"That's good for us. Plus, we were just on our way to see you. So you saved us a trip down."

"If it's about last night's shooting, it's going to be a bit delayed. Got in early today because they want us up and running on the second floor ASAP. Knowing how this place operates, it will be a lot more involved than they realize."

"Damn, I was hoping you'd have something for us to go on. I'm batting zeros right now."

"Well, there isn't much in the way of good useable evidence as of right now. With no casing and the round removed from the backstop wall, there's no ballistics to run for comparisons. Maybe the ME's office will be able to give you more."

Kelly slapped the notepad against his palm. "Let's hope so. I'm still waiting to hear back from them on the autopsy schedule."

"I guess that means we can head back into the office, and I can finish my morning cup in peace," Mainelli said.

"You can finish it in the car."

"Why? Where are we going now?"

"Back to the liquor store. I want to look at it again with fresh eyes. Do a little daylight canvass of the area."

"Patrol did a canvass last night. Should've been documented in the supplementals."

"It was. But it was late. People around there don't like to talk to uniforms. Might get something today that they missed."

Mainelli huffed.

"Jimmy, you don't have to come. I can handle it myself."

Mainelli rolled his eyes. "I'm coming. Ya know you nag more than my wife."

"I'll be sure to pass that along next time I see her."

The two entered the elevator as Charles wheeled his cart down the hall toward the new and improved forensics lab.

Mainelli handed Kelly the keys. "You can drive since you're so dead set on getting your ass back to the scene we left just a few hours ago. I'm going to relax and enjoy what's left of my coffee."

"Enjoy your break. I think we're going to be in for a long day."

7

Tyson's Market looked different in the light of day. Strange how the dynamic energy of a crime scene could amplify things. The building seemed smaller than it had last night. With the foot traffic of police and onlookers gone, it was just a store once again. The police tape had been torn down after the processing, but a bit of the yellow plastic hung loosely in a trashcan set up outside the entrance.

Kelly parked on the street and got out. Mainelli followed, tossing his empty cup into the trash atop the police tape as the two walked inside.

"I'm sorry, but we're closed for the day." A dark-skinned man stopped sweeping and looked at them. He was an older gentleman in his late fifties or early sixties. His hair was mostly gone from the top of his head and the bare portions of his scalp glistened with sweat. A thick mass of neatly combed gray hair lined the sides.

Kelly pulled on the chain around his neck to reveal the badge under his shirt. "We understand. Just following up from last night."

The man looked nervous, eyeing his broom as if he were

holding contraband. "I'm sorry. I thought that I could clean up. I was told the police were done here. I wouldn't have—"

"You're fine. We just wanted to take another look around in the daylight. Make sure we didn't miss anything last night."

Relief swept over the man's face. "I've only just started. Haven't really got around to the other side of the counter yet."

"You didn't happen to find anything when you started sweeping?"

The man shook his head. "Like what?"

"A shell casing."

"What's a shell casing?"

Sometimes Kelly forgot how little the general public knew about some things he took for granted. "It's a small metallic cylinder about this big. Brass, usually gold or silver in color." Kelly held up his thumb and index finger for a visual reference.

"No. Nothing." The man stretched out his arm. "Feel free to do whatever it is you need to do."

"Thanks."

Kelly and Mainelli again stood in the spot where the shot was presumably taken. They repeated the process of calculating the possible trajectory the casing, if ejected, would've traveled.

After several minutes of crawling around on the floor using the sunlight pouring in through the plate glass of the storefront, they came up with the same results. Satisfied he hadn't missed the casing, Kelly stood and dusted off his pants.

Mainelli rubbed at the corners of his eyes and then folded his arms. "We good here?"

"Seems that way."

Kelly exited the store. It wasn't yet eight a.m., and the heat was already stifling. During a heatwave, the city air tasted like the filth and grime had been baked into a potpourri of awfulness. Standing outside on the curb in front of the open door to

Tyson's Market, Kelly caught the lingering scent of death in the stagnant air around him.

"Ya know, now that Cliff Anderson is getting the boot from our team, I'm the senior man."

Kelly turned to look at his partner. The limited exertion of the last few minutes inside the store had left his white shirt damp with sweat. His thick black hair, normally slicked back and held by some type of heavy-duty pomade, fell loosely across his face.

"Your point?"

"All I'm saying is, maybe I should be the one guiding this thing. Feels like we are spinning our wheels this morning."

"Like I said back at the office, I can do this on my own." Kelly leveled a gaze at the man. "I get it. I'm still the new kid around the office. But it isn't like I'm new to the job. I've got my ways of doing things and you obviously have yours."

"Listen, Mike, I don't want to butt heads with you."

"Let's do a quick canvass. There were several addresses listed in the patrol supplementals where no contact was made. I'd like to check a few of them just to fill in the holes."

"Fine."

Mainelli's body language spoke volumes. He looked like a toddler being forced to go to the doctor for an annual flu shot.

Kelly looked at the list of addresses he'd written in his notepad, then around at the buildings surrounding the store. It took him only a few seconds to locate a multifamily unit across the street. Two of the three residents had answered and spoken with the patrolman who conducted last night's canvass. Neither claimed to have seen anything. The third-floor tenant was not contacted, either because they hadn't been home or refused to answer for the police. The building had a perfect vantage point into the store and offered the best probability for a witness.

Walking across the street with a sense of purpose, Kelly

bounded up the five steps to the porch landing. He turned the knob to find the door locked. Three doorbells were neatly stacked along the right side of the door frame. The nametags aligned with each button were sun-bleached and faded, making them illegible. Improving his odds of somebody unlocking the door, Kelly pressed all three simultaneously. A soft chime could be heard from the first floor. A dog barked loudly from somewhere on the second.

Kelly waited.

"Look. If they didn't want to talk last night, chances are nothing's changed in the last few hours."

A buzzer sounded and Kelly pulled the doorknob. Opening the door, he looked over at Mainelli and smiled. "Guess we're about to find out."

Kelly knew Mainelli was probably right about the first- and second-floor residents. If they'd spoken to the patrol guys last night and stated they didn't see anything, they'd unlikely add much today. But he wasn't here for them. The third floor held his interest.

Arriving at the third-floor landing, Kelly waited for Mainelli, who trailed behind. His labored breathing was canceled out by the stomp of his footsteps.

Mainelli took the final step, shaking his head in frustration. The dampness of his shirt turned the white fabric translucent. He arched back with his hands on his hips as he fought to gather himself.

"I should've stayed in the car."

"But then you would've missed your morning workout."

Kelly knocked on the door, striking it with enough force to leave no doubt as to whether or not he was heard.

He waited and listened, straining to hear over Mainelli's wheezy rasping.

A creak of a floorboard told him somebody was inside. He knocked again, slightly louder than the first time.

"Boston PD. We'd like to talk with you."

Silence followed.

"Maybe nobody's home." Mainelli shrugged as he pushed back his hair, using the sweat to increase its hold.

"I heard something." Turning his attention back to the closed door, Kelly leaned in closer. "Please come to the door. I can hear you inside. We don't want to take up much of your time. Just need to talk to you about last night."

A shadow swept across the light seeping out from under the door. A metallic click and turn of the knob. The door opened a few inches, the chain still locked in place.

An older man's face appeared in the gap. His eyebrows fanned out in long wisps.

"A little early for you to be banging on my door."

Mainelli chuckled softly behind Kelly.

"My apologies, sir. We're just following up on something that happened last night."

"Badges."

"Excuse me?"

"Badges. Let me see them. I've got to make sure you aren't some phonies."

Kelly held up his badge.

The old man squinted, giving the shield a careful evaluation. He nodded his acceptance but didn't remove the chain's latch.

"What is it you want to know?"

"There was a shooting at the market across the street. A young clerk was killed and we're trying to see if anybody saw anything."

"I was asleep."

"I didn't tell you what time it happened."

The old man crinkled his eyes.

"I didn't see anything."

"You were asleep, or you didn't see anything? Seems to me like you're not exactly sure which."

The creases around the man's brow deepened. He pursed his lips, as if battling to keep the words from escaping his mouth, but said nothing.

"Look, I understand not wanting to talk to the police. I get it. We don't need to put your name on the report. I can put you down as an anonymous party."

The man made a strange hissing sound like a punctured bike tire deflating. "Not too hard to put two and two together."

"And who would be doing that math?"

"People who kill people."

Kelly softened his tone and leaned in closer. "Sir, if you saw something that will help us, I can make sure you are protected."

"Protected?" The man smiled for the first time. His thin lips parted, exposing his pearly white dentures. "The Boston Police can protect me? I don't know what neighborhood you think you're in. But one thing's for damn certain—the cops don't run the streets."

"I grew up not far from here. Dot born and raised."

"Then you should know better than anybody. Conner Walsh runs this neighborhood. Protection and otherwise. Nobody's going to talk to you around here."

"Walsh's crew runs the corner store?"

"If you're asking me that, then you already know the answer."

The old man shut the door, locking the deadbolt in place.

Kelly turned. A smug, condescending look was evident on Mainelli's face.

"At least we now know the store was under Walsh's protection."

"And what does that give us, Mike?"

"A problem. A big one."

"How's that?"

"Because Walsh's going to be looking to even the score. Our clock is ticking a lot faster now. Best bet is to find the guy who hit the market before one of Walsh's goons does."

"Looks like we're not going to get anywhere with the canvass."

"Probably right. We have at least one witness. She gave me a little last night. Maybe she will be more willing to talk with us today."

"Are you talking about the stocker?"

"Yeah, she doesn't live too far from here. Probably a twenty-minute walk."

Mainelli's eyes widened as he wiped the sweat from his brow. "Ain't no way I'm walking."

Kelly laughed. "I can see I've crossed the invisible line of your patience with our morning's fitness regime. Don't worry, we'll drive."

The two walked out of the triple decker and back to their car. Kelly took one last look at the storefront before tossing the keys over to Mainelli.

The Caprice's air was on full blast by the time Kelly took his seat on the passenger side. Mainelli had unbuttoned the cuffs of his shirt and had his wrists pressed to the vents. After a minute or two of his cool air treatment, Mainelli was ready to go. He put the car into drive just as Kelly's phone vibrated in his pocket. It was Sutherland.

"You in yet?"

"Been in. Mainelli and I are back on location at the market. Just finished up a secondary walk-through and a follow-up canvass. Why? What's up?"

"I got a call from the ME. You guys are on the docket for the morning slot with the slab docs."

"What time?"

"Head over there now."

"Do you know who's performing the autopsy?"

"Does it matter? Just get over there so you don't lose your place."

"On our way." Kelly ended the call and slipped his phone back in his pocket.

Mainelli looked over at him as he slowed for traffic. "What's up?"

"Change of plans. Miss Burke's going to have to wait. We're heading to autopsy."

"Great. I start my day smelling like puke and end it smelling like death."

8

The Office of the Chief Medical Examiner's waiting area was refreshingly cool, and Kelly watched as his partner's ruddy cheeks returned to their normal olive coloring.

Mainelli flapped his collar, fanning the temperature-controlled air into his damp shirt. "I hope this takes all day. Wouldn't mind it one bit."

Kelly, a man not normally concerned with appearances, found himself straightening his shirt and patting down his hair. Out of the corner of his eye, he caught his partner giving him a funny look. But before Mainelli bothered asking why, the door to the secure wing of the building opened and his unasked question was answered. Standing in the doorway was forensic pathologist Ithaca Best. Her shoulder-length jet-black hair had a glossy shine that caught the light, giving it a shimmer.

Mainelli nudged him and whispered through the side of his mouth, "Tuck your tongue in, Romeo."

Kelly blushed and cleared his throat. "I was hoping you'd be helping us out today."

"I looked at the file that was sent over. No round or casing found for comparison?"

"Definitely not a paint-by-numbers kind of murder."

Kelly walked up to the woman who was nearly as tall as he was. Her slender form was disguised under her lab coat and scrubs.

She smiled as he got closer. "You guys ever catch a simple case?"

"Not lately," Kelly offered.

"I think it's his so-called Irish luck. Cases didn't seem so complicated—aw, what's it been—say six months ago." Mainelli punctuated his jest with a second jab to Kelly's ribs.

"Or maybe all your cases were this complicated, but you were too thick to realize it."

Ithaca laughed. "Now, boys, do I need to put you two in time-out? Or shall we go see if our dead friend has something to tell us?"

Ithaca smelled of honey and mint, like freshly steeped herbal tea. Kelly was grateful for the fragrant blast as she moved past him and led him down the corridor.

"Kelly, you called this one in for expedite?"

"I did. Needed to push things along. I've got some concerns with the missing evidence. The lack of any effective leads is going to slow us down. I'd hoped you'd be able to give us something to go on."

"No witnesses either?"

"One. We were on our way to see her when we got the call to head over here."

"Did you take a peek at the clerk yet?"

"Yeah. I did some prelims while I was waiting on you. Figured I'd get an idea of what we're going to be looking at. Not sure how much this morning's examination is going to give you in the way of evidence."

"Only one way to find out."

Ithaca stopped at the door to the pathology room. She used her key card to log in and unlock the door. The three entered.

Several of the tables had bodies actively being worked on by other pathologists and their teams. Ithaca walked through the center of the room that was divided into two rows of metallic beds. She didn't speak to her coworkers, who were deeply involved in various stages of their death investigations. Kelly heard the hushed speech as they recorded their findings. No other cops were present. Not all autopsies called for it. Murder was the exception.

Tucker Grayson's body lay separated from the others on the farthest table on the right. An opaque plastic sheet covered him from the neck down.

Ithaca donned a surgical mask and retrieved a pair of light blue powder-free nitrile gloves.

Mainelli reached for a box of large gloves under the wheeled metallic tray table where her instruments were set. Kelly caught the box as Mainelli tossed it to him, and both men donned gloves as well.

The synthetic material didn't breathe, and even in the cold room, Kelly felt the sweat begin to pool inside the gloves. He looked at Mainelli, whose sausage fingers were packed tightly, and laughed. "You know they make them in extra-large too."

"Too late. Ain't no way I'm going to try and peel these things off now. Took me too long to get 'em on."

Ithaca held up the recorder and activated it. A red light flashed, indicating the official beginning of the autopsy.

"Today is Wednesday, July 10, 2019. I, Doctor Ithaca Best, pathologist for the Massachusetts Office of the Medical Examiner, will be performing today's autopsy of Tucker Grayson, age twenty-two. Detectives Michael Kelly and James Mainelli of Boston Police Department's Homicide Division are in attendance and will be observing the procedure. Time on the clock reads 10:07 a.m."

Ithaca removed the plastic sheeting and set it on the floor beside the table. The clerk lay naked on the cold hard metal. His mocha skin now had a bluish-purple tint. His face was distorted from the round, causing his left eyeball to bulge out. Otherwise, no signs of injury.

"Single gunshot wound to the head. Entry is through the forehead approximately one inch above the bridge of the nose. Exit wound is located on the back of the skull."

Ithaca photographed the entry wound from several angles. She laid a thin, plastic, disposable L-square ruler beside the hole. "Measurements show the entry to be roughly three-eighths of an inch in diameter. The bullet pierced the frontal bone of the skull." She took photos with the ruler in place before removing it.

Ithaca then examined the remainder of the body but noted nothing unusual. Kelly focused on the hole in the clerk's head.

Ithaca removed the bags from Grayson's hands and squatted low to visually investigate them. She lowered a magnifier and closely examined each finger.

Kelly saw the meticulous approach and offered, "From the report, we don't have any indication there was a struggle or contact with the attacker. We bagged them as a precaution."

"I'm not seeing anything, but that doesn't mean it's not there. I'll swab the fingers and take clippings."

Ithaca set about swabbing the man's fingers, using a new swab for each. She paused each time to tag the swab as potential evidence before moving on to the next, then repeated the process with the fingernails. Kelly assumed the tedium of this would drive Mainelli nuts, but looking at the man, there was no trace of annoyance. He was enjoying his time in the cooler.

Kelly was losing hope the clerk's body held any clues as to the shooter's identity.

Ithaca completed the task as Kelly finished adding some notes to his pad. "You boys ready to help me with the flip?"

Kelly nodded.

Mainelli chuckled. "Heads or tails?"

Kelly slipped his pad in his back pocket, freeing his hands to assist. "No tech's helping you today?"

Ithaca thrust her chin in the direction of the other pathologists. "Little backed up. But no worries. I've got you two to help."

"Lucky us." Mainelli looked down at the body. "Where do you want me?"

She moved around to the head of the table. "Mike, if you'd be so kind as to place your hands here and here." Ithaca tapped the man's left shoulder and left side of the head near the ear. "Jimmy, if you would support the roll at the hip."

Kelly did as instructed and placed his hands in position.

"Just great. Mikey here gets the guy's head and I get to roll his johnson my way. Fair trade."

"I'll make it up to you. Maybe buy you lunch. How does hot dogs sound?"

"I'm going to have you roll him toward you nice and easy. Pull him to his right side and hold."

The iciness of the dead man's skin penetrated the synthetic rubber of the glove. It was a strangely satisfying sensation, the cold combatting the warmth of his shrink-wrapped hands. He pulled. Grayson's body was rigid, having spent the night in cold storage, and moving him proved more difficult than anticipated. Putting a little extra muscle into the movement, Kelly rolled the man to his side with Mainelli's assistance.

Ithaca grabbed her camera and the L-shaped ruler.

"Exit wound is located on the upper portion of the occipital bone just beneath the parietal." She photographed the wound and then went back to the tray and picked up clippers. She shaved off the hair surrounding the wound prior to taking the measurement.

"Size of the exit wound is slightly larger than the entrance, measuring just under seven-sixteenths of an inch in diameter. No observable bullet fragments."

Kelly maintained his hold on the body while Ithaca moved down the man's backside.

Mainelli held the man's thigh but averted his eyes from Grayson's genitalia.

"I'm not seeing anything else. You can roll him onto his back now."

Mainelli sighed. "Thank God."

Kelly rocked the dead man back into a supine position on the table and released him. The cool sensation on his hands lingered a moment longer.

Ithaca hit pause on her recording device. "I've still got to remove the skull and weigh the organs. You are more than welcome to stick around for that, but I'm not so sure it'll be worth your time. Cause of death is pretty much clear-cut. I'll document additional findings, if any, and send them to you in the official report."

"Any thoughts on the type of caliber used?"

"Hard to say with any certainty. But I'd venture a small caliber. In my experience, a twenty-two wouldn't have been capable of creating that exit hole. It'd most likely have rattled around and been lodged inside the brain somewhere. My best guess would be a nine-millimeter or thirty-eight. Could've even been a forty-caliber round, for that matter."

Kelly peeled off his gloves and jotted in his notepad. His damp skin stuck to the paper. "Well, that narrows it down to about a million possibilities."

Ithaca frowned. "And the report said no shell casing was found?"

"No. And no bullet either."

"What do you mean, no bullet?"

Mainelli chimed in, "Looks like whoever did this was smart enough to dig out the bullet from the wall it was stuck in."

"You've got a headshot victim where the killer policed up his brass and removed the lead from the scene? Not a good start."

"Like I said before—Irish luck."

"I'm not sure that's any kinda luck I'd wish for."

Kelly smiled and shrugged. "Well, without it, I'd have no luck at all."

"Sometimes it's good to step back and get perspective. Ever do that?" Ithaca asked.

"I've got my daughter. She helps. Boxing too. Sometimes a couple rounds in the ring clear my head."

Ithaca chuckled. It was a sweet, lyrical giggle. "So, getting punched in the head helps clear yours? Ha, I'll have to take your word for it. I was thinking something more along the lines of dinner."

"Dinner?"

Mainelli had a big shit-eating grin on his face and cocked an eyebrow at Kelly.

"You do eat? Everybody has to eat sometime. Even Homicide detectives." She tilted her head and pulled down her face mask. A tinge of blood from her gloves marked the light blue of her mask. Ithaca took off her gloves and wiped the sweat on her white lab coat. She pulled out a notepad of her own and scribbled in it. "I know a great place."

"Are you asking me to dinner?"

"Don't tell me a girl's never asked you before?"

"I can't say that I can think of a time when."

She grinned. "Then I'm happy to be the first." She tore out a page from her pad and handed it to him.

Kelly was dumbfounded. He took the slip of paper and saw she had written her phone number. He stood between Tucker Grayson's body and Ithaca as a bone saw whizzed behind him.

"So, what's it going to be?"

"I think I'd like that. When were you thinking?"

"Tonight. How's eight sound?"

"Let's make it nine."

"Deal."

Kelly tucked her number into his pocket and turned to leave.

As they walked out of the room, Mainelli leaned in and whispered, "You just got Doctor Death's number. Some guys got all the luck."

"Don't be jealous. I'm sure you've got some vomit to clean up when you get home."

Mainelli shook his head and chuckled. "Where to next, Romeo?"

"Let's check in on the witness. Right now, she's our best chance. Hopefully, she's more talkative than she was last night."

9

Muriel hung her keys on a hook by the door and locked the two deadbolts. She walked into the small one-bedroom efficiency apartment she called home. Today was shaping up to be a very different day for the hardworking woman. She'd eaten her lunch among the dead as she always did, and then found herself with something foreign to her: time.

In a spur-of-the-moment decision, Muriel had done something out of character. She splurged on herself and stopped by a nail salon on her walk home. She chose a fleshy pink coating for her nails. The subtle color would be barely noticeable to anybody else, but to her it was radiant.

Now, back home with her lunch eaten and nails done, Muriel debated on what to do with herself next. She thought about putting the kettle on for some tea, but the oppressive heat of midday deterred the idea. She didn't have an air conditioning unit. She had never seen a need for the luxury item since she was home so little. There was only a set of box fans, one in the living room and one in her bedroom. Neither seemed to be having much effect on the stifling atmosphere.

Tyson's Market was closed for the day while the owner's

family worked on getting it cleaned up. She was told she would be able to return to work once everything was done. And so, for the first time since she could remember, Muriel Burke had a day off from stocking and cleaning. Sadly, she didn't know what to do with herself.

Taking a seat in the worn recliner, she sat in the quiet and listened as the fan struggled to move the thick air. Death had given her a break and she decided to enjoy it. Pulling the wooden handle, careful not to damage her newly painted nails, she released the footrest. Feet elevated and her body in a semi-supine position, she closed her eyes and prepared to revel in her first ever siesta.

A loud knock on the door startled her, rousing her from her moment of bliss. Muriel waited, hoping whoever it was would give up and go away. She assumed it was the police following up with her. No need to answer. She didn't plan to tell them any more than she had last night.

She lay there, remaining still.

Three more bangs on the door, this time louder than before. If it was the cops, she thought it rude of them to be so persistent.

"Ms. Burke, I'd like to take a moment of your time and talk about last night. I know you are home."

She reset the chair to its original position and stood up. The recliner springs squeaked loudly as her weight lifted, releasing the coils' tension. Walking to the door, she peered through the peephole and eyed the man standing there. He had dark, neatly combed hair. He was clean-cut and wearing a white button-down shirt untucked at the waist. His hands were in his pockets and he had a casual air about him. It was not the detective she'd spoken with outside the store nor anybody she recalled seeing before.

"I'd like to be left alone, if you don't mind. I really don't have anything else to say to the police," she said through the door.

"Good. Because I'm not with the police."

Muriel thought for a moment and then felt a jolt of excitement. It was probably one of Mr. Walsh's employees coming to pay her off. Missing a day's pay at the market made the prospect of another hundred-dollar payment even more appealing.

Her hand dawdled near the locks for only a moment longer before she made up her mind. Unlocking the two deadbolts and opening the door, she stood face to face with the man. Without the distortion of the fisheye lens, she could see he was a man of impressive physical appearance. Chiseled muscles lay just beneath the thin layer of the cotton-blend fabric of his shirt.

"Ms. Burke, may I come in for a moment. I promise not to take much of your time."

He was well-spoken and regarded her with a warm smile, lowering her perpetual sense of dread. "I was just about to take a nap."

"Like I said, this won't take but a minute of your time. But what we have to talk about is best said in private."

This last statement solidified in her mind the purpose of the visit. Muriel stepped back from the door, allowing the man to enter. He walked past her, his broad shoulder gently brushing her as he moved into the living room. He paused momentarily and peered in the open door of the bedroom as he passed. Gesturing toward the small two-seater couch, he asked, "May I have a seat?"

"Of course." Muriel resumed her spot on the recliner as the man sat on the small loveseat. She didn't extend the footrest.

With the only two pieces of furniture now occupied, her apartment felt crowded. She hadn't had another person there since her father died. The man's presence made her uncomfortable in her own home. She now regretted letting him inside. She wanted nothing more than to complete this conversation and get back to her peace and quiet. Last time Walsh's crew paid her to keep silent, they had shown up at the store. But then again, the store was now temporarily closed, so it made sense they would come here. Maybe the most unsettling thing about this unannounced visit was the fact that the Irish mob knew where she lived.

"I didn't see anything. I know how this works. And I want you to know that I didn't say anything to the police."

"Now, Muriel—you don't mind if I call you Muriel, do you?"

"I suppose not." She thought about asking his name, for conversational purposes and general politeness, but decided against it. Probably better for her to know as little as possible about the man sitting in her living room.

He leaned back and stretched his arm wide, resting it on the back of the loveseat. The raised arm's position exposed the top handle or grip of a gun. Seeing the weapon, Muriel was even gladder she hadn't asked the man's name.

He must've realized she'd seen the weapon because he looked down at his hip where it was tucked in his waistband. He made no effort to shield it and offered no apologies; in fact, he smiled.

"Don't be alarmed, my dear. I'm not here to hurt you. I just need to know what you know. Maybe you can help me figure some things out. Does all this sound reasonable?"

Though she was normally steadfast and calm, Muriel's nerves were rattled by the man sitting before her. Her words didn't hide her worry, and she stammered slightly as she said, "Sounds fair."

"Good. I would like us to get off on the right foot, though, and to do that, I need you to be one hundred percent honest with me. And in the short time we've talked, you've already lied once."

"I didn't lie."

"Shh. We'll get this sorted out. Don't you worry. You did tell me you didn't say anything to the police. But we both know that isn't completely true. Isn't it?"

Her face contorted. "I tried to keep my mouth shut, but they pressed me. I just wanted to get home, so I told them just a little something to get them to leave me alone. I'm sorry."

The dark-haired man gave a dismissive wave of his hand. "What is it that you told them?"

"That I saw the man kill Tucker."

"And?"

"And that he had a tattoo on his neck."

"See. That wasn't so hard."

Muriel fidgeted with the tattered armrest cover, pulling at a loose thread. With stress consuming her, she no longer worried about damaging her pretty nails. "Is Mr. Walsh mad at me?"

"Who said anything about Walsh?"

Heart in throat, she swallowed hard. "I just thought you worked for him."

The man took his arm off the back of the couch. As he leaned forward with his elbows on his knees, the gun disappeared from view. The look in the man's eyes was terrifying. "And what if I do? Are you going to tell that to the cops when they stop by?"

"No. Never!" Her voice pitched and she squirmed in her seat, causing the old springs to squeak. "I helped him before. I told them who robbed them the last time. I understand how things work around this neighborhood."

"Why don't you tell me about that."

"Tell you what?"

"How things work."

Her breathing had changed with the rapid beating of her heart, and she suddenly felt it difficult to breathe. The muggy air didn't help the situation. "Mr. Walsh runs protection for the store. If something happens, we tell him, and he takes care of it."

"Do the cops work for Walsh?"

She wasn't exactly sure if this was a trick question. "Um—no."

"But yet you still told them about the shooter. You told them about the tattoo. You gave them information that would've been valuable to us. What happens if somebody with a tattoo on his neck ends up missing or dead? Where do you think they'll point the finger?"

Her eyes began to water. "I'm sorry. It was a mistake. I just wanted to go home."

The man paused and began gently caressing the smooth skin of his chin. This silence, no matter how brief, terrified her. When she'd first opened the door, she was secretly giddy at the prospect of extra money. Abandoning all hope of a payday, she now worried if she'd keep her life.

"You look absolutely terrified, my dear. It's not my intention to scare you. But my job is a very important one. And I'm very thorough in what I do."

She nodded. "How can I make this right?"

"Is there anything you think might help locate the person responsible for shooting up a store under our protection?"

"The tattoo was two letters: C and B. Not sure what it means. But maybe that will help?" The prospect of reward money started to enter her mind again. If he was asking questions, maybe she was valuable to him.

"Do you think you'd be able to recognize the person if you saw him again?"

Muriel shrugged. "Maybe, but it would only be by the tattoo. I never saw his face. It was covered with a bandana."

"There's nothing else?"

"No."

"Well, I think that's all I need from you for now." The man stood. He adjusted himself after spending the last few minutes on the low couch. Towering over her, he straightened his shirt, pulling it over the weapon.

He pulled out a folded wad of cash from his front pocket and began flipping out the bills. She counted six twenties. Twenty more than she'd received the last two times she assisted Walsh's crew.

He stretched out his hand, the crisp bills neatly stacked on his open palm. "Muriel, you've been a real gem. Thank you."

She reached out for the money, and then something in the man's words sent a chill down her spine. She froze, fingertips delicately quivering against the edge of one of the bills. She tried to hide her panic.

He smiled, handing her the money. Without another word, he walked to the door. With the distance each step created, Muriel felt her tension begin to fade.

And then, instead of opening the door, he did something that brought back her fear tenfold.

He turned the latches with a thud, locking both deadbolts in place.

10

It took a little over forty-five minutes to drive from the ME's office to Muriel Burke's residence. Traffic slowed them but so did Mainelli's need to stop for a sandwich. At least the loud grunted chews replaced his partner's incessant teasing of his upcoming date with the pathologist.

Burke's complex was a rectangular building near the corner of Upham Avenue and Wilbur Street. The red brick exterior's base was tagged in graffiti. Not the renderings of a street artist but of taggers whose barely legible scribblings would pass for a first grader's handwriting. Kelly noted the patches of white where the building's super occasionally made a weak attempt to cover it up.

"Hopefully, she's more talkative today than she was last night. Didn't give me much in the way of info, but I felt she had more to tell. Something in the look she gave when she told me about the tattoo. Maybe it's nothing, but definitely worth a shot."

Mainelli wolfed down the last bite of his sandwich. A smidge of mayo was on the corner of his mouth and Kelly considered not telling him, payback for the last three-quarters of an hour while he endured his taunts. He decided to cut him a break and gestured to his lip. "Looks like you just earned twenty bucks working the corner."

Mainelli took the hint and wiped the dregs of dressing from his face. "Let's hope she's more open than the old guy from earlier. And let's hope she's not on the top floor. I think I'm finally recovered from the last climb."

Kelly poked at Mainelli's soft waistline. "You know, Jimmy, you're more than welcome to come with me to the gym anytime you feel like it."

"Yeah right. And let you and your knucklehead childhood friends use me as their personal punching bag. No thanks."

"Just saying. A few rounds wouldn't kill you."

Mainelli stepped out. "Says who?"

A homeless man was picking out a partially smoked cigarette from a nearby trashcan as they walked up the concrete steps to the thick glass door entry. It was unlocked and led into a space containing a metal callbox. Kelly pulled on the inner door, but it was secured.

Mainelli went over to the callbox, pressed the button labeled *Burke*, and waited.

Nothing. He pressed it again. No response.

Mainelli then began pressing buttons at random. "Somebody's got to be home in this place."

A low-tone beep and click sounded. A raspy voice crackled through the intercom. "Who's buzzin'?"

"Boston Police. Trying to get up to apartment 3A."

The person didn't respond. A moment later the door to the first-floor hallway opened and a heavyset woman wearing a faded floral nightgown cautiously approached. Her ensemble looked as though she'd knitted it herself from a used couch. She held a yellow and brown tabby. The cat looked to be on the last of its nine lives.

She coughed loudly, a smoker's cough. Clearing her throat, she snarled, "Let me see the badges."

Kelly squared himself to the woman. The badge dangling from the chain was centered on his chest. Mainelli indulged the woman, turning his right hip toward her and displaying the badge and gun clipped to his beltline.

The cat woman pulled the door open and turned away.

"Thanks," Kelly offered.

The woman said nothing as she waddled away.

"3A." Kelly offered Mainelli a consolatory shrug. "At least it's not the top floor."

His partner shook his head and rolled his eyes.

Kelly led the way up the staircase to the third-floor entrance. Entering the hallway, they were overwhelmed by a heavy mustiness. The worn carpet was damp, and the walls were sweating. Apparently, management didn't splurge on air conditioning for the common spaces.

"My God, it's like a damn swamp in here," Mainelli griped.

The two made their way to 3A. Kelly knocked on the door. No stirring from inside.

He knocked again. A door opened from the apartment on the opposite side of the hallway. They turned to see a well-dressed younger woman in a blue pants suit. She exited with a small brown leather attaché case in hand.

"You guys are back again? Must be something important."

"What do you mean, back again?"

"Sorry. I just assumed you were with the other guy. He came banging on the door not too long ago. I peeked out my peephole."

"What guy? What'd he look like?" Kelly asked, concerned.

"Like you, I guess. Only saw the back of him. Well-dressed, dark hair. Why? Is there a problem?"

"No."

"She keeps to herself. Not used to seeing visitors at her door." In that moment, as the woman finished locking her door, she must've finally noticed the badges. "Oh, I didn't realize you guys were cops. Is Muriel okay?"

"Yeah, we just wanted to talk with her."

"I've got to run. I'm late for a job interview."

"Thanks for the heads up about the other guy. Sorry if we startled you." Kelly felt it best to minimize the concern in the nosey neighbor's mind.

She darted down the dank hallway and disappeared through the stairwell door.

Kelly unholstered his sidearm. "Got a bad feeling about this."

Kelly gripped the doorknob and turned it slowly. Mainelli took up position behind him with his weapon drawn at the low ready.

The door was unlocked. Once open, Kelly pressed it wide with his foot. "Muriel, this is Detective Kelly with the Boston Police. We spoke last night. My partner and I are coming in to make sure you're okay. Say something if you can hear us."

Kelly listened before moving forward. The only sound was a fan working overtime in the heat.

With Mainelli at his back, he entered the tight hall leading into the efficiency apartment. Two steps in, Kelly was able to see down the hallway and into the living room. Protruding out from behind a recliner were a woman's bare feet.

Kelly moved quickly into the room, visually sweeping and clearing the kitchen and open bedroom as he went. Mainelli was tight on his heels.

Rounding the corner into the living room, Kelly saw the woman sprawled out on the floor, a lamp cord around her throat. The soft blue coloring in her face indicated the high probability of death, but he knelt down to search for a pulse. Finding none, he stood and backed away from the body.

The two completed a more detailed search of the apartment to make sure the killer was no longer inside.

Kelly and Mainelli then retreated to the hallway, not wanting to further contaminate the crime scene.

Returning his gun to his holster, Kelly pulled out his cell. He called dispatch and relayed their findings.

The second call was to his sergeant. "Sarge, we're at the corner store robbery witness's apartment."

"She give you anything to go on?"

"No." He looked back into the apartment. "She's dead."

11

"Where's Charles?" Kelly asked the arriving tech.

"He's coming. Just lagging behind a bit. Probably stuck behind a ton of unpacked boxes."

Trent Dawes was relatively new to Boston's Crime Scene Response Unit. He'd come to BPD's Forensic Group only a few months prior to Kelly's arrival to Homicide. Dawes was in his late twenties, but his freckled face made him look younger. Kelly didn't know much about the kid. He'd assisted on a few cases but had never taken the lead. Dawes seemed bright enough, but in the short time Kelly had been working the death beat, he'd developed a rapport with the senior-most technician. Ray Charles's experience was second to none, and Kelly found himself learning something new every time they worked a scene together.

Kelly had cut his teeth on the Faith Wilson murder, and it had been Charles who'd helped him put the forensic pieces of the puzzle together. Kelly felt strongly that every murder deserved the highest quality investigators. He didn't like the idea of working the scene in Charles's absence, but time was of the essence. A second body lay before him, and he knew without a doubt more would follow if he couldn't get a handle on this case. As of right now, he felt the investigation slipping through his fingers.

"Shall we get started?" Dawes asked. He opened a metal clipboard and clicked his pen into the ready position. "Give me the details of the actions you took upon entering."

"We spoke to a neighbor who said a man had been here before us. I became concerned and checked the door to see if it was unlocked."

Dawes scribbled notes onto the pad. "Were you gloved?"

The question wasn't accusatory, but it still stung. He knew his grip on the knob could've potentially contaminated possible latent prints. "No gloves."

Dawes made note of Kelly's admission. "Go on."

"I turned the knob and opened the door. We entered, took a direct path to the body, and then conducted a secondary search of the apartment before backing out."

"Did you touch anything besides the doorknob?"

He nodded. "Yes. The decedent."

Dawes looked up from the clipboard. His eyebrows arched upward. "You touched the body?"

"Had to confirm she was dead."

"It wasn't readily apparent?"

Kelly noted a hint of judgment in the young tech's voice. He wished Charles were there. He'd already told the senior man his rationale in confirming death, even in the most obvious of circumstances. But he didn't feel like retelling the Anita Tandy story, when the blood-covered woman he'd believed was dead reached out and grabbed his leg. "I always check."

Dawes shrugged it off dismissively. "Where was the contact made?"

"I checked the pulse by touching two fingers to the right side of her carotid. Nothing else in the apartment was touched or disturbed while inside. Minus the doorknob, which I already told you. You have my prints and DNA on file, so elimination shouldn't be an issue. I marked our time of entry in my notepad." Kelly looked at his notes and then his watch. "Which was forty-seven minutes ago. Mainelli's started the crime scene log. Nobody's been in or out since." Kelly rattled off the information in rapid-fire succession.

Dawes bit the end of his pen and absently bobbed his head as he processed the information. He then uncapped the lens of the camera strapped around his neck. "I'm going to start with taking the overalls and then work my way inside. When I've got the photos done, I'll call you in. Hopefully, Charles will be here by then to assist in bagging and tagging the evidence."

"Do your thing."

Dawes stepped back from the door and snapped the first photo. "To be honest, I hope he runs a little late. I'd like to have an opportunity to prove myself. Tough being the new guy."

"Trust me, I know. Take your time and do it right," Kelly said.

"Well, don't take too long. It's hot as blazes and there's no A/C in there." Mainelli wiped a layer of sweat from his forehead using his damp sleeve. Beads of moisture immediately returned. "Or out here." He then began fanning himself with his notepad. "She's going to be pretty ripe soon, and I'd prefer to be long gone by then."

Dawes stepped back from the door. Kelly and Mainelli moved behind him, ensuring they stayed out of the picture. The tech then moved into the apartment, stopping every few steps to snap several pictures.

Dawes took his time and, from what Kelly saw, did a thorough job of the photography. He disappeared around the corner and worked deeper into the living room. Several minutes passed before he returned to the hallway.

"Detectives, prelims are done. If you guys want to come in now and start identifying items of evidentiary interest, you're more than welcome to begin."

Mainelli and Kelly both signed the logbook, noting the time of re-entry. Mainelli then handed it off to the young patrolman who'd been assigned the job of maintaining it from there on out.

The three men entered the apartment.

From clearing it earlier, Kelly knew the layout, but now he entered with a different mindset. Before, his sole purpose was the preservation of life; now, he walked through the short, narrow hallway methodically looking for any potential evidence that might lead them to the killer. The idea of more is better. He'd rather collect thirty items of interest and later find most were unrelated than pick up only a few to learn he'd missed a critical piece of the puzzle.

Muriel Burke kept a tidy home with minimal clutter. It was as if she had barely lived there. The kitchen looked undisturbed. No dishes in the sink. No plates on the table. All the cabinets were closed.

Kelly entered and walked to the sink area. He looked at the surrounding counter and in the metal basin. Both were bone dry. He'd hoped maybe the killer had washed up and a chance of trace DNA would be present, but it seemed not to be the case. In fact, he guessed the faucet hadn't recently been used at all.

Mainelli seemed distracted and Kelly saw him look at his watch for a second time since they entered the apartment. "Everything okay?"

"Yeah. Babysitter messaged me. Tony's still throwing up. He's running a high fever."

"Gabriella's not able to get home?"

"Not today. She's got her promotional interview today. End

of day." Mainelli exhaled loudly. "What can I say? My son's got impeccable timing."

"Look, I get it. Cut out of here. I've got this."

"You sure?" His face brightened and he perked up. "I hate to stiff you. Pun intended. Hate to leave you with Freckles here."

"Funny. Seriously, go. I'll fill you in later." Kelly thumbed over at the young tech. "Plus, Dawes here doesn't sweat nearly as much."

"You're sure?"

"Go. I'll catch a ride back with one of the patrol guys. Don't worry about it."

"Thanks."

Mainelli hustled out of the apartment, tearing off his Tyvek booties as he crossed the hallway threshold. His departure left Kelly and the freckle-faced Dawes to the task at hand.

Kelly moved into the living room and stopped near the recliner. Its footrest was extended, which, coupled with her position on the floor, led him to believe she'd been seated at the time of the attack. Maintaining a level of detachment was necessary in his line of work, but seeing her lying on the ground with her feet bare made him sad for the woman.

The supplemental report containing Burke's information stated her position as a stocker for the corner store was one of two jobs she worked. Her thick, swollen ankles indicated most, if not all, of her long days were spent on her feet. Yet, feet up in her recliner she was attacked and killed. A hard life met with a bitter end. And Kelly felt an overwhelming sense of purpose to make right what he could.

"Detective Kelly, I'm going to swab the lamp cord. Let's hope the doer didn't wear gloves. The grip strength and force used to strangle her lends itself to a high probability of transfer DNA."

"Agreed. And please call me Mike." Kelly edged himself

around her body, making an effort not to come in contact with her.

The index and middle fingers of her left hand were snared between the cord and her neck. "Looks like she put up a fight. Got her fingers in before it was cinched down."

"Hell of a way to go. I've got a laundry list of ways I don't want to die and this ranks in at number five."

Burke's right arm was outstretched over her head with the palm open. Kelly rounded her head and squatted low. He leaned forward and got within an inch of her right hand, studying the fingertips carefully. "Looks like our fighter might've got a piece of our perp. I need you to get some shots of her hands and then bag 'em."

"Sure thing."

"Knock, knock."

Kelly looked up to see Sergeant Sutherland hobble into the room. He stood and wiped a bead of sweat from his brow.

"Where's Jimmy?"

"Kid's sick. I think he's got to run him to the doc."

"I'm working hard on getting Anderson's replacement. Hoping to have somebody in his seat sooner rather than later." The big sergeant seemed to be suffering from the heat as badly as Mainelli. "I can lend a hand if you need."

"I think I've got it from here. Dawes said Ray will be along shortly."

Sutherland looked down at the dead woman. His face held no reaction. As a longtime member of Homicide, death, in all its forms, was now an unremarkable thing. He sighed loudly. "This is a real problem. The only potential witness is dead within hours of a murder she saw. I don't like it. Not one bit."

"Neither do I. Maybe she'll still be able to help us out."

Sutherland looked at Kelly cockeyed. "Please don't tell me

you're able to communicate with the dead. All I need is some ghost-whispering cop in my unit."

Kelly gave a soft chuckle and pointed down at Burke's outstretched right hand. "Looks like she might've got a piece of the bastard who did this. We'll know more once her body is on the table."

"When you called me, I immediately reached out to the medical examiner's office and asked them to move this case to top priority. I'm doing my best to bulldoze a path through the bureaucratic red tape and expedite any potential evidentiary leads. You let me know if you run into any roadblocks."

"Will do."

With that said, Sutherland turned and headed back out the way he'd come. His damaged knee caused the heavyset man to step unevenly. The injury, a shattered kneecap, occurred a few years back while chasing a perp. Sutherland now spent as much time battling with the medical disability board to get his rating changed as he did supervising the unit.

"I want updates as they come in," Sutherland called out from the hallway before departing.

12

"You ready to do this?" Lincoln White was his usual cool and collected self. But the man's violent temper always rested just beneath the pristine surface of his flat demeanor.

"Don't really have much of a choice, do I?" Brayden asked with enough false bravado to hopefully mask his fear.

"Everybody has a choice. It's the consequences that drive us. And I'm guessing, because you're here now, that you've weighed yours and made the right one."

"If you say so." Brayden sat in the back of the beat-up Town Car.

They were parked on the one-way street at Lexondale Avenue. Somebody had opened the hydrant down the street on Hilltop. Water sprayed out onto the street, and the kids playing at Martin Park left their playscape to dance in the improved water feature, cooling themselves off from the day's oppressive heat. Brayden remembered doing the same in his youth. He also knew it was only a matter of time until the fire department would arrive to put an end to this party.

The sight of the children laughing and playing did little to calm his nerves. His stomach butterflies had returned, and their invisible wings beat madly inside him.

White flicked him in the knee to get his attention. "Listen carefully. I'm going to tell you how we do business. You need to understand you won't be able to pull any bullshit with us. We can smell it a mile away. And we've got eyes everywhere."

Brayden turned his attention back to White's steely-eyed glare but said nothing.

"Brooks here is going to give you a full search. We've got to make sure you didn't bring anything with you. No contraband when we meet. That means no needles, and definitely no drugs. You got anything on you before we run your pockets?"

Brayden looked down at his front pocket and gave an impish nod. Part of him was embarrassed at having to admit he was dumb enough to show up to a meet with a cop holding a kit. The other part of him was worried they'd toss it and he'd have to find a new one.

"Take it out and put it on the seat beside you. Brooks is a pretty easy-going guy, but if he gets poked by one of your dirty ass needles, I won't be able to stop the hurting he'll put on you."

Brayden removed the capped needle he'd picked up earlier from the clinic. He then removed a clear plastic bottle cap and tie-off shoestring from the depths of his front pocket.

"We're going to drive around to a spot with fewer eyes and get set up."

The Town Car drove away from the park. They sat in silence until White pulled onto a service road off Gallivan Boulevard, an access point for the Codman Yard train service area. At this time of day, it was unoccupied. White pulled up alongside a small rectangular substation that looked like a doublewide trailer. The spot was secluded from view, and Brayden realized White and his narc guys must use this as one of their staging areas. He assumed they had places like this throughout the city.

Brooks got out. He didn't look as much like Magnum P.I. today. He wore a tight black T-shirt that stretched to fit around his oversized biceps. He opened Brayden's door and stood aside.

Brayden faced the bull of a man and exited. Although he was taller than the stocky man, the cop's size intimidated him. Without any pleasantries, Brooks spun him in the same unfriendly way he'd done on the previous night when he shook him down for the three bags. The cop's hands began the systematic process of searching him. No place was off limits, and the man spent time digging around his groin area, pushing and manipulating his testicles. "Find something you like?"

Brooks squeezed hard and Brayden instantly regretted making the comment. Brayden knew from experience a lot of cops didn't go to this extreme during a shakedown and therefore missed one of the best hiding areas for drugs. Brooks was obviously not one of them. And by his search methods, damn near strip-searching him, Brayden was convinced the man missed little if anything.

"You smell like shit."

"Thanks. It's a new cologne. You should try it."

The man shoved him back into the car. Not much of a bedside manner, Brayden thought to himself as he resumed his seat.

White put out his hand. "Let me see your ball cap."

Brayden handed over his faded Sox cap. His greasy hair flopped into his eyes.

"This is going to be activated as soon as we drop you off." White held a needle with a balled end. He pushed it into the fabric of the hat under the brim.

"What the hell is that? You didn't say nothin' about wearing a damn wire. Are you serious? You're going to get me killed."

"It's a micro camera. We use them all the time. Nobody will notice."

"I don't want to wear no micro camera crap when I do this. Ain't happening!"

White twisted in his seat, filling the space between the front seats, and leaned closer. "Do you really want to test my patience? I'm sure you've heard stories about me, either on the street or from your saintly brother."

Brayden mentally strained to hold his ground against the intimidating man. A failed effort. He looked down at his feet and bobbed his head in solemn acknowledgement. Brayden knew Lincoln White's reputation. Everybody in the drug world did.

"And what have you heard?"

Brayden shrugged. "Things."

"C'mon now. We're all friends here."

Brayden looked up to see White's broad grin twisting up into a snarl. His eyes had a wildness to them. A face that would give Jack Nicholson a run for his money in the creepy department.

"What do they say about me?"

Brayden mumbled some indecipherable gibberish. He wasn't even sure himself what he said.

White slammed the bottom of his fist on the gray leather of the center console. "Speak up! What. Is. It. They. Say?"

"You're dangerous."

"That's not what I'm looking for. I know that. I want to hear you say what they call it when people cross my path?"

"A Whitewash."

White retreated with a look of smug contentedness. "That's right. And do you know why they call it that?"

"Because nobody ever sees them again."

"I guess it's safe to say you get it." He turned away and stared out the front windshield.

Brooks took his place in the void between the seats. "You're going to wear the camera. I will activate it before you get out of the car and turn it off when you get back in. Don't say a word to me or White once the camera's on, and keep your head down when you get back in this car until I shut it off. Is that clear?"

"When they see this video, they'll know it's me. I'll be good as dead."

"How good a memory do you think these dealers have? To them you're just another junkie. A thousand more just like you will come and go before this video would ever be released in court. And more than ninety percent of the cases get pled out, so it's likely nobody but us will ever see it."

"It just feels wrong."

"Don't give me your code of honor line of crap. Some honor among thieves story. You're a two-bit junkie, one bad batch away from your last day. Save the bullshit for someone else."

"With friends like you, who needs enemies?"

"Okay, funny guy, here's the way it goes. We're going to drop you a couple blocks away from the meet location. They sell out the back of the bar. We've had some trouble getting a good buy into the place. And that's where you come in. I need you to face the dealer during the exchange. I want his face on that video when the deal is made. Got me?"

"If you've had trouble in the past, what makes you think I'll be able to pull this off?"

"Because you grew up with him."

"Who?"

"Tommy Sullivan."

"Whoa—hold on. Tommy Bones? You want me to buy into Conner Walsh's crew? Are you out of your mind? You might as well put a bullet in my head right now. A Whitewash ain't nothin' compared to what those guys will do if they ever find out."

White cracked his knuckles but didn't turn. He only stared

back through the rearview mirror. If looks could kill, Brayden had just taken two to the chest.

Brooks snapped his fingers in front of Brayden's face. "This isn't some democracy here. Get it out of your damned head that you got some kind of choice in this."

Brayden wanted nothing more than to grab the man's thick wrist and snap it, but looking down at his frail condition, he knew without a doubt it would end badly for him.

"You grew up with Tommy, right?" Brooks continued.

"A couple houses down. But I'm guessing if you're asking, then you already knew that."

White impatiently drummed his fingers on the steering wheel. "I know everything that goes on around here. Everything. That's something you need to think hard about. There can be no lies between us. For as long as we decide to use you."

"I thought it was a one-and-done? You snatched me on a couple bags of dope and what—I owe you for the rest of my life?"

"I didn't say the rest of your life. I'm saying you owe me until I say you don't."

"If you say so."

White stopped drumming. "I just did." He gritted his teeth. "You Kellys think you're something special. Well, I'm here to tell you, you're not. That goes for your self-righteous brother as well. Don't give me a reason to prove that point."

Being in White's presence for this little eye-opening meeting of the minds made it readily apparent Mike would've deplored working with the man during his time in Narcotics. He could imagine the butting of heads that must've taken place between these two.

Brayden offered no counterargument. No attempt to defend his family name or his brother's honor. He resigned himself to his circumstance and to the two men who now held the keys to

his invisible shackles and the unknown amount of time he'd
been sentenced to their servitude.

Brayden hissed, "Then what are we waiting for?"

Brooks pulled out three twenties from an envelope marked
buy money and handed them to Brayden.

He folded the bills and stuffed them into his pocket where
the kit once was.

"You're buying a bundle."

"A bundle doesn't cost sixty."

"You haven't bought from them before. They may highball
you. I don't want you having any reason to come back for more.
Whatever you don't spend comes back to us. Is that clear?"

Brayden nodded.

"Don't do anything stupid like trying to skim a bag off the
top."

"What if he shorts me?"

"There better be ten bags in that bundle when you get back
in this car. All I'm going to say about that."

"Anything else?"

"Just be your charming junkie self and I'm sure everything
will work out great. Remember, you do this shit on a daily basis.
No need to be nervous. It ain't like you got to worry about us
cops busting you. So, relax."

"Sure. Relax."

"Easiest money you'll ever make." White smiled at him
through the rearview mirror. "You might actually find you like
working for us."

"One last question. What if the camera doesn't work—ya
know, malfunctions or something?"

Brooks rolled his eyes, the annoyance clear on his face. "We
tested it before we picked you up. It's working fine. Plus, we've
got eyes on you and the place the whole time. You won't see
them, but trust me, they're there."

Brayden rubbed his sweaty palms against the oily filth of his jeans. "Let's get this over with."

White backed out of the spot.

Brooks turned to face front. "Now that's the spirit. Welcome aboard."

13

Music poured from the open doors of JW's Irish Pub. Brayden had spent many a night bellied up to the lacquered wood of the bar and knew most of its patrons by name, if not reputation. It had been a while since he'd set foot inside. Any money he had lately went to other things. Well, to one thing. And that was the reason he was in his current predicament.

He'd known drugs were pushed out of the bar. Although, knowing this particular establishment belonged to Conner Walsh, he'd always avoided getting his fix from here. Felt it was safer to strike out in other parts of the neighborhood. But his shitty luck had brought him here now, and he hated the idea of it. Not everybody from the neighborhood, especially his friends who frequented the watering hole, knew about his habit. And he was worried about exposing himself to their judgment.

Brayden wasn't going in the front door. There was a secondary brick building set back behind the main pub. He knew Walsh and his crew did much of their business there. And that's where he was instructed by White to make contact.

A cold buy was always problematic. Dealers didn't like walk-ins. Especially dealers moving weight. Which Brayden knew was the case.

A walk-up made dealers suspect for several reasons. And it raised questions.

Brayden wanted to turn back, but knew his fate was sealed if he did. He tucked his hands deep in his pockets and walked head down to the back of the building.

He passed a middle-aged man wearing paint-stained cargo pants and an identically coated T-shirt. The man wobbled slightly as he smoked a cigarette and held a glass filled with dark beer. His weathered face drew up into a crinkled smile as he warily eyed Brayden as he passed.

Brayden ignored the drunk man's glance and continued to his destination.

The one-story back building was small, tucked neatly behind the main bar, and looked like an office front to a storage facility. And maybe at one time it had been used for that purpose. A larger building was attached on the left with a metal roll-up bulk delivery door. Brayden found himself wondering what type of deliveries had been received through those doors since Walsh bought the space.

The concrete walls were painted pale sandy beige. No sign hung above the door. No indication as to what the building was used for. One window was set into the right side, but its glass was painted black.

Brayden walked to the door. A small surveillance camera was tucked in the corner of the flat roof's slight overhanging lip, angled directly down to the spot where he now stood. He dipped his head, hoping the hat would block his face from view.

His heart thumped wildly. Regardless of what White and Brooks said, there was nothing easy about this.

He worked to control the tremble in his hand as he knocked on the door.

Brayden pushed his hands into his pockets and fumbled with the money he'd been given. A screech of metal on concrete came from somewhere inside.

"Who's knocking?" a thick, angry voice called through the closed door.

"Brayden." He choked on his words. "Here to see Bones."

"Brayden who?"

"Kelly."

Something scraped along the metal of the door, followed by a loud thud. He heard two mechanical clicks of a deadbolt release before the door opened.

Standing in the threshold was Tommy Sullivan. At six foot eight inches and weighing roughly three hundred pounds, the man was intimidating under normal circumstances. But now, with the additional mental burden of Brayden's task, he seemed even more formidable. Then he saw the scar underneath the big man's left eye and remembered the day when Michael had given it to him. They were teenagers at the time, but Sullivan was already close to his current size. He couldn't remember what started the fight, but he did remember how it ended: watching his older brother lay out the giant with a single right cross.

"Christ. Look at you."

"Good to see you too, Sully." Most called him Bones, simply because the big man had broken so many of them in service to Walsh over the years. But Brayden knew him before all that and therefore called him by his childhood nickname.

"I wish I could say the same." Sullivan eyed him up and down, then looked back over his shoulder.

Brayden couldn't see past the man. "You servin' today?"

"Not sure what you're asking. Bar's around front. You're in our warehouse area."

"C'mon, Sully. Don't be an asshole. You know what I'm asking for."

The big man leaned forward, his bulk towering closer. "Did you just call me an asshole?"

Brayden looked at the man's balled fist. "No, I said don't be an asshole. Big difference."

The fist opened and Sullivan stepped back slightly. "You were always a smartass. Looks like nothing's changed."

Brayden thought about giving his classic retort, *better than being a dumbass*, but decided not to push the larger man's patience. "So, how about it?"

"Do you know what your brother would do if he found out? I don't need him breathing down my neck."

Brayden knew the man meant he didn't want Michael kicking the crap out of him again. Knowing how deeply the childhood beat down had scarred the mob's muscle gave him a sense of pleasure.

"Look, I'm hurting, man. My guy's blowing me off. I need to get right."

Sullivan looked out to the alley lot. The drunk painter was now gone.

"Step inside." The behemoth moved aside, opening the door just wide enough for Brayden to slip past.

Brayden entered. His eyes took a moment to adjust to the dim light. A back room had its door slightly ajar, and inside, he could see several men huddled around a table. They were old-timers, and at first glance, they looked to be playing a hand of poker. Upon closer inspection, Brayden realized that was not the case.

Several white packages were stacked neatly in the center of the round card table. One package was open, and the crew worked diligently to divide up its contents into smaller bags. A feeble man with wispy chalk-white hair peered out through coke-bottle glasses. Seeing Brayden, he stood and slammed the door shut.

"Don't mind the old bastards. They get nervous anytime somebody new comes in."

"I see that." Brayden fidgeted with the money in his pocket.

"What do you need?"

"Bundle."

"That's it? Shit, man, this ain't no corner hustle operation. People don't come here trying to cop some piddly bundle."

Brayden looked over at the closed door and then back at Sullivan. And in that moment, he was struck by an unplanned opportunity. One he hoped would clear his obligation with White. "Look, Sully. I've got a guy. He wanted me to come get a sample of the product before he went all in."

Sullivan laughed. "You've got a guy? You don't even have a place to take a freakin' shower, but you've got a guy."

"Forget it." Brayden turned to leave. "I just thought we could make some good cash together. I'll catch you later."

The big man grabbed him by the shoulder. "Hold on. Where you runnin' off to?" His laughter subsided, but his face remained bright red. "Tell me what you've got lined up."

"I'm not going to lie to you. I need to get straight. But I've recently met this guy. He's a junkie too, but he's got cash. Like crazy money."

"A junkie with cash. I'd like to see it."

"I'm being real. He got hit crossing the street. Some rich prick in a Beamer whacked him when he was walking on the damn crosswalk."

"No shit?"

"No shit. Up on Adams."

"So, what? He got some type of settlement?"

"Exactly. Fifty."

"That's it? Seems like getting hit by a car would pay more."

"I guess when your lawyer stiffs you, you end up with less."

Sullivan shrugged indifference. "Guess so. What's your point?"

"He's blown through some of it but not all. Told me he wants to buy a brick."

"You're telling me one of your junkie friends wants to buy a brick of powder. He'd be dead in a week."

Brayden laughed. "I know. That's what I told him too. But he says he wants to go into business for himself and try his hand at moving the product."

"How much cash does he have on hand right now?"

Brayden could see the big man's mental wheels begin to churn. "Enough for a brick."

"How do you know? I haven't told you how much."

"I've been around long enough to know it'll run for about $15K. And I know he's good for that. Hell, maybe he's got enough for two if you price it right."

Sullivan got closer, dipping down to ear level, and whispered, "I think you might be onto something. Give me a day or two to figure things out and then I'll reach out to you. Gotta cell?"

"Of course."

"Stop by the pub tomorrow during the day. See Cormac. He'll be tending. Tell him you're there to see me. He'll give you the details."

Brayden bobbed his head in acknowledgement. "So, we've got ourselves a deal then?"

"Looks that way." Sullivan eyed the door.

Brayden got the not-so-subtle hint it was time for him to go. He cleared his throat. "How about that bundle?"

Sullivan gave a disappointed shake of his head. "Pathetic. You just brokered a deal for some real weight and here you are begging for some piss amount of dope."

"Like I said, gotta get straight. And I need to bring my buddy a sample of the goods." Brayden fished out the cash White had given him.

Sullivan eyed the wad of cash in his hand. "Really? What do you take me for?"

Brayden felt a wave of panic set in and his stomach bunched. "I—don't—"

The oversized mitt of a hand reached out and swallowed Brayden's. "Keep your chump change. I want to see the real money. Wait here for a sec."

Sullivan let go of Brayden's hand and retreated to the back room where the old men were still busy cutting up the product. He came back out a few seconds later.

"Here you go." Sullivan tossed the banded bundle.

Brayden wasn't expecting the airborne delivery and failed to catch it. He scrambled to pick it up. He thumbed the wax bags, counting the bundle to ensure there were ten and remembering the not-so-veiled threat made by Brooks if he came up short.

"Are you kidding me? You're counting to see if I shorted you?" Sullivan pursed his lips and looked as though he were about to explode. "I'm talking about moving some Ks your way and you think I'm gonna pull some shit on a bundle?"

Brayden cowered slightly while simultaneously hating himself for the weak display. "Sorry. Force of habit."

Sullivan didn't respond. His large frame brushed him as he opened the door. "Don't forget. Tomorrow. Cormac at the bar."

Brayden stuffed the dope into the same pocket as the buy money he never used. "Tomorrow it is." He stepped outside.

The door slammed shut and Brayden could hear the four-by-four wood brace being slipped back into place, followed by the thud of the deadbolts.

He walked away, following the path White instructed him to.

Ten minutes of walking and Brayden came to the pick-up location. The black Lincoln Town Car sat idling behind the apartment complex.

Brayden entered the backseat and closed the door. The blast of air conditioning was refreshing, and he could feel the heat prickling his skin diminishing.

White didn't turn to face him. He kept his eyes forward. Brooks did the same. And then Brayden remembered the rule. Don't look at them with the camera and don't speak until it's off.

He dipped his head, removed the Sox cap, and silently handed it to Brooks, brim down.

Brooks held up a finger, signaling him to remain quiet. White's stocky partner fiddled with the hat and pulled the camera out from the brim. A second later the hat came sailing back, landing on the seat near the spot where his needle kit still rested.

"So, let's have it." Brooks held open a small plastic bag with the word *evidence* in red letters at the top.

Brayden retrieved the bundle from his pocket and dropped it in.

"How much did he charge you?"

"Nothing."

Brooks spun in his seat to face him. The movement shook the boxy car. "Nothing? Did you not understand a thing we said to you before you stepped out?"

"I did. I saw an opportunity and things kinda just happened."

"What opportunity? What are you talking about?"

"I talked up a deal. A key of dope. Maybe two."

Brooks cocked an eyebrow and looked as though he was torn between laughing and uncontrollable rage. "How does a sick little junkie broker a deal with the mob?"

Brayden shrugged. "You're the one who said I could do the

cold buy because I was from the neighborhood. Maybe you didn't see my full potential."

Brooks leaned in, but White gripped his shoulder and pulled his pit bull back. "Let's see what he has to say. It might be the break we've been looking for."

The glimmer in White's eyes unnerved Brayden to the core.

14

"How long until you think you'll be able to get me results on the swabs?" Kelly asked, leaning on an unpacked stack of boxes.

"They're top priority on my list. But as you can see by the boxes you're leaning against, we're not up to full speed yet. So there'll be a bit of delay." Raymond Charles sipped the tepid coffee in the thermos his wife had given him.

"I don't mean to press, but—"

The salty senior crime scene technician gave his version of a smile. "Yes, you do. And I would too if it were my case. My hands are tied with this transition to the new digs. As soon as the lab is up and running the way it should be, I'll be processing those swabs we took from the dead woman's fingernails."

"If you had to guess?"

"Two days. Give or take."

"Thanks, Ray." Kelly looked down at the mug on Charles's desk. "I'll bring you a cup of Dunkin' next time I stop by. Seeing you suffer through your wife's home brew is killing me."

Charles raised his mug in mock cheers and gave a throaty laugh.

Kelly left the new office space of the Crime Lab Unit and

made the short return trip down the hall to his own office. Entering Homicide's secured door, he saw Sergeant Sutherland hovering near his cubicle.

"Sarge, you looking for me?"

"Lieutenant's been asking for a status report. News about the dead witness has made its rounds and the higher-ups want to be kept in the loop."

"The scene's done. Looked pretty clean minus the nails. Maybe some transfer on the cord. But I'm betting whoever goes out of their way to kill a witness is smart enough to wear gloves."

"I've spoken with forensics. Anything you want is billed top priority."

"Thanks. I just spoke with Ray. They're still getting the new lab in order."

Sutherland frowned. "I thought that was supposed to be done before the move."

"Apparently so did they. Not much we can do about it now."

"Did he give you a timeline on the forensics?"

"Couple days. Maybe sooner." Kelly looked at his watch. It was nearing three p.m. "I'm going to cut out for a bit. But I'll be back later to write my supplemental report."

"Everything okay?"

"Yeah. Embry's taking off with her mother for a little vacation to the Cape. I wanted to spend a little time with her before she goes."

"Then what are you sitting around here for? Get going."

Kelly tossed his notepad on the ever-growing pile and headed for the door, hoping to beat the start of rush hour.

Kelly pulled out in his department-issued blue Caprice. The

steering column vibrated non-stop and the engine made a strange ticking sound. But compared to his last car, a beat-up Impala, it was a dream. Most importantly, the air conditioning worked.

He made decent time and only got hung up for a few minutes by rubberneckers slowing for a fender bender on the opposite side of the road.

Sprinting up the steps and onto the porch, he heard his daughter's infectious giggle. Kelly peeked in the window to see her seated across from his mother, the two enjoying a wild game of Go Fish. He took a second to absorb this moment, mentally recording the exchange between the two girls he loved most in his life.

There was no way of making a surprise entrance with the loud squeak of the front door. He'd been meaning to put some WD-40 on the hinges but knew it was a bigger project than applying a dab of lubricant. The frame had shifted over the years and the door was out of alignment. The angled pressure caused the metal-on-metal creak every time the door opened or closed. His mother told him to leave it alone, saying it was better than any home defense alarm system.

Hearing the door, Embry bolted out of the kitchen at break-neck speed. "Daddy!" She leapt off the ground a few feet in front of him. He caught her midair and the two embraced.

"I missed you too, my sweet."

She released her hug and slid down his body to the floor. "I thought you said you were going to come home last night?"

"I did. You were asleep. And I had to go back in before you got up." He mussed her hair. "But I'm home now. Want to hit the park for a little bit before your mother comes to pick you up?"

She answered with a big smile and went to grab her sneakers from a bin by the door. Kelly's mother ambled in from the kitchen. Months had passed since the fall that broke her hip, and the recovery was slow. The doctor told her that while it would take another six months before she would be operating at full capacity, she would never be quite the same.

She walked up and gave Kelly a gentle kiss on the cheek, then said with a wink, "Your coffee was a bit strong this morning."

"Late night and early morning. I needed a little extra boost today."

"That job's going to be the death of you."

He laughed. "I guess it'll be a pretty easy case to solve then."

"I'm making meatloaf tonight."

"I can't stay for dinner. After Sam picks up Embry, I've got to head back in to finish up a bit of paperwork."

"It's always work with you. Take some time to appreciate the life you've got."

Kelly looked down at his daughter as she looped her shoelaces into a double knot. "I know, Ma. It's why I came home. I'm doing the best I can."

She patted his cheek gently. "I know that. But it's my job to worry."

Kelly leaned in closer to his mother. He lowered his voice to keep Embry from hearing his next words. "There was a pretty bad robbery at Tyson's Market."

"I know. I saw on the news. Just terrible."

"I don't want you closing up the store by yourself. Make sure Reyansh is around, and lock the door ten minutes early."

Her normally serene face went rigid. "You didn't catch the person responsible yet?"

Kelly sighed. "It's not like TV, Ma. But I'm working on it." He looked back down at Embry, who was scrambling to her feet. "We're going to spend a little quality time before I head back to the office."

Kelly gave his mother a kiss on the forehead and then

followed Embry out the door. She was already bounding down the porch steps toward the sidewalk as he closed the front door.

Embry skipped ahead. Kelly watched the carefree girl bounce along, taking care to leap and dodge over the cracks in the sidewalk.

The playground was only two blocks from the house. Once in view, Embry looked back at him, smiled, and then broke into a run. Kelly didn't bother trying to keep pace and just enjoyed the moment.

She did her typical laps through the playscape obstacles until the heat wore her energy down to a manageable level. Kelly stood under the shade of a nearby maple and watched.

Embry approached in an exaggerated slump of exhaustion. "Dad, let's swing."

Kelly took up the swing next to his daughter and gently pushed off against the woodchip-covered ground. Embry was already kicking and leaning with a relentless fervor that propelled her higher with each pass.

"Dad?" she asked as she swung past.

"Yes."

She began to drag her feet and slow herself, bringing her momentum to a near stop before looking at him with an uncanny seriousness not often seen in his daughter. "What is it like to be around dead people?"

"It's like being around people who are alive, they're just a lot quieter."

She brought her swing to a full stop and rolled her eyes. "Seriously, Dad."

"That's a tough question. I guess I'd describe it as surreal at times."

"What's surreal mean?"

"Kind of weird. Strange." Kelly thought for a moment, trying to put into words the experience of dealing with the dead and phrasing it in a meaningful way for his eight-year-old. "It's serious work. The families of people who are murdered look to guys like me to help them find justice."

"What if they don't have families?"

Kelly held back the gut-reaction chuckle tickling the back of his throat at the literal takeaway from his last statement. "I seek justice for them all. It's my job to speak for the dead. To help them find peace."

Embry bobbed her head slowly as if processing his words.

"Why do you ask?"

"Because of the smell."

Kelly pulled up his shirt, dipped his head, and took a deep sniff of the fabric. He caught the unique funkiness left after spending several hours in the non-air-conditioned apartment of Muriel Burke. "That's something definitely unique about working with the dead."

"Surreal." Embry smiled at her use of the new word.

Kelly returned his daughter's smile. His phone vibrated, and he hated it for interrupting the shared moment. He pulled it out and saw the incoming text message from his ex-wife. *Getting an early start. I'll be by in half an hour.*

"Looks like we get a few more minutes at the park before we've got to head back and get you packed up for your trip to the Cape."

The bright-eyed smile faded. "I wish you were coming."

"Me too. But things are different now."

She looked down and kicked at the woodchips.

"Look on the bright side. When you get back, I should be all done with this case and we can spend a lot more time together."

Her head perked up, and just like that, she was back to her happy-go-lucky self. Kelly took this moment to absorb as much of his daughter's energy as possible, knowing he'd need it to fuel the darkness of the task ahead.

15

"No worries. I understand. I explained it to Sutherland."

"I appreciate it, Mike. His temp's down but he'll be out of school for a few days. My wife will be home with him tomorrow."

"I'll catch you up then. Not like we have much to go on yet. A possible caliber size for the weapon is up for debate. Sutherland's got us top billing at the ME's office, but I still haven't gotten the word on Burke's autopsy. I bothered Ray about getting us the results of the swabs, but they're a hot mess over in forensics right now with the move. So, as of right now, we're about as well off as we were when you left."

"You sure you don't need me to come back in? I could make it there in about half an hour."

"Not worth it. I won't be here."

"Oh, that's right. It's your night to get your head kicked in."

"That too. But I'm also meeting up with Ithaca afterward."

"So, you're doing it?"

"I guess. What could it hurt?"

"Michael Kelly on a date. Never thought I'd see the day. Thought you chose to up and join the priesthood."

Kelly laughed. "I'll catch you in the morning."

"Don't stay out too late," Mainelli taunted, and ended the call.

Kelly stood up from his desk and walked to the closet where he kept a couple extra outfits. Working with dead bodies tended to call for a backup wardrobe. He grabbed a pair of jeans and a polo shirt. Stuffing the spare clothes into his gym bag, Kelly headed for the door.

"You cutting out?" Sutherland peeked his head out from the lieutenant's office.

"Yeah. I finished up the supplemental from the Burke scene. You need something before I go?"

"No. Just wanted to let you know Anderson's replacement will be joining our ranks tomorrow morning."

"Who is it?"

"Now what fun would that be if I ruined the surprise? I've got very little excitement in my life."

Kelly shook his head. "You've got a strange way of amusing yourself."

"Tell that to my wife."

Kelly turned into the hallway. On his way out he stopped by the new forensics lab. His key fob granted him access. The fob's digitized chip also logged every entry in and out of any of the facility's secured doors, an additional security device and a way of managing the integrity of the sensitive space. Being a member of Homicide granted him access to most of the building, minus supervisory spaces or specialized units like Organized Crime and Narcotics.

Kelly entered. The lab's open floor space had a new-car kind of smell. Fresh and sterile.

Ray Charles was lecturing Dawes near the junior technician's cubicle. Kelly couldn't hear the specifics of the senior man's rant, but the words "protocol" and "court" were used.

Kelly surmised he was trying to instill the importance of methodically approaching a scene and keeping the case's big picture in mind.

"Ray, I'm cutting out for the night. Anything you need from me before I go?"

Charles turned toward him. Dawes gave Kelly a grin, obviously grateful for the interruption.

"I hate moving. I'll retire before I ever move again." He kicked an open cardboard box at his feet. "Told those bastards to leave us in the basement. But no—they had to go and apply what they think is common sense and put us on the same floor as the rest of you lunatics."

"Those bastards being our bosses?"

"I know the real reason. Some fat ass complained about having to hoof it downstairs any time they needed something."

"Maybe you're right."

"No maybe about it." Charles pulled a handkerchief from his pocket and wiped the cloth across his brow, removing the sweat from his dark forehead. "And if your real reason for stopping back in is to see if I've had a chance to get to the analysis since we last talked—the answer is no."

Realizing the man's temper was nearing the boiling point, Kelly decided to bow out and leave him to resume scolding Dawes.

"Have a good night, Ray." Kelly then looked at Dawes. "And nice job processing the Burke scene today, Freckles."

Kelly headed out of the secure space, hoping his comment gave the new technician some reprieve.

The smell of sweat and leather mingled in the thick humidity of the gym. No air conditioning for Pops. It wasn't used in his day and it wouldn't be tolerated in the forging of his current stock-yard of fighters. A couple old standing fans oscillated in the corners, but did nothing to combat the heat exacerbated by the effort put forth by the pugilists earning their keep.

Kelly's pores opened up, releasing the floodgates his Caprice's A/C had held back. He welcomed it. Setting foot on the hardwood floors instantly transported him back to simpler times. A time when life wasn't so complicated. Not to say he didn't face adversity in his youth. He did, the worst being the death of his father. But the gym had saved him from slipping too deep into the dark place. Pops had saved him. The gym owner's steady resolve pushed Kelly to fight against the pain. The disciplined regime promoted a sense of purpose, and he would be forever grateful to the man. Pops had transformed himself from coach and mentor to father figure.

To this day, Kelly thought of Pops as a second father. And the gym as his second home.

Edmund Brown, the Harvard-educated principal, and Donny O'Brien, Catholic priest, were trading blows in the ring. Kelly was late. And he assumed Bobby wouldn't be there. He hadn't shown up to their Thursday night fight sessions since the incident in the parking lot. Usually a good fight solved things between the two of them, but the last time had been different.

Bobby had information on the man who'd murdered Kelly's partner eight years ago. The permanent red card on his Murder Board. Bobby either was too scared or too deep with Walsh's crew to expose the person responsible. Their childhood loyalty had been tested, and it came up short. The two hadn't seen each other or spoken since.

Kelly didn't speak about it to Brown or O'Brien. And his two childhood friends knew better than to ask.

The buzzer chirped one loud beep, signaling the last ten seconds of the round, or the Hard Ten, as Pops referred to it. It was the time in a match when boxers unloaded every last bit of energy, knowing a minute rest was close. Some great bouts were won and lost in those precious seconds. But watching his two friends in the ring, it was readily apparent neither man had much in his tank. Each let loose a combo at the same time. Since they were exhausted and completely gassed, it ended up looking like a gloved game of patty-cake.

The final bell rang out. Three loud electronic beeps signaled the bout's end.

Both men lumbered to the ropes and draped their bodies lazily over the top rubber-coated rope, using it to support their weight.

"Don't let Pops catch you. You'll be doing another round." Kelly waved his finger in mock disapproval.

Brown picked up his water bottle and squeezed a long stream of water into his mouth. "Maybe we'll drag you in here and play a little two-on-one."

"Come on. How would that look? Me beating up two grown men at the same time. And one being a man of the cloth." Kelly smiled at his own joke. "It'd be downright shameful is what it would be."

O'Brien wiped his sweat onto his towel and then flung it at Kelly. "I drank holy water today. Don't force me to call upon my divine strength when the Lord's work is needed elsewhere."

"If that was God helping you in the ring just now, then the world is in far more trouble than I originally thought."

Brown and O'Brien slipped between the ropes and hopped down to the floor. They walked over to Kelly and gave a quick tap of the gloves. A boxer's respect.

Kelly began wrapping his hands. "Where's Pops tonight?"

Brown bit at his laces and loosened his glove. "He's at Walpole. Ray's up for parole in a few months. He's trying to help him get ready for the hearing."

"How long has it been?" Kelly asked as he looped the canvas strap through his finger and back down around his thumb.

"Coming up on twenty," O'Brien said solemnly. "I'm not sure how Pops will take it if he gets turned down again. You got any pull with something like this?"

Kelly shook his head. "No. Not really. When it gets closer, I can try and reach out to a couple people. But the parole hearings are very tightly controlled. And most of the decision rests on whether the victim's family supports it. From what I gather, they've vehemently protested against Ray getting an early release in the past. Not sure what's going to change this time."

Brown sighed. "I can't believe it's been twenty years. I can still remember that night."

"I don't think any of us will ever forget it," Kelly said. "Hard to believe, knowing Ray the way we did."

"That's why this is so difficult for Pops. I don't think he ever believed his son was guilty. You work these cases now, Mike. Do you think it's possible to screw up and get the wrong guy?"

"It happens. A guy in my unit, Cliff Anderson, just got tossed for screwing up evidence on a bunch of cases. So sure, cops are human beings and we've got some who are incompetent like in any other job. But those guys are few and far between."

"But they exist." Brown put his glove out and Kelly yanked it off.

"True. And they ruin it for the rest of us."

"Ever thought about taking a look at the case? Seeing if there was something else missing?" Brown asked.

Kelly nodded. "I plan to. But I'll be honest. Cops don't like when other cops start digging around in somebody else's cases."

"But it's Ray. That's Pops's son. And that makes him family." Brown had a way of looking deep into Kelly's soul.

"I know, and I will. I promise to do it before the parole hearing. If nothing else, maybe I can give Pops some peace of mind about the case. Regardless of the outcome."

"You also need to fix whatever is between you and Bobby." O'Brien laid a gloved hand on Kelly's shoulder.

"What is this? Guilty burden day at the gym. Feel free to unload all your troubles on me tonight. Not like I'm trying to solve a double murder or anything."

O'Brien gave him his priestly look, as if he were preparing to listen to confession. "That's awful. I really don't know how you do it."

"Same as you. You take the load of all those sinners who burden you with their problems. It's all about compartmentalization. Keeping things separate."

"True. But all the death you see has got to take its toll."

Kelly finished wrapping his second hand and then began slipping his bag gloves on. "And as for Bobby, he and I have got some things to work out. Things that can't be settled in the back lot."

O'Brien must've seen the seriousness in Kelly's eyes because he didn't push the subject any further. "Well, I've got enough energy for another round or two in the ring if you want."

"I saw you in there. And no you don't. But it doesn't matter anyway tonight. I'm just going to do a little bag work to burn off some steam and then I've got to cut out early."

"But I've got a full cooler. And everybody knows Ed's not going to drink it."

"I can't. I'm meeting someone."

Brown perked up. "Meeting someone? Do tell."

"It's nothing. Just somebody from work."

Brown's eye cocked up and his smooth dark skin rolled up into a big smile. "You're being awfully coy about this. Is it another cop?"

"Somebody we know?" O'Brien chimed in.

"You guys are worse than a bunch of schoolgirls. No, it's not a cop. And no, you don't know her."

Both men surrounded Kelly, folded their arms, and waited. He knew these guys better than he knew himself and was confident they'd hound him until he spilled the beans. "Fine. Her name is Ithaca Best. And she's not a cop. She's a pathologist with the ME's office."

"Michael Kelly is going on a date with a doctor?" Brown burst into laughter.

"What's so funny about that? And it's not a date."

"Then what is it?"

"Just dinner," Kelly offered dismissively.

Brown, still chuckling, said, "Well, if there's a candle on the table, then you, sir, are on a date."

Kelly stepped around the two men. "If we're done with the inquisition, I'd like to get a little workout in before I go."

Brown gave Kelly a hearty slap on the back as he passed. "See you next week. Unless you've got another date lined up."

Using the ring timer to initiate his first of three heavy bag rounds, Kelly squared up to the faded leather and readied himself. As the buzzer sounded, he unleashed a barrage of blows, each strike finding the sweet spot where years of abuse had softened the bag. The shockwave from each impact felt good, and the release helped clear his mind of the day's tragic start.

Kelly glanced in the window as he walked up to the door. Ithaca was already seated at a table. He gave a quick sniff of his shirt. He hadn't had time to shower after his workout at Pops's. He managed to wipe himself down with a wet towel and throw on a second coating of deodorant before dressing. Probably not the best way to start off a date. But by not making a big deal about the dinner, he felt it lightened the mood.

The restaurant had an open layout and lacquered wood tables scattered throughout the dining space in an intentionally haphazard manner, giving a relaxed atmosphere. A fireplace was set along the back wall, and Kelly imagined it would be a great spot to visit in the winter months. The bar, separated from the main room by a decorative half wall, was packed. Each stool was filled, leaving several patrons standing.

Kelly pulled open the door and was met by guitar music from a live band using the space between the bar and main room as its stage. The acoustics were loud enough to be heard throughout, but not so overwhelming that diners were forced to yell their conversations.

Ithaca had her back to the door and didn't see him arrive.

He looked down at his watch. It was five minutes past the hour. He hadn't intended on being fashionably late. The Fairmount Grille wasn't far from Dorchester, but he had failed to account for the inevitable traffic delays even after rush hour.

"I hope you weren't waiting long?"

She turned her head and raised her glass. "I'm already on my second glass."

His eyes widened. "Wait—what? Didn't you say nine?"

"Wow. I hope your suspects can't dupe you so easily." She gave him a consolatory smile. "Just teasing. I got here about ten minutes ago. Left straight from the office."

"Me too. Well, not exactly; my office by way of my gym."

"Good to know I'm not the only one who keeps an extra set of clothes at the office."

Kelly took a moment to really see the woman seated before him. The only contact they'd had since he joined Homicide had been in the presence of the dead. Seeing her now, dressed in an emerald silky blouse and tightly fitted jeans, he realized how drop dead gorgeous she was, which set his nerves on edge.

"You look nice." *My God, did I just start off with "you look nice?"* he berated himself.

"You clean up well too." She gestured to the seat across from her. "Sit. Have a glass. Not sure what you drink, so I took the liberty of ordering their house merlot. Pretty damn good if I say so myself."

Kelly sat. He made sure his untucked shirt covered the pistol stowed on his hip. His badge, typically hanging from a chain around his neck, was now clipped onto his belt near the gun. The metal ridge of the badge poked into his oblique and he adjusted it. He called his current ensemble his "casual look."

"Nervous?"

"Me? Nah. I get asked out all the time by good-looking

doctors. In fact, as soon as we're done here, I've got another hot date lined up."

She giggled in the same flighty manner she'd had during the autopsy. "You were fidgeting. Wasn't sure if it was pre-date jitters."

Kelly leaned in, not wanting any nosey patrons to hear. "It's this stupid badge and gun. I hate wearing this rig when off duty. But it's not like I've got much of a choice."

"Then why do you? I mean you're off, right?"

"Yeah. Not that simple. Actually, I get asked that question quite a bit. I guess some people assume it's because us cops have some ego thing attached to it. Maybe that's true for some, but not most. Maybe early in my career, I could have been carrying it for the power of it. But now, I carry it because of Kelly Malone."

"Who's Kelly Malone?"

"He worked the Eleven before I got there."

"The Eleven?"

"Dorchester. C-11 is the district designation. But those of us who work it just call it the Eleven."

"Sorry, I didn't mean to interrupt. You were saying about Malone?"

"He was a beat cop. Good, not great, but the guy did his job well enough. We rode together a few nights when I was new to the streets. He had this thing about leaving his duty weapon in his locker at the station. Something about not bringing his work home with him. Anyway, one night he stopped by a convenience store on his way home to pick up some ice cream for his pregnant wife. His shit luck, it was being robbed."

Ithaca pursed her lips. "What happened?"

"He went into automatic drive. Full cop mode. I guess in that moment, when faced with the armed threat, he reacted as if he were still in uniform. Maybe it was that his shift had just ended and his brain hadn't completely switched off yet. Whatever the reason, Malone called out 'Drop the gun' and went for his."

"But you said he didn't take his gun home."

"Exactly. He went to draw and found he was grabbing nothing but the clothes he was wearing. It's called a slip and capture. Under duress, our brains resort to the ingrained reflexes. His did just that. The perp must've seen the movement and fired."

"He died?"

"Worse."

"What's worse than death?"

"In my experience, plenty. In Malone's case, he's in a wheel-chair for the rest of his life."

Ithaca sat back and grabbed for her wine. "I guess that story would make any cop carry off duty."

"Especially if you saw him lying in that pool of blood on the floor of the convenience store, the tub of ice cream next to his body."

"You did?"

"First on scene. I was working a double that night." Kelly filled his glass with the merlot. "Life-changing stuff right there."

"I bet."

Kelly took a sip and changed the subject. Nothing like starting a first date with a depressing cop story. "This place is nice. How'd you hear about it?"

"My friend Chris owns it. We went to school together. Smart guy. Could've been a fantastic doctor. But after graduation he decided the medical field wasn't what he was looking for out of life and went into the food industry."

"Looks like he's doing well for himself." Kelly surveyed the décor and then turned his attention back to her.

"He was. Apparently one of his financial backers pulled out earlier this month. He told me tonight, before you got here, that he's shutting down next month. Starting over after six years has got to be tough. But if anybody can bounce back, it's Chris."

The comment made Kelly think of his failed marriage and his hurdles in rebuilding a life out of the ashes. "What about you? Are you happy with the career path?"

"Well, only downside is I work with a bunch of stiffs." Ithaca chortled. "Bad joke. I'm filled with them. But I do love it. Something about piecing together the last seconds of somebody's life. It's like a human jigsaw puzzle."

"It's important work you're doing. Speaking for the dead takes a special breed."

"Seems like you've grown attached to the work. I remember when we first met, I wasn't sure about a guy who came from the macho world of SWAT and Narcotics. Didn't know how the death beat would take. But you really seem to have a knack for it. Homicide suits you."

Kristen Barnes had said those same words to him. He found it strange to think of her now while with Ithaca.

"You never know how something's going to fit until you try it on."

"And how would you say being in Homicide fits you?"

"Like a glove."

A waiter appeared holding a tray with a plate of nachos. "Compliments of the house."

"Tell Chris we said thanks."

"Look at you, high roller status."

"To be honest, I think he had a bit of a crush back in the day." She looked back toward the bar and waved to a well-dressed man speaking with a guest. He smiled back and gave a friendly wave in return.

"Maybe it's not wholly diminished."

"Nah. He's a great guy, though. Give you the shirt off his back in a pinch. But it never happened back then and it's not on my radar now." She punctuated her statement with a sip of her wine.

Something out of the corner of his eye caught Kelly's attention. A man seated alone at a nearby table was eyeing the room. If Kelly didn't know better, he would guess the guy was casing the place. Maybe looking to rob it. A little crowded for something so brazen.

He focused on the man's hands. A lot could be learned from body language. Sometimes, a person's actions, subconscious or not, told a great deal about what they were thinking. The man Kelly was watching kept his hands on the table. Typically, robbers repeatedly checked their weapon before engaging in the crime. Reassuring touches helped prepare their mind for its deployment.

Nothing the man was doing indicated he was armed. But something was definitely off. He didn't fit the atmosphere. His gaunt face. The way he nervously tore at the napkin. There was a glass of water and an empty basket of bread on the table in front of him. No dinner plate. No drink. And Kelly recognized the desperate look. The guy was dope sick.

Kelly flagged the waiter who'd just brought the comped dish.

"Are you ready to order, sir?"

"Not yet." He shot a glance at the man and lowered his voice. "How long's he been sitting there?" Kelly cast his eyes in the lone diner's direction.

"Too long. At least forty-five minutes. Maybe more. Hasn't ordered anything. Said he was waiting for a friend."

"Thanks."

The waiter looked confused. "Is he bothering you? I can ask him to leave."

"No. It's fine." He gave a disarming smile. "We'll be ready to order in a few minutes."

The waiter headed back into the kitchen area.

"You guys really can't shut it off, huh?"

"God knows I try. But I've learned to accept that once you understand human nature in its rawest form, the world never looks the same."

A table of four finished and walked toward the restaurant's exit. They were laughing loudly and totally engaged in a story being told by a woman with purple highlights in her hair.

The gaunt man looked around nervously. His feet bounced up and down as he tore off a bit of napkin, adding it to the pile of shredded pieces he'd created. As the purple-haired woman and her entourage departed, his gaze focused on the vacated table and the cash tip sticking out of the black leather bill holder.

Kelly stood. "Give me a minute. I'll be right back. I've got to step outside to make a quick call." He moved to the door and out into the warmth of the evening air. He pulled out his cellphone and held it to his ear. Kelly watched the gaunt man out of his peripheral through the window while standing off to the side of the door. He nodded and did his best to pretend he was listening intently to somebody on the other end of the line.

The gaunt man stood. His movements were jerky as he walked to the table. He nervously rubbed at the back of his neck and kept his head down as he approached. The man snapped down at the bill holder and swiped up the tip. Nobody noticed. Nobody but Kelly.

The thief then made his way to the door.

As soon as the man exited, Kelly put his phone away and snatched him by the elbow. The man spun to face him, completely caught off guard by the interruption. The frantic look in the man's eyes made it apparent he hadn't noticed Kelly until now. All that time to case the place and he missed the cop sitting one table away. The embodiment of crap luck.

The thin man yanked his arm back but failed to break Kelly's grip. "Get the hell off me, man! What's your damn problem? You got a death wish or something?"

"Cough it up."

The man squirmed and wriggled to free his trapped arm. It was a pathetic attempt. The weakness of the man's desperate effort to free himself was a clear indication of how far gone he was. "What the hell are you talking about? Are you crazy, man?"

Kelly saw the man ball his free hand. Moving at much faster speed than the addict, he quickly twisted the man's body and forced him away from him. The contorted position made it impossible for the man to land a punch. He had become a human marionette and Kelly was pulling the strings. "Don't be stupid. I'm not going to hurt you. At least, I don't want to. But that's going to be up to you. You're not leaving with that waiter's hard-earned money."

"The hell you say! You're crazy!"

"Am I?" Kelly lifted his shirt, exposing his badge tucked neatly along his hip. The butt of his Glock added to the impact of the display.

The man's head sank and the tension in his body went slack. Kelly felt the resistance drain in the arm he continued to hold firmly. The addict was a vision of defeat. And one he'd seen too many times to count. One he'd seen in his brother the last time the two had spoken.

"Look, I'm not hauling you off to jail. I'm not even calling this in. But the money's not going with you. Understand?"

The gaunt man gave him a sheepish look. "You're not going to arrest me? Why are you cutting me a break?"

"Because everyone deserves one of those every now and again."

The man's balled fist had loosened, and he shoved it into his pocket. Kelly tensed. Hands in pockets could go south fast if what came back out was a weapon. But in this case, when his hand reappeared, the crumpled bills of the tip money were bunched inside his fist. Without looking up at Kelly, he pushed his hand out and opened his palm.

Kelly took the cash, damp from the man's sweaty palm, and released his grip on his elbow.

The man gave Kelly a look, split somewhere between hate and gratitude. Without saying a word, the drug-sick thief took off running down the street. Kelly lost sight of him as he disappeared in a gaggle of pedestrian traffic.

Kelly watched him go and couldn't help but think of his brother. He hadn't seen Brayden in months, and their last conversation had been strained at best. He still hadn't been able to corner him on his comment, *Maybe it's time you knew the truth.* His brother was chasing his addiction, and Kelly had been temporarily written out of his life.

Letting the thought go with a sigh, he turned his attention back to the restaurant and the woman patiently waiting for his return.

He gently brushed her shoulder as he passed by. "Sorry about that."

"Everything okay?"

"It is now."

Kelly didn't sit back down, though. Instead, he walked over to the waiter, who was busy tending to a table. He tapped him on the back and interrupted his lively recital of the chef's special. The waiter turned. Kelly handed him the wad of cash and pointed over to the table where the purple-haired woman had been. The waiter gave him a hearty handshake and was on the verge of giving Kelly a hug as he backed away.

Returning to the table, Ithaca raised her hands in confusion. "What was that all about?"

"That guy stole the tip off the table."

"The creepy one?"

Kelly wondered what Ithaca would think of his brother if she ever met him. *Would she consider him creepy too?* he asked himself, unable to gauge the answer to his inner monologue's question. Or more likely, he just didn't want to allow the probable answer to enter his mind. "Yes, that one."

"And you got it back?"

"I did."

"And how'd you go about doing that?"

This time it was Kelly who gave a coy grin. "I can be very persuasive when I need to be. I'm all of a sudden really hungry. You're the frequent flyer around here. What's good?"

"They've got a lot of comfort food on the menu. But I usually come here for the burgers. The Fairmount burger was nominated best of Boston. It comes with a bacon aioli, bacon, and smoked Gouda cheese," Ithaca said without opening the menu.

"That sounds great. I'm sold."

Just as Ithaca caught the waiter's attention, Kelly's phone began to vibrate. He looked down at the caller ID and frowned.

"Problem?"

"Work." Kelly maintained his frown as he swiped the answer button. "Hey, Sarge, what we got?"

"Another store just got hit. The Lexi-Mart at Talbott and Welles."

"Another body?"

"Yes. The shooting just went down. Scene's still being secured as we speak. It sounds pretty chaotic down there. I want you on location ASAP. Looks like we got another witness. This time let's try and keep them alive long enough to find the bastard who's doing this."

"So we're assuming it's the same guy?"

"We're not assuming anything. That's why I need you to get your ass down there as soon as humanly possible."

"On my way." Kelly ended the call and looked at Ithaca. "I'm sorry. I've really gotta go."

"I get it. No need to apologize. Sounds like we'll both be busy for the next couple days. Let's try this again when the dust settles."

"I'd like that."

Kelly threw down some cash on the table for the wine and headed for the door. He looked back at Ithaca before disappearing into the night.

17

The Lexi-Mart was a bodega-style market in a small strip of businesses on Talbot Avenue near the corner of Welles. The mini mart was bookended by a tax office and The Lady of the Eternal Light Gospel Church, neither of which were open. And from the tax office's boarded front window, it looked as though it was permanently closed.

A barrier of yellow tape surrounded the strip of businesses and spilled out into the street, shutting down the westbound lane of Talbott. The red and blue lights from the sea of cruisers and two ambulances danced along the walls of the neighboring houses.

Kelly parked outside the tape and exited the vehicle. Only twenty minutes ago he'd been at a swanky restaurant in the company of a beautiful woman. Work had instantly teleported him to this bizarre scene. *Surreal.* Embry's new word perfectly described the feeling.

He approached the scene slowly, scanning the area. Kelly wanted to make sure he was taking in the details. He could see broken bits of glass along the sidewalk. There was a void where the upper pane of the door should have been except for a few spider webbed chunks clinging to the upper corner. The scene looked nothing like the shooting from the previous night. And at first glance, Kelly doubted the connection.

"What the hell happened here? It looks like a war zone." Kelly surveyed the shattered glass storefront.

"Shootout from what I can tell from that guy over there." The patrol officer pointed toward a man on a gurney being loaded into the back of an ambulance. "He interrupted a holdup."

"He was armed?"

"Yeah. He's apparently a PI. Told me he was set up down the street trying to get some juice on a cheating wife. He heard a gunshot and decided to try and be a hero."

"How'd that work out?"

"Took two rounds. One in the shoulder and the other grazed his arm. I'm no doctor, but it doesn't appear to be life-threatening. The medics are stabilizing him and should be transporting him soon."

"And the other guy? The robber?"

The patrolman shrugged. "Escaped. Hero said he got off a few rounds but wasn't sure if he hit him. I did the initial scene walk and didn't see any blood trail or anything like that to indicate he found his mark."

"What about the clerk? You said the PI heard a gunshot."

"Dead. One shot, right between the eyes. Young kid. Twenty-one, I think. Josh Daniels. Lives in the neighborhood." He swung his arm outward, gesturing to the perimeter tape. "We went pretty wide with the scene. We weren't sure how far it extended. Let me know if you want me to adjust it once you've taken a look."

"Will do. Thanks." He gave the patrolman a slap on the shoulder. Kelly watched as the ambulance pulled away with the wounded PI onboard. "Good work. Make sure you get an initial statement from our hero."

"Johnston will be riding in the ambulance. He'll try to get something out of him on the ride and will take the formal statement once the guy's cleared surgery. It'll be in the supp as soon as he's got it."

"Who's running the show tonight?"

"Sergeant Cooper."

Kelly scanned the group of uniforms clustered outside the perimeter by one of the SUVs and picked out the salty sergeant from the crowd. Sergeant Dale Cooper had been one of Kelly's favorite supervisors during his time working the Eleven. Cooper had also been the one who stepped up on his behalf a few months ago during a pursuit Kelly was involved in. The crusty sergeant had gone nose to nose with Lieutenant Duff in defense of Kelly's actions that day.

He walked over to the man. "Hey, Sarge. Looks like I caught this steaming turd tonight."

"Why does that not surprise me? What do you need from us on the patrol side?"

"I just got a quick brief, and I know Johnston is riding with our injured shooter. I'd like somebody to stay with the guy at the hospital and retrieve the bullet as soon as it's removed from his shoulder."

"Consider it done. Anything else?"

"This case, if it turns out to be related to the one from the other night, is getting the red-carpet treatment. So when the bullet's out, call immediately. One of the crime scene guys or I will come get it. If it's the same guy, then we've got our first potential lead."

"You know who the dead kid is?"

"Josh Daniels. Name doesn't ring a bell. Should it?"

"Probably not. But his brother's should."

"Who's that?"

"Luke Daniels, head of the Corner Boys. That local gang of misfits who've been terrorizing the Dot the last few years."

Kelly let the information assimilate into his mental case file. And the first thought that popped into his mind worried him greatly. *Retaliation.*

"What was the PI using?"

"Snub-nosed thirty-eight."

Kelly retrieved a pair of latex gloves from his crime bag in the trunk and grabbed his camera. He closed the trunk, donned the gloves, and made his approach. He picked a path and began methodically moving toward the store's entrance, systematically snapping photos every few steps.

The initial walk-through of a scene was as important as anything else he'd do. And he didn't take the task lightly, gathering his initial impression when details were at their most undefined point.

The cracked sidewalk was littered with glass. Kelly saw droplets of blood trailing off toward the recessed door of the tax office. Based on the info from the patrolman, it most likely belonged to the private investigator. Looked as though he took refuge in the doorway.

Kelly called over his shoulder to Cooper, "I take it this is where our guy was?"

"Yup. He was still in that spot when we arrived."

Kelly moved and stood near the spot where the first bit of blood was noticeable, careful not to step on any visible evidence. He positioned himself facing the storefront. From where he stood, the PI would've had a limited vantage point into the store. The windows were covered with poster advertisements that would've obscured the visibility.

"Don't go stepping in anything and ruining my scene."

Kelly turned to see Ray Charles standing behind him.

Dawes was also standing close behind. He smiled at the sight of the duo. "Bet you're happy as me to be here."

"We were still at the office. I told you I'd have that place up and running."

"Couldn't have come sooner. This case is quickly spiraling out of control."

"Are we guessing it's related?"

"Looks that way. Possibly some type of retaliatory hit. Good thing is, this one got interrupted." Kelly held up the camera. "I just got started on the initial walk-through. Care to join me?"

The three began moving toward the door.

Kelly noticed something along the curbing. The silver-coated cylinder, roughly the size of a small thimble, lay in a weathered crack. A shell casing. He immediately stepped back. "I think we've got something. Looks like our perp didn't have time to pick up his brass." He squatted low and snapped several pictures from multiple angles. Dawes did the same. Redundancy was the lifeblood of investigatory excellence.

Kelly got close enough to see the etched markings on the back end of the casing. 9mm.

Dawes placed a placard, marking the evidence. It would be photographed again when the full scene had been mapped and then again when it was removed and tagged.

"This scene has already given us more than the last two combined," Charles said as he added to the rough sketch in his pad. He'd be using a crime scene mapping program to create a computerized 3D replica of the scene, but the man was old school and always started with a hand-drawn notation. "Let's head inside and see what other gifts our doer has left us."

Kelly took the lead and gingerly gripped the corner of the door handle with his gloved hand to avoid any area most likely used by the perp when he entered.

The store was cool compared to the mugginess outside.

Nothing looked disturbed inside the main space. There were only two condensed aisles spaced tightly together. The counter was to the left of the door. Kelly made his way over and saw the clerk sprawled out, not unlike the one from Tyson's Market on the previous night. But as Kelly walked around toward the access door, he noticed another casing. "Doesn't seem like we're dealing with the same shooter."

"What makes you say that?" Dawes asked.

"There wasn't a casing at the first one. Either he used a revolver, or he picked up his brass. I'm guessing because the guy removed the round too, he cleaned up his evidence trail. Not seeing the same care here."

"Makes sense. I mean, if this is a retaliation, it would make sense it'd be a different shooter."

"I guess it was wishful thinking. Ya know? Kill two birds. Now what I've got is three bodies. And potentially two, or possibly three, different doers. Looks like my workload just tripled." Kelly rubbed a knuckle against his temple. "Not like my team isn't short-staffed or anything."

"All you can do is take it by the numbers. The case will work itself out over time. They always do. You'll drive yourself crazy trying to control the uncontrollable," Charles said.

Kelly nodded at the man's tempered wisdom. "Spoken from experience."

"She is the best teacher." Charles tipped his pen in the direction of the dead man. "How about we see what our friend here has to say."

Dawes dropped another placard. Kelly moved around to the back of the counter and had a much clearer view of the dead clerk. His body was flat on the ground. Kelly paused at what he saw before him.

Josh Daniels's arms were folded across his chest, as if he'd already been prepared by a mortician for viewing. His left hand lay across his right and underneath was a green rose. "Well, this day just got worse."

"Is that what I think it is?" Charles said, peering around Kelly in the tight space.

"It is."

Dawes, unable to see from his position, moved to the front of the counter and peered over. "What's with the green rose?"

"Looks like a message is being sent." Kelly stepped away from the body and back out onto the main floor. He pulled out his phone to call Sutherland. "Big problem, Sarge. Body's got a green rose. Looks like Walsh's crew just sent their response to last night's shooting."

"We've got to get a hold of this thing before it spirals out of control."

"I'm afraid it's going to get worse before it gets better. I need to meet with the Organized Crime guys on this. I'll reach out to Sharp."

Kelly ended the call, then set about processing the rest of the scene with Charles and Dawes. He thought about the potential he'd felt starting this night with Ithaca, and now it was ending at a murder scene. A BPD Homicide Cinderella story. And his carriage had definitely turned into a pumpkin. *Surreal.*

18

"You look like hell. Have you been here all night?"

The words startled Kelly and he sat up. A piece of paper clung to his face. Disoriented, he removed the document and rubbed his eyes. The incandescent ceiling light caused him to squint. Rubbing his eyes and yawning, he strained to see the numbers on his watch. 7:30. Kelly stood and stretched his arms wide. "Guess so. Must've passed out. Please tell me you brought a coffee."

"Now what kind of partner would I be if I didn't?" Mainelli held the medium-sized D&D regular in front of his face.

Kelly snatched it and gulped the hot liquid. "The kind who leaves me to work a scene by myself."

"Look, man, I'm sorry about that. After finally getting Anthony to sleep, I went lights out. My phone died and I missed the call. Nothing like waking up to a barrage of angry voicemails from Sutherland."

"Shit happens," Kelly offered groggily. "How's little Tony feeling today?"

"Better. Temp seems to be under control now. And it looks like I got to clean up the last bout of projectile vomiting that hit the floor last night." Mainelli eyed the stack of paperwork serving as Kelly's makeshift pillow. "But seriously, Mike, I owe you for last night."

"Under the bridge. I'll get you up to speed on the case."

Mainelli looked around the office. "Did Sutherland tell you who we'll be getting to replace Anderson?"

Kelly shook his head. "No. I think he enjoys teasing us with the anticipation. But anybody would be better. Whoever it is, I hope they get here soon. This case is quickly getting out of control."

Mainelli pressed his girth into Kelly's cubicle space and propped his rump on the edge of his desk. "Before we get started, I'm dying to know. How did it go?"

"How did what go?"

Mainelli rolled his eyes. "Really? The date. How did it go with our esteemed pathologist? Did sparks fly? Is she to be the next Mrs. Kelly?"

Kelly shrugged. "Okay, I guess. For the few minutes we had together. Didn't get too far. The shooting kind of messed things up."

"Dumbasses with guns have a tendency to do that. The joys of working the murder beat. Do you think there'll be a second date?"

"Maybe. We'll see."

"Where should I put this?" A female voice interrupted the banter.

Both men turned abruptly to see a smiling Kristen Barnes holding an oversized cardboard box.

"Kris?" Kelly gave her a double take. "What's up?"

"Boys, meet your new partner." Sutherland popped his head out from his office, smiling ear to ear. "I told you I'd get you your extra man—excuse me, woman."

"You're the replacement?"

She shrugged, box in hand. "Looks that way. I've had my fill of sex crimes. Plus, I figured somebody needed to look after you."

Mainelli hopped off the desk, taking some of Kelly's paperwork with him and spilling it onto the floor. "Drop that right over here," he said, skirting around the cubicle wall to the spot that Cliff Anderson once occupied. "Welcome to the show."

Barnes placed the box on the desk with a thud.

Sutherland walked over. "Get Kris up to speed on the case, and then I want to meet in the conference room for a debrief on the two shootings. Captain's been up my ass ever since the wit got whacked."

"You know, boss, you don't need to try to talk mobster on my account," Mainelli jested.

"I thought you Italians only understood when I did."

Proud of his jab, Sutherland retreated to his office before being forced to engage in any further display of wit.

Barnes looked at the two men of her new unit. "So, where are we at?"

Mainelli laughed. "Well, Mikey here was just about to spill the beans on his date last night."

Kelly's face reddened. He could feel the warmth. "Shut up, Jimmy. She meant the case."

"I know what she meant. But I'm just following the boss's orders and getting our new partner current on *all* things pertinent to this investigation. I mean, if you're going to be lovestruck and preoccupied, our newest addition to the team needs to be aware."

Barnes leaned on the cubicle wall. "Let's have it, Mike. Who's the lucky girl?"

And there it was. A slight hint of something in her voice. Barely noticeable, but definitely present. *Was it jealousy? Why would Barnes be jealous? It's not like anything had ever really happened between us,* he thought to himself. But there was certainly an unspoken chemistry when they had last partnered up. He'd written it off then but couldn't help thinking of it now.

"It wasn't really a date. Just friends. No big deal." He eyed Mainelli. "Jimmy here is just upset because he spent most of yesterday catching puke in a bucket. Comparatively, anything would seem like a romantic outing."

"It was with one of the pathologists from the ME's office," Mainelli added, apparently unwilling to drop the onslaught of stress this conversation was causing Kelly.

"Oh really? Which one?"

"Ithaca Best. And, like I said, it wasn't really a date."

Barnes gave a nod of approval. "She's cute. Never thought of you as the doctor type, though."

"She asked me." His face was burning hot now, and he knew there was no way the two didn't notice his change in complexion.

"That's how they all start."

Now Barnes was baiting him. "How about we focus more on the quickly mounting stack of bodies this case is accumulating and less about my personal life."

Mainelli held up his hands. "Whoa. Looks like we struck a nerve. He's probably just miffed because last night's shooting interrupted the conclusion of his date—correction, 'dinner with a friend.'"

Kelly sighed and opened a file folder. "Something's off with these robberies. I just can't put my finger on it."

Barnes leaned over his shoulder. Her hair brushed his cheek and he smelled the sweet scent of caramel and honey.

"What's the connection?" Barnes asked.

"Looks like the first spurred the second, but it doesn't really add up. The first shooting took place at Tyson's Market, a store under the protection of Walsh's crew. And the second looks like Savin Hill's answer. A retaliation."

Barnes picked up the case file containing the photos from the Talbott shooting. "What's the connection to the second store? Why'd they shoot up that one?"

"The leader of the Corner Boys' younger brother works there. He's the vic."

"So, what doesn't add? Seems pretty clear to me. Walsh's guys were pissed about the other night and sent a message. Street justice. Like some alpha pissing contest, marking their territory."

"My problem goes back to the first shooting."

Mainelli rolled his eyes. "Here we go. Mike's convinced there's a lot more to this than meets the eye. I feel like you're going to go all conspiracy theory on us."

Kelly waved the first case's folder in the air. "You don't think it's strange the shooter at Tyson's Market took the time to retrieve the bullet from the wall and police up his brass before departing?"

Mainelli offered a shrug. "Maybe he's smart. Maybe he's watched too much TV. There's about seven thousand spin-offs to *CSI* on the air and you know these turds eat the stuff up."

"I don't see it. From what I know, the Corner Boys are street thugs. Not trained assassins. That first one looked more like a planned hit than a robbery."

Barnes looked at the two men and then weighed in, "It does seem a bit odd. I've worked a lot of low-level street thug crimes and can't remember a time when I've seen them take the time to retrieve a bullet. Most would just dump the gun. Or sell it."

"So, we've got a hit on a store protected by the most powerful organized criminal ring in Boston. And then we've got this second shooting, which looks like the beginning of an all-out turf war." Kelly rubbed at the crick in the back of his neck and took a long sip from his cup, neither helping to clear his mind enough to see the answer clearly.

Mainelli interjected himself back into the debate. "This is going to sound crazy, but what if Walsh put a hit on his own store? Made it look like the Corner Boys."

"Why would he do that? The heat it would bring down on his crew would be immense."

"I guess. But it's been done before. Feign an attack and you get the support to show force. Maybe he's been pushing his crew to make a move on the Corner Boys and needed some added motivation to get it going?"

"It's a pretty wild theory."

Barnes's brow scrunched. "If what you're saying is true, what evidence do we have to connect the two?"

"Not much from the first shooting. The second, on the other hand, was a proverbial treasure trove of evidence." Kelly drained the last bit of coffee and tossed it in the nearby trash can. "Patrol brought the round retrieved last night to the lab. Charles will be getting it processed soon. It was recovered from our do-gooder PI, who stepped up and literally took one for the team. That plus the casings recovered put us in pretty good shape evidence-wise."

"You still don't have anything to compare it to from the first shooting," Mainelli offered. "Even if we locate the shooter and gun from the second shooting, it's unlikely we'd be able to stick the Tyson's Market body on him. Unless we get a confession."

"Ithaca said the wound was most likely consistent with a small caliber handgun. And that's what we found last night."

Mainelli huffed. "It ain't enough to hold up in court."

"We don't even have the shooter yet. Let's worry about court when we get there." Kelly appreciated Mainelli's willingness to play devil's advocate. It was essential to have multiple opinions when approaching an investigation. Time and evidence would whittle down the truth.

"All right, for the moment let's say we've got one shooter out there stirring the hornet's nest," Barnes interjected. "If what you said is true, we've got a much bigger problem on our hands. We're looking at the start of a gang war."

"I've already got a call in to Sharp over at Organized Crime. Maybe somebody in his group has some intel that will steer us in the right direction."

Barnes looked at both men and then gestured toward the door. "Only one way to find out."

Kelly stood outside the door to the Organized Crime office. His fob didn't have access permission. The solid wood door had no window. Centered at eye level was a placard that read *Secure Access: Authorized Personnel Only.* Kelly had knocked and was now waiting idly by with Barnes and Mainelli.

The door opened and Kelly was surprised to see Lincoln White. He met the man's eyes. No warmth was shared by either man.

"If it isn't Saint Michael?" White offered sardonically.

"Early for somebody who spends his nights abusing the civil rights of junkies."

A flash of anger shot across the older man's face. He pushed past, brushing shoulders with Kelly, who leaned in slightly. The firmness of his stance knocked White off balance.

White muttered some inaudible rant as he headed down the hall toward his office.

Barnes looked wide-eyed at Kelly. "No love lost there."

"Guy was a prick when we worked together in Narcotics. And nothing's changed that." Kelly exhaled the tension he felt at seeing the man and added, "Karma's a bitch and he'll get his one of these days."

Sharp popped his head out from his office and waved. "Mike, come on back."

Kelly and his team moved through the office toward the man. The space was about a quarter of the size of Homicide's; with only six detectives and Sharp as the supervisor, the auxiliary intelligence unit didn't need as much room. The detective cubicles were clustered in the center, their walls lined with pictures and maps. Sharp had access to digital databases but still believed in the old way of visually organizing and charting criminal activity.

"Jim, thanks for taking the time to meet with us. Been a crazy couple days on our end and I was hoping you'd be able to help."

Detective Sergeant James Sharp directed them to the seats scattered around the office as he pulled up his chair and put his feet up on his desk. He grabbed a rubber ball and began bouncing it off the wall above his computer. "I heard it's gotten a bit wild west out there. What can I do to help?"

"I know you've been working on Walsh's crew for a while. And when it comes to him, you're the expert around here."

He bounced and caught the ball. "I guess, but all that hasn't amounted to much in this office. That guy's remained untouchable no matter how hard we press. Walsh has got deep pockets and connections that make the most senior of politicians seem out of touch." Sharp held the ball for a moment, his face growing serious. "And don't for a second think he doesn't have people on the inside here. Why do you think we work in a secured space?"

"Be that as it may, we've got three dead bodies in the past two days, and we're convinced it's going to get a lot worse if we don't get a handle on this thing fast."

Sharp's feet came down from their relaxed position as he sat up and pulled himself closer to his desk. His face was all business now. "My guys have been working round the clock since the first shooting."

"And? Anything we can use?"

"As far as the shooter or shooters? No. Not yet at least."

Kelly stretched his back, still not fully adjusted from the awkward sleep position. "We're waiting on forensics, but I was hoping you'd be able to give us a head start."

"Shut the door," Sharp said.

Mainelli reached back and pushed the door closed.

"I've got a guy on the inside."

"I figured you had a snitch. Heard anything?" Kelly asked.

"Not a snitch. A cop."

Kelly was shocked. "You've got someone undercover? How the hell did you pull that off?"

"Not easily. It took a long time." Sharp sighed. "Longer to get him to the place he's at within the organization."

"Can you contact him? Reach out about this?"

"That's the thing. It's harder than it sounds. Not like I can just call him." Sharp looked worried. "I've got ways to reach out, but it's up to him to make contact. Deep cover work requires a full immersion."

"I didn't think it was even done anymore," Barnes offered.

"It's not. This project received special approval."

Kelly leaned in. "Jim, if you could get us in contact with him, it could really help. We've really got to know what he knows."

"It doesn't work that way. You're never going to contact him. We can't risk any exposure." Sharp put the rubber ball in the top drawer of his desk. "I couldn't arrange it even if I wanted to."

"And why's that?"

"Because we've lost contact. He's been unreachable for a few weeks."

"Aren't you worried he could be dead?" Mainelli asked.

"We've picked him up on surveillance. So we know that's not the case, but his lack of contact is of concern. The higher-ups are considering pulling the plug on the op. But with the shootings, they're holding out a little longer."

"Is that normal? Your guy going off the grid for that long?"

Sharp shrugged. "Sometimes. Working in this type of assignment makes things complicated at times. Meetups get missed. Check-in calls go unmade. I try not to panic every time he's off schedule. Although, under the circumstances, it's a bit frustrating."

"That's an understatement. You've got a guy embedded in Walsh's crew and there's war being waged on the streets of Dorchester. And all you can say is it's a bit frustrating?"

"Well, it's not like I can go down to Walsh's hangout, barge in, and say, 'Excuse me, Mister Mob Boss, I just need to borrow one of my operatives for a moment.'"

"Not what I meant." Kelly grit his teeth and fought the rage bubbling inside. "You don't have an emergency recall signal. A coded message that brings him in."

"We do."

"And?"

"I used it. The other day after the first shooting. Told him it was time to come in for a debrief."

"What did he say? Or do?"

"Nothing. He never responded."

"Send it again. And I want to be there when you meet up with him."

"I'll send it. But no way in hell are you going to be there for the meet. I'm not compromising my guy for some bullshit murder investigation."

"Bullshit murder investigation? Have you lost perspective? I remember when you were one of the good guys."

"Still am." Sharp sat back in his chair and folded his arms. "You're trying to solve a couple murders. And I know you think it's important. But you're not seeing the forest for the trees. I'm looking at the big picture. I'm going after the gang responsible for more deaths than you'll ever work in your career in Homicide. Hell, I'm working to prevent future murders by the case we're working." He gave a smug look. "So, Mike, you tell me who's doing the greater good?"

"More people are going to die if we don't get access to what your guy knows. Doesn't that matter?" Kelly asked in frustration.

"I know you don't see it now, but there are more important things at stake."

Kelly's brow furrowed. "More important than murder?"

"Yes." Sharp eyed all three visitors as if to ensure his simple yet complicated message was personally received. "Now, if you'll excuse me, I've got things to do. And you've got a killer to catch."

Kelly walked out with Barnes and Mainelli and they huddled in the hallway.

She gave him a baffled look. "What was that all about?"

Kelly hunched his shoulders. "Don't know. I've known Sharp a long time. Never seen him act that way."

"Looks like we just keep running into dead ends." Mainelli's stomach rumbled. "Maybe we should get some breakfast and mull this over?"

Kelly shook his head. "I've got a better idea."

"Better than food?"

"Let's see if we can find Sharp's guy."

Barnes reeled back slightly. "Not sure that's a good idea. Exposing a deep cover guy could be disastrous. I'm all for catching the bad guy, but that's a career-ending move."

"I didn't say anything about exposing him. I just want to know what he knows."

"Even so. You heard Sharp, that guy's been off the reservation. He can't even contact him."

"And that's where you're wrong. Sharp lied to us. Something tells me his guy is still in contact with him. No way the bosses would allow him to remain undercover with the neighborhood about to go to war. Not unless his guy is still feeding him intel."

Mainelli shook his head. "Why would he lie about that?"

"We're going to find out."

"How do you plan to do that?"

"We are going to follow him."

"You're going to follow a detective sergeant of a specialized unit?" Mainelli's whole body was saying no. "Count me out. No way am I getting caught up in some witch hunt. Especially one with career-tanking implications."

"Nobody's making you come. Stay here and wait for Charles to process the evidence, but I'm going."

"Me too." Barnes winked.

"You guys might as well turn in your shield and gun now."

Kelly ignored him as he and Barnes headed down the hall. Kelly called back, "Keep us posted on the evidence."

"What do I tell Sutherland if he asks?" Mainelli's voice was more shrill than normal.

"Tell him we're out doing police work."

Barnes lowered her voice to a whisper. "What's the plan?"

"I'm still figuring it out as we go." He offered a conciliatory wink. "What's the worst that could happen?"

"With you, sky's the limit."

19

"We know what we've got to do. The truce is over. Bring me that bastard! Bring him here so I can put a bullet in his damn skull myself."

Adam Murphy, the oldest of the Murphy brothers and Luke Daniels's most trusted soldier, spoke up. "I get it. You're pissed. Rightfully so. But still—you want us to bag Conner Walsh?"

Daniels stared at the man. His eyes were glassy and blood-shot, a direct correlation to the lack of sleep and amount of alcohol in the gang's leader. His words slurred together, the sound of it only adding to his visible anguish. "Did I stutter? His crew killed my brother. Shot him down like a dog. What'd Josh ever do to anyone?" He rubbed his eyes, further reddening the already blotched puffy surface underneath. "He was a good kid. Never hurt a fly. So, you tell me—what the hell would you do in my shoes?"

Murphy's face was affectless, a trademark that garnered him the nickname Slab. "I'd kill 'em all."

Another man, Simon Lynch, added his two cents. He was a tall, thin man with deep, sunken eyes. He'd fight if he had to, but Daniels had added him to the gang's roster for his intellect.

He was their numbers guy. In the Corner Boys, because of their small numbers, everyone had to pull their weight when a problem arose. So Lynch would be asked to temporarily trade his calculator for a gun. And seeing the slight tremor in his hands, this was obviously something he had trepidation in doing. His voice stammered as he said, "He's going to be well protected. Ain't like we can walk into his bar and snatch him. That'll be a guaranteed death sentence."

Daniels spit on the floor. "I don't care who and how many you've gotta kill to bring him to me, but if I don't see him down on his knees in front of me within the hour, there's going to be a problem. And if I get word that any one of you chickened out, it'll be you who'll be on your knees."

There was a commotion among the group of seven as they began to gather up their tools for the job. Small hushed discussions broke out among the men as they loaded their weapons. All but sixteen-year-old Ryan Murphy, the youngest member of the group and brother to the crew's enforcer. By default, with his older brother's propensity for violence, the group assumed Ryan would carry a similar zeal for bloodshed. The opposite couldn't be truer, and he absolutely hated being part of the Corner Boys. But growing up in his neighborhood, with his brother, the choice was made without him having a say. Ryan did his best to stay low and do the bare minimum to keep in Daniels's good graces and away from his brother's brutal punishment. But looking around the room, he could see doing so today would be impossible.

Adam approached, tucking a black handgun into the front of his jeans. "Ry, it's a big day for you, little brother." Adam had a wild-eyed grin that exposed the gold tooth replacing one of many that had been knocked out over the years.

Ryan swallowed hard and did his best to put up a macho front. At times like this he usually tried to stay near Lynch. Two cowards together didn't make his fear and repulsion to violence so obvious. But today, Adam had taken notice and was forcing him into the spotlight. "What do you mean by 'big day?'"

"Time to earn your keep." Adam pulled a second pistol from the back of his waistband. "This is for you. Checked it already. One round in the chamber, five more in the clip. All you've got to do is point and squeeze."

Ryan hoped his older brother couldn't see the quake ripple through his body. He'd only held a gun once before and that was just out of curiosity. He'd never fired one. And the thought of doing so at other people, gangsters or not, sickened him. But knowing the beating that would follow if he refused, Ryan took the gun. He delicately balanced the weapon in his palm, scared it would accidentally go off.

"Don't be afraid of the damn thing, for Pete's sake. You look like a little bitch the way you're holding it." Adam swatted the side of Ryan's head. A love tap compared to his typical beatings. "Grip it proper. Like this." Adam withdrew his gun and held it in front of his brother. "And you only put your finger on the trigger when you're ready to shoot. That way you don't blow off your wee Irish pecker."

"I know how to hold it," Ryan lied. False bravado was better than none.

"You're poppin' your cherry today. I want that clip empty when you hand it back to me."

Ryan felt dizzy. Bad enough he was carrying a gun. Now he was being ordered to use it. Killing a person had never been something he wanted to do. His brother had done it. Years ago, when he was thirteen. Knifed a kid in the heart. Did most of his teenage years in the juvenile detention system, where he met Daniels. Where they formed an unbreakable bond.

Ryan saw the look in his brother's blue-gray eyes. He'd have no choice in the matter. Nothing in Ryan Murphy's life had ever been left up to him. Adam said he had to empty the gun. He didn't say anything about hitting a target. How could he be expected to be a good shot if he'd never used a pistol before? It was the only possible saving grace to this horrible ordeal. He'd fire over their heads and hope he didn't accidentally hit anybody. He'd do his best to make it look good for his own sake.

"When are we going?" Ryan asked, hoping his brother didn't pick up on the tremble in his voice.

"Soon as we get the word from the lookout. Gotta confirm the big man's there before we roll out."

Ryan stuffed the gun into his pants like he'd seen his brother do. He did his best to make sure the muzzle wasn't pointing toward his junk. The metal dug into his waist uncomfortably.

Adam slapped him hard on the shoulder. "Just point and shoot. Simple as that."

"If you say so."

Ryan joined the others who were slowly working themselves into a fever pitch of anticipatory excitement. The only member who seemed to be on his level of worry was Lynch, but the skinny boy did a better job of hiding it.

Today was shaping up to be the worst in his sixteen years of bad luck. He sat on the worn couch, avoiding the spring protruding through one end, and began the waiting game, hoping the lookout never called.

20

The bar floor around Walsh's stool was littered with lollipop wrappers. He looked rabid, his bloodshot eyes darting wildly over the men loosely surrounding him. His thin white hair was slicked back, and if Bobby had to guess, the leader of the Savin Hill Gang hadn't slept since he last saw him. Seeing Walsh in such a frenzy was a rarity, and it made Bobby tremble.

"Who the hell authorized anybody to make a move on those stupid bastards?" His bloodshot eyes scanned the room. "Who!?"

Speaking during one of Conner Walsh's rants was a guaranteed death sentence and every man in the room knew it. Every man in the room kept his mouth closed.

"Nobody's leaving this room until I have the name of the son of a bitch who shot that halfwit on Talbott last night," he seethed, taking a slow sip from the tumbler on the bar. "Nobody's walking out of here at all if I don't get an answer." His tone dropped but the seriousness of his words couldn't have been more profound.

O'Toole looked just as baffled as Walsh but controlled his temper, one of the reasons the man had been so valuable to

Walsh over the years. O'Toole managed to remain calm during these moments and therefore served as good counsel. He was the yin to Walsh's yang. But this morning, O'Toole seemed as nervous as the rest of the crew.

"Fitzy, go down the line until I have my answer."

Fitzpatrick pulled out a pistol from his waistband and walked to the first man. He stopped short and turned to Walsh. "No need to."

"What did you say?" Walsh pushed himself off the barstool and stood rigid.

"I said, there's no need to. 'Cause I already know the answer."

"And who pray tell would that be?"

Fitzpatrick squared himself to the self-proclaimed King of Boston. "Me."

Walsh looked stunned. Momentarily and uncharacteristically at a loss for words. His eyes widened.

The men nearest Fitzpatrick moved away, clearing a path for whatever tumult was to follow.

"You, my most trusted soldier, directly disobeyed an order. What was unclear about the meeting yesterday? Danny, did I not say we were going with your suggestion?"

O'Toole shifted on his stool. "You did. I'd already reached out to the kid who runs their crew. That little shit, Luke Daniels. He was supposed to come to the table this afternoon so we could sort this thing out."

Walsh folded his arms and eyed Fitzy like a lion preparing to devour a gazelle. "Did you hear that, Fitzy? Did you hear we were going to meet with them?"

Fitzpatrick didn't answer. He didn't move. The gun was still held down by his thigh.

"Now you're telling me you went out and shot one of their

own? Worse, you shot his mentally handicapped younger brother! There's no coming back from this. No way to reason with them. No way to make this right. Not without a blood payment."

"Those pricks needed to be taught a lesson. They needed to have their nuts snipped before they got big balls."

Walsh flexed his neck from side to side with an audible cracking sound made more dramatic by the hushed silence of the room. "When did you start thinking for yourself? When did I open the floor to free thought within this gang?" His voice began to rise in volume and intensity. "What on God's green earth made crossing me seem like a good idea?"

"I did what's best for us. I sent the message that needed to be sent. And the one you were apparently too weak to send." Fitzpatrick rubbed the outside of the gun's trigger housing with his index finger.

Bobby noticed and subtly slipped his pistol out from the small of his back. He kept the weapon hidden from view. He could feel the beat of his heart and the tingle of adrenaline pumping through his extremities.

Walsh turned his back on the man and grabbed his glass off the bar. He drained the whiskey in one gulp and then hurled the empty tumbler sideways across the room. The glass shattered against the wall and several of the men flinched. Fitzpatrick did not. Neither did Bobby.

Walsh then began walking the room, pacing slowly and leveling a steady gaze at each man he passed. It was said Walsh could bore deep into a man's soul. Some whispered rumors he was the devil incarnate.

"I'm not sure what's happening here. I brought many of you up from when you were kids running the streets with no pot to piss in. Here you are now. Made men. My men. And yet how many of you knew about this and didn't tell me."

One by one Walsh's inner circle bowed their heads in shame.

"I'm left with a difficult decision." He poked Fitzpatrick in the chest, knocking him back a step. "Do I clear out my ranks and begin anew?" He looked around and then settled his gaze back on the man who'd usurped his authority. "Or do I make an example of the one who took it upon himself to try and take matters into his own hands?"

The group offered no answer.

Bobby noticed something he'd never seen before among Walsh's inner circle. They weren't overtly backing their leader. It was a silent mutiny. Typically, others would chime in their support. In the silence, Bobby felt an unease. An imbalance in the world he knew, one he'd spent the better part of his life in. And he didn't like it.

"The others have seen it." Fitzy took his turn to eye the other members.

Walsh's eyes narrowed, and a low whistling sound seeped out from between his clenched teeth like a kettle near boiling. "The others have seen what?"

"You've taken the easy left instead of the hard right. In years past, a shooting on our turf in a store under our protection would have been dealt with swiftly. Now here you are, complaining that I handled the business end of things."

"Say what you really mean!"

"You're getting weak. And this crew runs on strength. You built it that way. I just don't think you have it in you to keep it operating in the same way."

O'Toole cleared his throat. "Times are different now. Can't go around blowing things up every time we send a message. We've got to be more subtle. Cops and officials aren't as easy to bribe as they once were. Not with all that social media crap. That's why we agreed to approach this more delicately. Have the

Daniels kid come in for a meet. Give him a chance to turn over the shooter. That's real power. Not that botched shooting gallery you pulled on Talbott."

"What do you mean botched?"

O'Toole's jowls flapped like a hound dog as he spoke. "You got spotted. That damn guy who shot at you."

"Doesn't matter. I was wearing a mask. There's no way he can ID me. Plus, he's laid up in the hospital."

"What about the gun?"

"What about it?"

"Where is it?" O'Toole eyed the pistol still bootlegged in Fitzpatrick's hand.

He followed the man's gaze down to the gun. "This isn't it, if that's what you're asking. I took care of the gun from last night. Nobody will find it." Fitzy then tucked the weapon into the small of his back.

"Enough!" Walsh interrupted. "You shouldn't have put that gun away."

Fitzpatrick looked unfazed by the veiled threat. "And why's that? You're going to kill me? Why? Because I did what you were too weak to do. Because I did what needed to be done?"

Bobby held fast with his pistol still gripped tightly behind his back.

"You think I'm dumb enough to come at you without an insurance plan? You should know me better than that."

Walsh paused, his anger still bubbling, but a visible line of concern was etched across his brow. "What are you talking about?"

"I took care of the gun. But not in the way you think. And it won't come back on me, because it's linked to you. I think you know why and how. And if you haven't completely lost your mind, then you'll be smart enough to let me walk out of here."

Walsh's eyes went wide. Bobby knew why. He was the only

other person in the room who knew exactly the leverage Fitz-patrick held. Several years back Fitzpatrick had proven his worth to Walsh by claiming he could steal the gun from Boston PD's evidence. The gun that would put Walsh away for life. Of course, at the time Walsh didn't believe Fitzpatrick was capable of pulling off the task. But a few days later, the gun, a Ruger 9mm with filed off serial numbers, disappeared from evidence. Fitzpatrick told Walsh he tossed it off the docks. But now, in light of his recent statement, it was readily apparent this had not been the case. The ace up his sleeve gave him the winning hand in this life-or-death round of roulette and Walsh must've real-ized it, because he turned his back on the man and sat facing the mirrored glass behind the bar.

"I'm leaving. We'll talk more once you've had a chance to think things over. It's time for you to step down. Let me know when you're ready to hand over the keys to the kingdom."

Walsh said nothing as Cormac placed a new glass on the bar in front of him and poured a double. He unwrapped a Tootsie Pop and stirred the amber liquor. The only sound was the clink of the hard candy as it rattled along the glass of the tumbler.

Bobby watched as Fitzpatrick left. The door slammed shut and the room remained silent. Even the normally loquacious O'Toole was left speechless as each of the senior members of the Savin Hill Gang contemplated the future.

21

They kept a distance six cars back and watched as the Organized Crime Unit's detective sergeant turned right into the Stop and Shop plaza from Popes Hill Street.

The parking lot was more congested than one would figure for mid-morning Friday, but the additional patronage aided in their ability to conceal themselves among the other vehicles. Kelly had kept a loose tail since their departure from the station. Following another cop around town felt strange. It was a long shot, but he was playing the odds that Sharp would be inclined to set a meet after their heated exchange.

Kelly continued to follow at a distance, driving deeper into the lot to where it widened near Freeport Street. The additional space gave them options for positioning once Sharp stopped.

Barnes kept watch from the passenger seat. "There he is parked next to the blue Mazda."

Kelly pulled into a spot two rows away. A Pathfinder provided concealment but also blocked some of the view. The two positioned themselves for the best vantage point and watched carefully.

"This reminds me of my narc days. Hopefully, we don't have

to wait as long. Drug dealer time was always an unpredictable thing."

"Any ideas who his deep cover guy might be?" Barnes asked.

"No. I tried looking it up in the database, but the electronic files related to OC and Narcotics are password protected. The hard copies are kept in Sharp's office. Don't think he'll be inviting me for coffee anytime soon."

"I guess it makes sense they'd put up restrictions. The mob's reach is a scary thing. Never know who's connected, or worse, on the take."

Kelly thought of Bobby. The favor he'd called in to help find a dead girl's killer. The favor resulted in an unforeseen dead body. And the consequences had strained their relationship, causing an ever-growing rift in their seemingly unbreakable bond.

Barnes sat up. "Strange that Sharp brought White with him if he's meeting with his guy. I thought he'd meet his UC alone."

"Me too. I guess it makes some sense that White's involved. Much of Walsh's money comes from the drug trade."

"What's up with you and White?"

"I didn't agree with his tactics. I think you've known me long enough and seen how I work cases to know that I'm willing to do what it takes to get the bad guy, but White took things to the next level."

"How so?"

"He was unnecessarily violent. That was never my approach for extracting information. I'm more of the 'get more by honey' mindset. I stopped him one time when he was giving an informant a beating when he didn't feel the guy was being truthful. He didn't like being interrupted. Needless to say, he found it more difficult to beat on me."

Barnes's eyebrows raised in surprise. "You went toe to toe with Lincoln White? How did I never hear about this?"

Kelly shrugged dismissively. "White only brags about his wins," he said. "And I don't brag at all."

Barnes twisted in her seat and stared at him intently. "I've got to know."

"Not much to say about it. As imposing as he looks, his jaw is made of glass."

"Stop being so coy." Barnes smiled. "Must've felt good."

Kelly joined her in smiling at the memory of laying out the Narcotics legend. "It really did."

Kelly refocused his attention on Sharp's unmarked and squinted hard. Sharp's vehicle was parked facing Kelly's, but sunlight and a tinted visor panel made seeing into the car difficult.

"Hold on. Looks like our guest of honor might've just arrived. Somebody just got in the back seat."

"I can't see through the glare of the windshield. Did you get a good look at him?"

"No. He came in from the other side. He was blocked by that minivan parked next to them."

Kelly reached across to the glove box. His forearm grazed her thigh as he opened the latch and pulled out a pair of binoculars.

"Could've just asked. Or were you trying to cop a feel?"

Kelly retreated. "I didn't ... sorry, I was—"

"Jeez, lighten up. Just messin' with you."

His face warmed again. "I knew that."

"Don't worry, I won't tell your girlfriend."

Kelly sighed, letting the comment slide as he retracted his seat. Leaning back, he brought the binoculars up to his face and peered out. Barnes adjusted her back as well.

"The glare's making it impossible to make out the guy's features. Strange—it looks like White's doing most of the talking. You'd think if he was Sharp's guy, he'd be taking the lead."

"Once we figure out who the UC is, maybe we'll have a better understanding of the reason. Could be a dope thing. Who knows?"

The minivan blocking their view drove away. "Maybe. Now that my line of sight is cleared up, we should hopefully get a look when he steps back out." Barnes put her hand out. "Hand me the binos, I think I'll have a better angle."

Kelly turned over the binoculars.

Barnes shifted herself and took up the lookout. "What's the plan after he leaves?"

"Follow, I guess. If the opportunity presents itself, we'll try to corner him when he's alone."

Barnes rubbed her temples. "It's my first day in Homicide. Nothing like ruffling a few feathers by snatching an undercover being managed by two of the most powerful cops in the PD."

A smile formed on Kelly's face. "At least you can say it wasn't a boring start."

"With you, I never thought it would be." Barnes's posture perked slightly. "We've got movement. Looks like the driver's side back door is opening. Should have eyes on the prize in a second."

Kelly resisted the urge to move into a better position, fearing the motion inside the car might draw attention from Sharp or White.

"He's out." Barnes inhaled deeply. "No way! You're not going to believe me when I tell you."

"Who is it?"

Barnes turned to face him. "It's Brayden."

Kelly was caught off guard at the mention of his brother. It took him a moment to process the information. "Doesn't make sense. Why would Sharp go into all this cloak-and-dagger talk about an undercover if he was using an informant?"

"Kind of obvious, isn't it? He didn't want to tell you because it's your brother."

"Having White here with Sharp makes more sense now. He must've picked Brayden up on a bust and flipped him. Why wouldn't Brayden just call me? Or White, for that matter?"

"I know you and Brayden are at odds right now, but you're still his older brother. And if the guy I knew from back in the day is still in there, he looks up to you more than you'll ever know." Barnes gave him a reassuring look and followed it with a squeeze of his forearm. "It's going to sound a bit cheesy, but when Brayden and I dated, he talked about you all the time. Mike did this—Mike did that. He worshipped you. You were his hero."

It'd been a long time since he'd felt his younger brother's adoration, or even a modicum of cordiality. Upon hearing Barnes's words, he was taken aback. "'Were' being the optimal word in that sentence. I don't think my brother still holds me in such high regard."

"He's your brother. Nothing's going to change that."

"I guess. So, you've got a reason why Brayden wouldn't reach out to me. But it still doesn't excuse White for not looking out. Regardless of his thoughts on me, we still wear the badge and that's supposed to extend to family. The Blue Code."

She released her grip on his arm. "Maybe White's blood doesn't run as blue as yours."

"Maybe I should test his jaw again and find out."

Barnes chuckled. "Well, should be pretty easy to snatch him up without drawing too much suspicion."

They watched as Brayden moved along the row of cars and out of view. "We'll wait for Sharp to drive away and then we'll go have a chat with my little brother," Kelly said.

Barnes then furrowed her brow and picked up the binoculars again. "Weird."

"What?"

"Somebody else is walking up to Sharp's vehicle. I guess Sharp wasn't lying." Barnes shook her head. "Now that's a face I haven't seen in a long time. Patrick O'Malley."

"I thought he took a task force officer position with one of the fed agencies a few years back. Those guys go off and we rarely see them again until their assignments are over. But I guess now it makes more sense. It's been at least two, if not three, years since I last saw him."

"Doesn't look much different from how I remember him. Except maybe a little more mobby."

"Not sure if mobby is a word."

Barnes laughed. "It is now."

O'Malley disappeared inside the vehicle, taking up the same spot Brayden had just vacated.

"How are you holding up?" Sharp asked with an air of genuine concern.

"Good as can be expected. Things are really tense right now. You couldn't have picked a worse time to call me away. This better be good."

"It's Kelly. He's working the bodies of the robberies and he's digging hard into Walsh."

"What'd you tell him?"

"Told him we got a guy on the inside."

O'Malley's nose scrunched and his eyes narrowed in anger. "You exposed me to Michael Kelly? What were you thinking? That boy scout is going to rip this thing apart."

"I didn't expose you. I exposed the idea of you in the hopes he'd see the light and realize there is more to this than just a couple homicides."

Still seething, O'Malley said, "How'd Saint Michael take the news? Did he immediately back down?"

Sharp looked at White. "Not exactly."

"Do you know what I've sacrificed for this assignment? Do you know the impact it's had on my life? I've spent years splitting my life. Sneaking around to see my wife. And now I'm losing her to cancer. I've given everything. We're too close to seeing this through to have Kelly screw it all up. How'd Kelly even end up with the case? I thought Cliff Anderson was supposed to get it assigned to him. If so, that idiot would still be sitting at his desk trying to type up the first case."

"There are some things outside of our control. Anderson was kicked out of Homicide recently. I guess his ability to botch an investigation finally caught the eye of his superiors."

O'Malley sighed. "Shit luck I guess."

"Seems so. In Anderson's unexpected exit, Kelly got the case."

"Make sure you keep him off my ass. I've got enough to worry about without him playing hero."

Sharp gave a pensive pause. "Maybe it's time to shut this operation down."

"What? Are you out of your damn mind?" O'Malley's fair skin reddened. "Shut it down?"

"Nobody was supposed to die. That wasn't the agreement."

O'Malley's face remained red, but his lips curled into a faint smile. "Like you said—some things are out of my control."

Sharp glared hard at the man. "I think it's time for you to come home, Patrick. We'll do what we can from here."

O'Malley looked away and grew quiet. "Home? I've got nothing to go home to. Karen is failing. It's stage four. Doctors have given her months at best," he whispered. "This is all I have left. Let me see this through. Let me finish what we started. At least then it won't all be for nothing."

White cleared his throat and interrupted the moment. "If you're staying—" He shot a glance at Sharp. "Then we're going to need some assistance from you with something."

O'Malley turned his attention to the man seated in the front passenger seat. "And what's that?"

"I've got a guy doing a buy into the crew. Decent weight. Two bricks of dope."

"I haven't heard anything about it."

White raised an eyebrow. "That's disappointing. I thought you were in the know. You're supposed to be the guy who knows the inner workings of things."

O'Malley leaned forward, his shoulders tense. "I guess you weren't listening to our conversation. I have bigger things going on right now."

O'Malley's retort didn't faze White, who continued matter-of-factly. "Take it easy, pal. I'm not the enemy here. Just trying to give us some alternatives should yours fall apart. Besides, I guess it makes sense you wouldn't know about the deal. My snitch brokered it with Sullivan. Looks like the low-level enforcer is trying to make a little money on the side."

O'Malley shrugged. "What's it got to do with me?"

Sharp leaned in close. "Because I said it does. We need this as a contingency. An angle to build a case outside of our planned agenda. And you're going to be there to make sure it goes down."

"Why are we worried about a little drug deal when we're so close to a much bigger opportunity?"

"Consider it an insurance program." White gave a crooked smile. "Do we have an understanding?"

"Sure," O'Malley said. "Who's the guy? Your snitch?"

White broke into a big grin. "You're gonna love this. It's Kelly's younger brother."

O'Malley ran his hand along his defined jawline. "That's

some twisted shit. Using a cop's brother on a high-level drug buy." He laughed. "But I love it."

White nodded. "I figured you would."

Sharp gave O'Malley a look of genuine concern. "No more screw-ups. No more deviation from the plan. Do you understand me?"

O'Malley leveled an intense stare at his supervisor. "Are we done here?"

"For now." Sharp carefully evaluated the man in the back seat. "Remember whose side you're on. You're a cop first."

"I haven't been a cop for a very long time." O'Malley opened the door and stepped out.

The meeting lasted less than ten minutes before O'Malley reappeared. Barnes, still holding the binos, said, "He's out. Moving toward a black Cadi parked a row away."

"The Brayden situation can be addressed later. We need to have a chat with O'Malley."

Barnes put the binoculars down. "He's in the Cadillac."

Kelly put the Caprice in drive and waited with his foot on the brake. Sharp pulled out of his spot and sped out toward the same entrance he'd come in. O'Malley moved toward an exit on the opposite side of the shopping plaza and pulled out onto Freeport Street. Kelly released the brake, and he and Barnes began to drift in the direction of the Cadillac. "If he's been able to stay deep cover in the most dangerous crime family in Boston, my guess is he can spot a tail a mile away."

"Well, you managed not to spook two of the sneakiest bastards in the PD. I'm confident if anyone can do it, it'd be you."

"I wish I had the same confidence in my ability as you do."

Barnes smiled. "I guess that's what makes us such great partners."

The Cadillac was a block and a half ahead. Kelly maintained his distance and tried to anticipate O'Malley's next move so as not to accidentally close the gap. He needed to get the man alone and away from any watchful eyes. He now had to avoid being spotted by members of both sides of the law, and Walsh, Sharp, and White had eyes everywhere.

22

"This is it. You ready?" Adam Murphy asked. The group had done several shots of whiskey while waiting for confirmation that Walsh was on location, and Ryan could smell the sourness of it on his older brother's hot breath.

"I guess." Ryan's stomach was in knots. He wasn't sure if it was from the forced consumption of alcohol or the all-consuming fear he felt. Most likely a combination of the two. Whatever the cause, he didn't like it. Being forced to shoot a gun at people seemed complicated enough without having to worry about vomiting beforehand.

Adam grabbed him by the ear and pulled him close, a painful attention-getter learned from their not-so-gentle mother. Twisting the cartilage of his left ear, Adam hissed, "Get your sorry head out of your ass! Shit's about to get real. And fast. Time for you to be a man."

The words were accompanied by flying spit droplets. Ryan winced at the unwanted shower. He wished he hadn't. Adam must've perceived it as weakness because he followed with a violent smack across the face. The impact caused Ryan's eyes to water reflexively. He shoved his brother with all the strength he could muster. "You're an asshole!"

Adam began slapping his own face like a maniac's version of The Three Stooges. "Good! Now that's the spirit!" He turned his attention to the group. "Boys, looks like my pissant little brother's got a little fight in him after all. Let's put some of that anger to use. Load up."

They were packed into a white utility van they'd stolen a few weeks ago. Daniels decided it would be the perfect car for a snatch-and-grab operation. The back space of the van was gutted. Benchless, the riders sat on the warped floorboards.

Ryan looked around at the bunch. Adam had moved away and was now facing him, but no longer paying attention. Lynch was close by and had spent the past few moments fiddling with his gun. Perry Dempsey, the biggest of them at roughly six foot two and weighing nearly two hundred and fifty pounds, was sitting shotgun in the worn, off-white leather passenger seat and was, ironically, carrying one. The driver, Deny Byrne, gripped the steering wheel tightly. The white of his knuckles did little to bely the tension. For being the only member tasked with staying behind with the van, Deny seemed to be on equal par with Ryan as far as nerves went. The only person absent was Luke Daniels, who today was acting more like Puzo's Don Corleone from *The Godfather* than the leader of a small-time street gang. He remained behind at the hangout, an abandoned warehouse on Aukland Street.

The distance between their starting point and the destination wasn't far, but it didn't feel like it. Each bump of the road jostled Ryan's unease to a frenzied state, adding to his paranoia surrounding the dangers ahead.

"Comin' up on it now. 'Bout a block away." Deny punched the steering wheel and made a strange whooping sound.

"People are going to be talking about what we do here today for years to come! Give 'em hell, boys!"

The rest of the group began pounding the metal walls of the truck in an out-of-sync fashion that sounded like an off-key garage band drum solo. The ruckus was amplified when they added drunken battle cries. Ryan looked on, silently observing the madness, completely incapable of bringing sense to the lunacy. His brother was the loudest of the group and took on a manic, deranged look Ryan had never seen before, frightening him.

The van skittered to a screeching stop. Ryan fell to his side. He righted himself as Adam leapt toward the rear and booted open the back door. His older brother reached back and pulled Ryan forward by the arm. "Time to show me you're worthy of the Murphy name! Do-or-die time, little brother."

With a shove, he was launched out of the van and stood facing the Irish tricolor green, white, and orange flag hanging above the main entrance to JW's Pub. The rest of the Corner Boys filed out behind, barreling into him. Ryan realized that to any bystanders watching them exit the van, the motley crew must've looked more like a gaggle of drunken partygoers than a team of gangsters ready to make a major play. This thought played heavily into his self-doubt as to the probability of a successful outcome.

As planned, Ryan reluctantly led the charge to the side door. As he traipsed along the alleyway, most of his momentum was spurred by his brother's continual shoving. The group was no longer hooting and hollering, and the drumming of his heartbeat replaced the cacophony with equal, if not louder, resonance.

Five feet from the black-painted steel door, Ryan stopped dead in his tracks. He was frozen by fear. His feet felt as though they were rooted to the concrete. Even with his brother's hard push from behind, Ryan remained in place. He could hear voices around him but couldn't make out the words. The door was already open, and he was staring at a massive hulk of a man with a bald head buffed to a bowling ball's shine. The mobster's eyes scanned the approaching horde, and it took a millisecond for him to recognize the threat. "Got trouble!" he hollered into the open space of the door as he drew a pistol from the small of his back.

Ryan looked on as if watching the events unfold through someone else's eyes. The other members of his gang swept by him, Adam now in the lead. The bald man wearing a black T-shirt and jeans did not retreat. Instead, he stepped out the door. Ryan saw the look of surprise on his face turn to a visceral anger as his lips curled up into a snarl. One of Conner Walsh's human guard dogs was preparing to bite.

The first shot rang out, cutting through his foggy distortion of sound. Ryan couldn't tell who fired the shot, but figured it was his brother.

The man in the black shirt jerked violently and his body twisted. He fell back into the bar and disappeared from sight. Before the door could shut, Adam, Lynch, and Dempsey flooded inside.

As the door closed behind them, Ryan listened as the dissonance of gunfire erupted from within.

His body, no longer frozen, was on the move, a sort of autopilot survival function. But he wasn't heading toward the bar or back out to the waiting van. Instead, Ryan ran toward a large green metal dumpster nestled on the opposite side of the alley. It was set back near the concrete wall of a tool repair shop.

He pulled out the small handgun his brother had given him and wiped the outside of its frame on his shirt. Ryan had seen enough crime shows to know to remove the prints. He opened the side slot to the bin. A foul stench of rotten waste filled the warm air as he tossed the weapon inside. It landed with a muted thud. Ryan peered in and saw the weapon had fallen between two large black trash bags. He hoped the black butt of the gun would blend in enough that it wouldn't be discovered until it was removed by a garbage truck.

The bar door opened again as gunshots continued to ring out. Ryan panicked and tucked himself behind the dumpster. Peeking out, he looked on as the chaos continued to unfold.

Lynch was the first back out the door, falling as he exited. The lanky man moved awkwardly on all fours for a moment before launching himself back to his full height. His gangly arms pumped rapidly as he ran toward the van. He was not a good runner. Even with the adrenaline dump, he seemed to move slower than the situation dictated.

Panic set in when the door began to slowly close again with no sign of Adam. Ryan felt helpless. The rapidity of gunfire began to decelerate like microwave popcorn in its final seconds before the beep.

Just before coming to a complete close, the door swung wide, slamming into the outside wall. Adam staggered out into the light with his arm slung around Perry Dempsey's thick neck. His head hung low and bobbed freely as Dempsey shuffled him along. Ryan could see his brother's blood-soaked shirt but couldn't tell the cause or extent of his injuries. It looked bad, though. Adam's legs were barely moving. Dempsey was doing the brunt of the work moving them down the side of the pub toward the street.

Dempsey continued to fire blindly behind him, indiscriminately loosing rounds. It wasn't effective in terms of eliminating the threat, but it did keep their pursuers from exiting the building. Tires screeched as the van backed wildly into the side lot. Lynch opened the rear doors as Dempsey's gun ran dry and members of Walsh's crew began to stream out.

Dempsey flung Adam into the back and climbed inside after him. The van peeled out onto the road, fishtailing as it entered the light traffic and almost colliding with a lime green beat-up Toyota Tercel.

The lot, only moments before a modern version of the O.K. Corral, was now plunged into silence. The members of Walsh's crew who'd ventured outside after the retreating survivors of the failed abduction began to casually back-peddle inside.

Ryan tucked himself deeper behind the dumpster and, for the first time since his father died, said a prayer.

23

Kelly watched as O'Malley cut into the parking lot behind a row of brownstones converted into businesses. He slipped the Caprice behind a Subaru parked along the curb a few spaces down from the entrance.

O'Malley remained in his vehicle. Kelly and Barnes waited.

"If he moves to head inside, let's try to intercept him," Kelly said. "Keep it casual until we can get him alone and then we'll pry a little deeper."

Barnes gave a subtle nod. "It's not like he's going to run from us. He's still a cop, right?"

"He's been undercover for a long time. Not sure what that does to a person. You and I have both done a little role playing in Narcotics and prostitution stings. Even under those brief circumstances, the character lines become a bit blurred. I can't imagine what staying in another persona for years would do to a person. Lots of good cops never were able to make the shift back. It's one of the reasons those Donnie Brasco-type assignments have gone by the wayside."

O'Malley hadn't moved. Kelly assumed he was waiting on something or someone. Maybe this was part of his routine. A place to cool off and settle his nerves before getting back into character and returning to his mobster buddies. Made sense he'd need a moment to compose himself. Must be terribly difficult to live two different lives, Kelly thought. Especially when one of those lives, if exposed, would be an unquestionable death sentence. There were a lot of unknowns with O'Malley. And Kelly hoped their conversation with the deep cover operative would answer some, if not all, of them.

His cell vibrated with an incoming call from Mainelli. He swiped to answer.

"Hey, Jimmy, you're on speaker with me and Kris. What do you got?"

"You're not going to believe this when I tell you, but Charles just finished up with the shell casings from the second shooting."

"And?"

"Remember that case a few years back where Conner Walsh was charged in the shooting death of Terrance May?"

Kelly remembered. He'd been in Narcotics at the time, but the potential conviction of Conner Walsh was pasted on the front page of every newspaper and television station. It was truly the talk of the town. He also remembered how an airtight case with rock-solid evidence had fallen completely apart. "Of course I remember. It was the only time where Walsh was pinned with a murder." Kelly actually knew of another time, but exposing that crime and its sole witness would jeopardize Bobby's life. And that was something he wasn't willing to risk.

"And you remember how it fell apart at court?"

"Well, for one, the star witness disappeared. And then, magically, so did the evidence."

"That's right. The gun used, with Walsh's prints and DNA, disappeared from evidence. The case disintegrated without it. And Walsh walked."

"Don't tell me?"

"Yup. It's one and the same. Charles is still comparing the round retrieved from the PI's shoulder to be absolutely positive, but—all things point to a big fat yes."

Kelly sat back. "I did not see that coming."

"That's all you can say? Mike, this could be the biggest case in recent history. We've got a chance to take down Conner Freakin' Walsh! Cut the head off the snake and completely dismantle the Savin Hill Gang."

"Let's not get ahead of ourselves. We still need to get a handle on this thing. Not like we're going to walk up to Walsh and ask for the gun. We've got to find the damned thing first." Something nagged at Kelly like an itch just out of reach. *Why would the gun be used again? Why now?* "Are we really supposed to believe Walsh shot the kid on Talbott? Doesn't make sense."

"Maybe whoever's using it now isn't Walsh, but it's got to be somebody in his crew, right?" Barnes added.

"Not sure. Seems like if Walsh knew that gun was still out in the world, he'd have gone to great lengths to make sure it was melted down or at the bottom of the Charles by now."

"That's it." Barnes was bright-eyed. The emerald green caught the sunlight and was dazzling. "There's no way Walsh knows that gun is being used again."

Kelly caught her drift. "Maybe it's time we had a little talk with the head of the Irish Mob. Maybe we can somehow use him to flush out our shooter."

"Sounds crazy to hear you say it out loud—but maybe a little crazy is what we need right now," Barnes offered.

Mainelli clicked his teeth. "First you follow the head of our Organized Crime Unit and now you're talking about going and having a sit-down with Walsh." He sighed loudly. "All I can say is, thank God I'm sitting here with Charles. At least one of us will be alive to tell the tale."

The radio built into the Caprice's center console began a barrage of chatter. Initially Kelly had tuned out the chatter, which, in Boston, was constant. But listening now, he heard the urgency in the voice, and then, "—all units in the area of Dot Ave head to JW's Pub. Code 99. Multiple reports of shots fired coming in. Unknown number of shooters. Unknown if it's still active at this time. Supervisors acknowledge the Code 99."

Animated responses filled the air as the patrol division confirmed receipt of the priority radio transmission.

Kelly looked at Barnes. "Sounds like we're going to get that meeting with Walsh sooner than we thought."

"If he's still alive," Barnes said flatly.

Kelly shot one last glance at O'Malley, who was still sitting in the Cadillac, before dropping the Caprice into drive. He waited until he was out of sight before activating his lights and sirens.

Kelly and Barnes raced through the mid-day traffic toward the pub. And for the first time in his police career, Kelly hoped Conner Walsh was still alive.

As they rolled up, the scene was still very much active. Uniformed patrol personnel had swarmed the area, and several men were cuffed and seated on the curb. Kelly released his badge from inside his shirt and walked up to one of the patrol officers standing with his gun out and held at the low ready.

"Still active?"

"Not sure, Detective."

"If we don't have an active shooter, it might be a good idea to holster that thing."

The young patrolman looked down at his gun. "Right," he said as he locked the Glock in place on his patrol belt. "We've got some detained inside and out. Ambulance is on the way. Two injured. Doesn't sound like we've got any bodies on this one. From what we've gathered, the shooters fled. Working on getting descriptions, but these guys aren't too helpful." He thumbed at the detainees on the curb.

Kelly recognized one. Tommy "Bones" Sullivan. The oversized giant he'd knocked out in his youth.

"Sully. Funny seeing you here," Kelly offered sarcastically.

The larger man cocked his head up, squinting against the sun, and spat. "You know me. I like my drink."

"Never knew day drinking to be so dangerous. Or maybe it's just the company you keep. Feel like telling me what happened here?"

Sullivan smirked.

"So, it's going to be that way?" Kelly started to walk toward the bar's main entrance. He stopped on the lip of the curb and stood next to Sullivan. Leaning down, he spoke in a hushed tone. "Remind me what the conditions of your parole are? I'd bet it says something about not being around guns. Hope I don't find something that's going to jam you up. Be a real shame to see such a stand-up guy have to go back in to finish his bid. How many years do you have left to serve if you get violated?"

Sullivan spat on the ground again, this time near Kelly's foot, but said nothing. Kelly didn't need him to. He could see the oversized man's demeanor change from one of arrogant cockiness to pure fear. He'd let the thought of possibly returning to prison settle in and marinate a bit while he looked around the scene. Maybe the Savin Hill enforcer would have a change of heart when they next spoke.

Kelly and Barnes entered the main door to JW's Pub. Even with the daylight pouring in through the doors, the inside was still dark. The smell of stale beer and cigarettes hung heavy in the air around him. He looked around, disappointed when he saw no sign of Walsh. And even more so upon seeing his best friend, Bobby McDonough.

Kelly made a beeline for him. "Bobby."

His friend was seated at a table with his hands cuffed behind his back. "Mike."

All of the gang members inside the bar were in handcuffs and seated separately, ensuring limited communication and preventing them from fabricating a cohesive party line on what had occurred. Kelly knew it didn't matter anyway. Nobody among this group would talk to the police.

"When the call came in I was hoping you weren't here." Kelly took a second to size up his childhood friend. "Are you hurt?"

Bobby seemed a bit shocked at the question, as if he hadn't expected his well-being to be Kelly's concern. "Yeah. Just grazed me."

In the dim lighting, Kelly squinted and noticed the tear in Bobby's shirt near the back left shoulder. There was blood but nothing of monumental concern. "We've got medics coming."

"I don't need a medic. It's nothing. Just a scratch." He wiggled his wrists and twisted slightly, bringing his cuffs into view. "But I sure wouldn't mind getting these things off."

"If you're tough enough to ignore medical attention, I think you can handle the discomfort of a pair of handcuffs. Not like it's your first time in bracelets."

"Nice. Kick me while I'm down."

"You know the deal. Not till we figure out what's going on here."

Bobby's face drew up into a snarl. "That's right. I remember now. This is your neighborhood too; the only difference is you bleed blue."

Hearing the words from their last fight a few months ago thrown back in his face jarred him. This was the first time the two had spoken since then, and the circumstances that now brought them together weren't lost on Kelly. He pushed past his friend and offered no retort. "Is anybody in this place going to tell me what the hell happened here today?"

"Couple youngins rushed up in here and tried robbing the place." Bobby didn't make eye contact when he spoke.

"Is that the line of crap you're going to feed me? A robbery gone bad?"

"It's what happened." Bobby looked at the flesh wound on his shoulder. "Amateur hour."

"I'm not buying it."

Bobby shrugged. The gesture was accompanied by a pained wince. "Buy it. Don't buy it. Doesn't really matter."

"It does matter. To me." Kelly shook his head slowly. "So, let me get this straight. A group of young kids came in here guns a'blazing. You get hit and somehow managed to fend them off? How? With what—stern looks and angry words? Where are your guns?"

"Guns? I'm shocked you'd think such things of me. I'm a pacifist. You know that. We all are around here." Bobby was now openly mocking him, feigning an overacted expression of disbelief. His reply was loud enough to evoke a chuckle out of the closest detainees.

"Fine. I get it. Somebody did a quick cleanup, and here we are, left with the steaming pile of bullshit you've concocted." Kelly scanned the room again. "Where's Walsh?"

Bobby shrugged and immediately winced again.

Kelly pulled up a seat next to his closest friend and lowered his voice to a whisper. "Don't nod. Don't react to what I'm about to tell you. Feel free to keep that smug look on your face, but I need you to listen carefully to what I'm about to say." Kelly waited, making sure he gave his friend time to process the request. Barnes looked on with a trace of concern etched into the lines beside her eyes. "I need to meet with Walsh. Privately."

"Ain't going to happen. You've made this request before. I told you the same answer."

"It's important."

"Oh—okay—well, why didn't you say so?" He blew out a hiss. "You're a cop. He'd never agree to it. He's never going to expose himself to a situation that could potentially implicate him. And if you try to bring him in for official questioning, his lawyers will have him pulled out of there before you've had a chance to offer him a cup of coffee."

"I need to find the shooter from the other night on Talbott. And I think he's able to help me with that."

"Don't know what you're talking about." Bobby's denial, an obvious lie, was delivered with less conviction than his previous retorts. He continued, "And even if I did, why would Walsh want to help you."

"That's the thing. I have some information that would benefit him. When Walsh finds out what I know, then he might be interested in talking."

Bobby cocked his head and furrowed his brow. "What do you mean?"

"Just tell him it'll be as important to him as it is to me. Maybe even more so for him."

"If it's so important, why don't you tell me, and I can relay it?"

"Because I need to be there when he hears it. Plus, I don't want you involved any more than you need to be. The less you know the better."

Bobby mumbled, "Or is it you just don't trust me anymore?"

"This goes beyond trust."

"I'll see what I can do."

Kelly stood and walked over to one of the patrolmen. "Any of these guys have a gun on them?"

"Not a one. We did a quick sweep when we cleared the place. Didn't see anything. Once we got them corralled, we did a secondary search. Goose egg so far. Maybe you guys will have better luck."

"Not their scene." Kelly heard the familiar voice and wasn't pleased.

He turned to see Jim Sharp and Lincoln White standing in the bar's main entrance. The bright sun at their backs cast the two men in shadow. Sharp stepped deeper inside. He paused with his hands on his hips in a superhero stance as he slowly surveyed the bar. His eyes came to rest on Kelly.

Kelly, still seated next to Bobby, engaged Sharp in a silent staring contest. "How so?"

"For starters, you're Homicide. And from what I can tell, there are no bodies."

"We've still got the unaccounted-for shooters and enough blood to make me wonder." Kelly pointed toward the side exit. Dark pools of blood marked the wood floor. "I'm pretty sure all that didn't come from Bobby's little flesh wound."

White had a self-righteous look on his face. "Tell you what, hotshot—you find a body and we'll gladly turn this shitshow back over to you. But until then, this belongs to us. We've got known members of a local gang involved—or at the least, victims of an attack. Either way, this is our area of expertise. Feel free to find your way out."

Kelly decided not to press the issue. With the two store shootings and Burke's apartment, he had enough on his plate without trying to process the bar. Plus, with the lack of cooperation by all present, the investigation was unlikely to yield much. He glanced at Barnes, who looked as though she was ready to pounce. "Let's get going."

"We could call Sutherland. He'll straighten this out," she hissed.

"Not likely. I'm sure he's already aware. And besides, we'd be spinning our wheels in here. Nobody's going to be talking. And it looks like most of the evidence has been removed or tampered with enough to drop this into the open-but-closed file relatively quickly." Kelly eyed Bobby. "Walsh will get our message. It's the best thing to come out of this."

"If you say so."

Kelly stood and put a hand on Bobby's uninjured shoulder. "Good seeing you're still alive. Stay that way."

"You too. Watch your back out there, Mikey."

Kelly headed for the door. Sharp and White parted as he and Barnes passed by. Kelly thought of his brother and the betrayal by both men, but especially White. He resisted the urge to slam his fist into the side of White's jaw again. The memory of dropping the man entered his mind, and the thought of it temporarily satiated his need to repeat it now.

They walked back toward their car. Police tape was being stretched across the street, effectively shutting down all traffic on both sides of Dorchester Avenue, the busiest street in the neighborhood. As they moved toward their Caprice, passing the alley between the pub and a machine repair shop, Kelly caught movement out of the corner of his eye. At first, he thought it was a small animal, a stray cat or dog. But on further inspection, he realized a person was tucked behind the lot's large dumpster.

Kelly subtly tapped Barnes's arm and stopped. "Don't turn your head now but we've got somebody hiding behind that dumpster along the side alley to our left."

"Okay."

"Let's take a casual stroll. I want to box him in before he can bolt. I really don't feel like making this a foot chase. I'd like to do this quiet. And, if possible—stay off Sharp's radar."

Kelly moved toward the dumpster and Barnes followed, both keeping their heads down as if they were looking for something on the ground. Not out of the ordinary for detectives to search the area for evidence after a shooting. Casings littered the concrete, but neither stopped to mark or tag the evidence.

Once close enough, he then veered toward the far end of the dumpster as Barnes, reading his move, covered the other end. The two effectively cut off the person's only possible escape routes.

Kelly brought up his gun, as did Barnes. "Hands. Show me your hands. Do it now!" Kelly delivered the message in a terse whisper so as not to draw the attention of any of the patrolmen, but his tone was forceful enough to command compliance.

"Please! Don't shoot! I don't have a gun. Please!"

"Listen to me carefully. Everything I tell you is critical to your safety. Do anything outside of what I tell you to do and you could get shot. Neither one of us wants that. Do you understand?"

The hidden man bobbed his head up and down slowly. His voice was weak and jittery as he muttered, "Yes."

"Crawl out to my partner. Keep your hands where we can see them at all times."

The man began moving forward on all fours. His side scraped against the back of the trash bin. He was just thin enough to navigate the narrow space. Thirty seconds later he emerged into the light. Kelly quickly saw he wasn't a man at all but a young-looking teen who looked shaken to the core. His body trembled as he remained on his knees awaiting the next command.

Kelly held his weapon pointed down, keeping it tight to his body so as not to draw any unwanted attention. "Stand up slowly and face away from my partner."

Barnes holstered her sidearm and guided the boy to a

standing position. Maintaining a firm grip on the boy's left elbow and right shoulder near the neck, she brought the boy's hands together at the small of his back and locked them into place with her left hand. After systematically patting him down for weapons while he stood frozen in place, she announced, "He's clean."

Kelly put his weapon away, holstering it beneath his untucked shirt. "What's your name, kid?"

His body, still turned away, was trembling. "Ryan—Ryan Murphy."

"You can turn around now." Barnes released her grip. As the boy repositioned himself, Kelly looked at his clothes. Dirty and soaked with sweat, but no sign of blood. "Are you hurt?"

Ryan kept his head down, slow-swinging it from left to right like a pendulum. "No."

"How old are you?"

"Sixteen."

"Are you going to tell us how you ended up behind this dumpster?" Kelly asked.

"I didn't want to be here. It was their stupid idea. Where I come from, choices aren't really given." He sniffled loudly.

"What street?"

"Aukland."

"No kidding. I grew up not too far from there."

Ryan made eye contact for the first time. "Yeah right. You're a Dot Rat?"

"Born and raised. Saxton Street." Kelly didn't bother adding that he still lived there. That after his marriage had failed, he'd tucked tail and returned home. But Dot Rat he was, and by the looks of his life to date, not much was going to change in that regard.

Kelly reached out and put a hand on the kid's shoulder. "I'm not the enemy here. My partner and I are really here to help. How about we take a ride?"

"I don't want to go to jail." The boy stepped back, breaking free of Kelly's hand, then turned as if he was about to run. Barnes immediately stepped into position, cutting off his escape route.

"Relax. No need to bolt on us. Jail is not what I had in mind. I was thinking more along the lines of getting something to eat." He gave Ryan a disarming smile. "Hungry?"

"I guess."

Kelly and Barnes strode out toward the street with their new acquaintance in tow. One of the patrolmen standing on the sidewalk gave Kelly a questioning look but was immediately interrupted by a supervisor redirecting him to a new task.

The trio slipped under the yellow tape and within a minute were pulling away from the crime scene, their best lead trembling in the Caprice's cushioned backseat.

24

"I heard about the shooting. Do you really think it's a good idea to try and set this deal up while things are so hot?" Brayden held the burner phone they'd given him and waited for White's answer.

"The shooting was other business. This is the drug trade. Do you think dealers get spooked every time there's a little bit of blood spilled? If that were the case, the cartels would be obsolete." White offered a frustrated grunt. "When I hang up the phone, I want you to reach out to Sullivan and get this moving."

"Okay."

White ended the call, and Brayden called Sullivan with the same burner he'd just used to talk with the head of BPD's Narcotics. The irony wasn't lost on him. His conniving scheming left him feeling dirty, but he was operating purely out of survival. Brayden thought himself more cockroach than human at this point. But they say a cockroach can survive a nuclear fallout. Maybe he'd manage to survive this.

The phone rang three times, and Brayden was preparing to hang up when he heard a voice on the other end.

"Who's this?" the gruff voice asked.

"Brayden."

"You pick a hell of a time to call. You've got shit timing. Guess you haven't heard about what went down today?"

Brayden considered reciting White's speech about cartels and the drug trade but felt it best not to have any knowledge of the shooting. Too many questions could follow. Better to play dumb. "Nah. I haven't heard nuthin'. Why, what's up?"

"Some crazy ass fools rushed the place and tried to roll us." Sullivan was the most animated he'd ever heard. Maybe the near-death experience had a euphoric after-effect. "Some balls. Who the hell comes direct at Walsh?"

"Anybody get hurt?"

"Not really. A couple guys got hit on our end. The other guys got the worst of it."

Brayden didn't want to ask for any further clarification. He was actually hoping the deal would be postponed or called off altogether. But he knew his luck, or lack thereof, and didn't hold out much hope. "If it's a bad time, I get it. We can do this when things slow. But I wanted to let you know my guy got the money together for those two keys we talked about."

Sullivan was quiet for a minute. "Shit, you think a little shootout is going to slow me down? Let's do this."

"You're in charge. When and where?"

"Tonight. Be ready. I'll hit you up with the location later. You feel me?"

"I feel you. It's all good. Don't worry, I'll be ready whenever you call." Brayden hung up first. He exhaled loudly and pulled a cigarette from his pack. He couldn't get it lit quick enough. After a few long pulls, his nerves calmed enough to make the follow-up call.

As he redialed White's number, he took a drag. White picked up the phone but said nothing.

"It's going down. Tonight. Not sure the time exactly."

"Where?"

"He didn't give specifics. Just said to be ready."

"I'll call you with the meet location so we can get you set for the buy. Keep this phone close and be ready to go at a moment's notice." White was quiet for a second. "You better not ghost on me."

"I won't. I'm good. Just want to get this thing over with. Be done with it."

"You know what's coming your way if you do?" Without waiting for an answer, White hung up the phone.

Brayden pocketed it. The ashen embers of the cigarette had burned down to the edge of the filter, and he could feel the heat of it on his grimy fingers. He dropped it to the ground and took another cigarette from the pack. His hand shook, and he wasn't sure if the tremors were from his dope sickness ... or fear.

"You still living on Aukland?" Kelly handed the cheeseburger and fries to the boy in the backseat.

The Caprice had aftermarket tints on the side windows, enough to completely wash out the kid's features from interested eyes. Even with the obscurity provided, Ryan still felt the need to slump down low. He snatched the bag and greedily rummaged inside to retrieve the food before taking a big bite. Chewing noisily and breathing through his nose, he looked up with a mouthful of burger. "Yeah. Well, sort of. My mom still lives there. So, it's my home until I can get the hell out." He looked at Kelly and Barnes and saw they didn't get any food. "What? You guys aren't hungry?"

"We're fine." Kelly watched as the kid chomped down again. The burger was already half gone. He knew the boy's body needed sustenance. Adrenaline did a number on an empty stomach. "You sure are, though, huh?"

Ketchup lined the outside of the boy's mouth as he gave a faint smile. "Thank you."

And there it was. Food remained one of the best ways to lower resistance, an offering dating back as far as the earliest of civilizations. Food was used as leverage in negotiations and interrogations alike. It wasn't a magic bullet for bringing about a resolution, but it laid the foundation for establishing rapport. The first step in effective communication.

Kelly pulled in behind an abandoned building and parked. "We could've gone into the restaurant, but I figured you wouldn't want to get seen with a couple of cops."

Ryan nodded as he stuffed some fries in his mouth.

"You want to tell me what happened today?"

He stopped chewing and swallowed the contents in his mouth. "I'm not like them. I'm no banger. It's not my thing. But like I said before, when you grow up the way I did—choices don't come easy. I didn't want to go. They made me."

"Who's they? Your brother?"

Ryan broke eye contact and began searching the bag for loose fries.

"I believe you. We both do. We understand your situation better than you realize. I'm just trying to figure out what's going on," Kelly prompted. "I don't want anybody else to get hurt if I can help it. There's been enough shooting and killing over the past few days."

"They didn't have nothing to do with those corner store murders."

"What about Tyson's Market? Somebody had a Corner Boys tattoo on their neck." Kelly didn't like the idea of exposing a case fact, but at this point it seemed the most tactful approach he could come up with.

Ryan stopped his search effort but left his hand in the bag. "Listen, I'll admit the Corner Boys aren't the best and brightest. My brother included. But they're not stupid enough to hit a store under Walsh's protection." He shoved a couple fries in his mouth and bit down with a crunch. "Besides, nobody from our crew has that tat on their neck."

Kelly glanced at Barnes. "Let's say what you're telling us is true and they didn't hit Tyson's Market. They were still stupid enough to go after Walsh in broad daylight."

Ryan nodded slowly. He pulled out a freakishly long floppy fry and began to nibble it. "One of Walsh's guys killed Luke's brother. I guess the killing sent him over the edge. Understandably. I hate my brother, but I'd be hard-pressed not to avenge him if somebody put him down. That's street code 101."

Kelly thought of his own mantra: Family First, Family Always. He understood the rationale better than most. "I get it. But what was the plan? Did Daniels really think you guys could just roll up into Conner Walsh's spot and kill him?"

"The plan was never to kill him—at least not at the bar. It was to capture him. Luke wanted to shoot Walsh himself." Ryan looked between the two attentive detectives. "Saying it out loud makes it sound even crazier. I want you to know I had no plans of doing what they asked."

"And what'd they ask you to do?"

"It was my brother's dumb idea. He wanted me to go in first and shoot up the place. Told me I had to empty my gun, or he was going to beat me." Ryan paused and gave a slight shudder. "He'd do it too. And it would be bad. They always were."

"You're a brave kid."

Ryan's head reared back. "Brave? I hid behind a freakin' dumpster while everybody manned up. Tell me what's brave about that!"

"You took the hard right instead of the easy left. You broke off from the group under a tremendous amount of pressure. That takes guts. And a strength few would have." Kelly knew the boy needed to hear it. He needed to feel some level of self-worth and confidence if he was going to continue the conversation. "So, yeah—I'd call you brave."

Ryan gave a barely perceptible nod.

"You told me you were forced to go to the pub on a half-cocked plan. What happened next? When you got there?"

"I got out of the van. They shoved me toward that side door. But when I got close, I—um, froze." His eyes watered. "I just stood there like a chicken shit."

"Hey, don't you beat yourself up over that," Barnes said. "Facing the pressure and danger you were under would have the same effect on most. Hell, it takes us cops a long time to learn how to control that fear. To use and channel it. There's no shame in freezing. Not sure I would've done much different if I were in your shoes."

"I wasn't going to shoot anybody. Even if I didn't freeze. I had a plan. I was going to fire the gun above everybody's head. I figured my brother would assume I was just a crappy shot. Nobody'd be sticking around to check for accuracy. If my gun was empty when I got back in the van, I'd be good. Considered one of the guys. And live up to my brother's ridiculous expectations."

"But you didn't," Barnes said. She had a softness to her voice that added a balance. "You didn't fire your gun."

"No, I didn't." Ryan sighed. "My brother stepped up and led the charge. When they went in, I ran and hid behind the dumpster."

Kelly watched as the boy seemed to shrink, his diminished physical presence an obvious outward display of feeling like a failure. Kelly needed to press on before the boy's waning willingness to share his story faded completely. "What happened next? Did you see or hear anything?" he asked.

"Lots of shooting. It was fast, like watching a time-lapse video where minutes are converted into seconds." The boy rubbed the top of his head, mussing his hair. "It really was a blur."

"It always is. Take a second and try to take your mind back to when they first disappeared inside the pub. What's the first thing you remember?"

"Gunshots. The door was only closed for less than a minute. Two at most. And then it popped back open."

"Who opened it?"

"It was Lynch." Ryan looked up as if he'd just crossed some invisible line of betrayal by mentioning his friend's name. "He didn't want nothin' to do with this either. He just got sucked in."

Kelly took the deflective comment in stride and continued. "Lynch opened the door. And then what?"

"He fell to the ground and then took off running. For a second I thought that was it. That Lynch was the only one to escape. But then came Adam and Dempsey."

"How many of your crew entered?"

"That was it. Just Lynch, Dempsey, and Adam."

"And they were all unhurt?"

Ryan was slow to shake his head. "Adam didn't look good. Dempsey carried him. Adam was covered in blood. But I couldn't tell how bad it was." Ryan's eyes watered again but no tears fell.

"Who's Adam?"

"My brother. Last I saw of him was when Dempsey loaded him into the back of the van. Then they drove off."

"What'd you do with the gun?"

"I tossed it in the dumpster. The one you guys found me hiding behind."

Kelly nodded. "Do you know where they are now?"

"They'd kill me if I told. Sure as shit. Bad enough I'm talking to you now."

"If your brother's hurt as bad as you say, I need to try and find him. Sounds like he's going to need medical attention."

"He'll never go back. He told me that. More times than I can count. Did a bunch of time for knifin' a kid a few years back. He swore he'd take his own life before he'd ever go back in the system. I've got to honor that. Least I can do. Since I wasn't there to protect him."

"It very well could've been you covered in blood if you had."

Kelly understood the fragile balance loyalty created and decided to let it ride for now. He got some valuable information from the teen. Most importantly, that the Corner Boys weren't responsible for the Tyson's Market shooting.

Ryan took the last bite of burger. "So, what happens to me now? You fed me and bled me for info. You gonna ship me off to juvie?"

"You sound like a bright kid with a crappy future. And if you let me, I'd like to help with that." Kelly looked over at Barnes. "I want to take you to see somebody who specializes in that sort of thing."

A few minutes later, Kelly pulled the Caprice into the familiar lot. His home away from home.

"A boxing gym?" Ryan asked. "How's a boxing gym supposed to help me out?"

"Just trust me on this." Kelly put the car in park, then exited without offering any further explanation. "Give me a second to talk to Pops and I'll be right back."

Barnes gave a wink of assurance as Kelly closed the door.

Kelly walked in through the rear entrance. The gym doors were always unlocked, day or night. The old proprietor of the pugilistic arts said the only time they'd be locked was when he was dead and buried.

A few guys were scattered about the floor running some drills. Speed work and agility came before the ring. And the few who were inside were putting in their time mastering the finer skills. But aside from those members, the place was relatively empty. Kelly walked to the back office where Pops, when not on the floor, typically sat and reviewed old matches. He was constantly studying the game, never growing so comfortable in his knowledge that he didn't seek more.

The door was open, but Kelly knocked on the frame out of courtesy. Pops's head lifted up from behind the small television. His neatly cropped hair had turned an ashen gray years back and gave him a distinguished look, fitting of the wisdom he bestowed. His dark skin seemed to never age or wrinkle, and had it not been for his gray hair, Pops could be mistaken for a person half his age.

"I've got a new kid I'd like to run by you."

Pops pushed himself back from his desk, not surprised by the interruption.

"He's been through a pretty rough day thus far and I think he'd benefit from some of your counseling. Your special kind of counseling."

Pops looked up from the disorganized pile of his desk. "Is he here now?"

"He is. Out in the back of my car with my partner." This wasn't the first youth Kelly had brought to see the man, and he was sure Ryan Murphy wouldn't be the last. "You watching some of the old fights?"

"No. Not today. Just going over my son's parole hearing paperwork. I want to see if there's anything I can do to help him this go-round. Out of my element with all this legal jargon."

"Oh, that's right, I heard it was coming up. It's supposed to take place in a couple weeks, right?"

"Yeah. Couple weeks." Pops's normally impassive face looked sad. Understandably so, but seeing it still threw Kelly for a momentary loop.

"It's a bit crazy right now with these shootings. But when I finish up this case, I'm going to take a look at it and see if I can help you out. Do me a favor and get something together for me to review in a few days. I want to see it from all perspectives. Maybe if we put our heads together on this, something will stand out."

Pops's face lit up. "You'd do that for me?"

"Absolutely. I'd do anything for you. I'm just sorry I haven't gotten around to doing it sooner. I've been meaning to look into it for a while now, but I've been slammed and it keeps falling to the wayside."

An invisible weight seemed to lift from the man's broad shoulders. "What about this kid? The one you brought to see me? You mentioned he was in a jam today? I'm assuming it's bad if he's in your cruiser."

Kelly nodded. "I'll let him tell you about it if he's up for talking. He just unloaded a pretty heavy burden."

"You know my way."

"I do. And that's why I brought him." Kelly looked around at the framed newspaper clippings of champions that hung on Pops's office walls. Most of the stories behind those successes were born from strife. Kelly eyed the frame containing a faded front-page photo of him standing victorious in his Golden Glove championship bout. "But he's not so different from me when I first walked in these doors, and look how I turned out. I just want to give him a better shot than he's got right now."

"I'll see what I can do. But you know my rules. I don't force anybody to stay who doesn't want to be here. The decision to be a part of this family has to be made willingly. It's the only way it works."

"I know that. Like I said, I at least want to give this kid a fighting chance."

Pops gave a rare smile. "Well, you know better than most that I do like the hard cases."

"Was I really that hard?" Kelly chuckled and thought about the many battles that came from training hard-headed young men like him.

"You don't know the half of it. I didn't have a gray hair on my head until you walked through those doors."

"Ready to make his acquaintance?"

Kelly walked out of the office with Pops and headed out the back door to the lot where his unmarked was parked. The same lot where he and his pals drank their post-Thursday night fight brews. And the same lot where he and Bobby set out to solve their personal differences. "Fighting solves everything" was an ethos that, up until that fight with Bobby, had held true. The punches thrown that night did little to reconnect the two men, born of different mothers but brothers all the same. Seeing him today reminded Kelly they still had much to discuss before they would ever get back on even footing.

Kelly walked over to the car, idling with the air conditioning on full blast, and tapped on the back-passenger window. Ryan startled when Kelly opened the door. "I want you to meet somebody. Somebody who helped me out when I was in a position much like yours." Kelly stepped aside, bringing Pops into view. "Ryan, I'd like you to meet Pops." Kelly then turned to the man he considered a second father. "Pops, this is Ryan Murphy."

The boy looked up at the gray-haired black man who stood before him, sizing up the chiseled muscles of a thirty-something-year-old. Momentarily shocked and confused, he asked, "You want me to be a boxer?"

Kelly looked down at the kid. A bit of ketchup was still smudged in the left corner of his mouth. "I don't want you to be anything you don't want to be." Kelly thumbed toward the gym. "A lot can happen inside that place. Not all of it has to do with throwing a punch. This is an opportunity. Take it for what it is. But I'll tell you one thing, this man here changes lives. And what goes on in there gives you strength to take on all comers. Life's not been easy for you. Not saying it's going to be from here on out either. I am saying, the skills, both mental and physical, will increase the likelihood you're properly equipped to handle it."

"And what if I tell you no?"

"Take it or leave it. Your choice. It's not a far walk from here to get back to Auckland. So, if that's where you want to end up, Pops isn't going to stop you. I'm not going to stop you." Kelly paused and saw the boy hadn't moved. "All I'm gonna say is everybody needs a second chance at starting over, but not everybody gets one. This is your chance to turn the corner. Consider it a crossroads, so to speak. Whether you choose to take a right or left and what you do with it and where you go is completely up to you. I leave everything from this point forward in your hands."

Kelly moved aside and Ryan stepped out from the vehicle.

Kelly closed Ryan's door and walked around to the driver's side. "Hopefully I'll see you around. Maybe some Thursday in the near future." Kelly gave Pops a wink and mouthed the words *Thank you.*

Ryan looked back at Kelly and Barnes one last time before walking toward Pops.

The older man stuck out his hand and Ryan took it.

Kelly and Barnes drove away.

As they pulled out of the lot, Barnes looked over. "Well, that was totally unexpected."

"This is my neighborhood, and what happens to these kids matters. If I can put him on the right path, maybe we won't be dealing with him on the professional end in the future."

"You know you can't save them all."

"I know. But it doesn't mean I shouldn't try."

"What's next?"

"I'll drop you back at the station. Something I've got to take care of."

Barnes gave him a dejected look. "Something personal?"

"I've got to find Brayden. I'm not sure how he's mixed up in all this. But I'm really worried about him."

"No need to drop me off. Let me help. Many hands make light work."

Kelly shot a glance at his partner. "This is something I need to do alone."

Barnes must've seen the seriousness in his face because she didn't push any further. "Maybe we should regroup this evening after you've had a chance to talk with Brayden. Just promise you won't hesitate to call if you need my help."

Kelly merged into the heavy traffic. "I promise."

25

"Sullivan called me. Said the deal is going to go down this evening. Wants to meet somewhere over by the Lower Mills. He told me to be close to the area and he'd call me again at 7:00 with the specifics." Brayden fired off the details in a rapid nervous barrage.

"Okay. Give me some time to get the money together. Head to the park where I picked you up last time. Be there in a half hour. And wait around until we get there."

"I'm going to have to walk. So, it might take me a bit longer than thirty minutes to get there."

"I don't care if you have to steal a car, bike, skateboard, whatever. You'll be there in thirty minutes. I don't need one of your bullshit junkie excuses. God help you if you show up bagged out of your mind. You need to be clean for this. I can't have you make some dopehead mistake."

Brayden didn't need to see the man to know the intensity in his face. He could picture White's crooked smile. "Don't worry about me. I'll be there."

"And don't tell anybody where you're going. None of your junkie friends, and especially your brother."

"My brother? Why the hell would I tell him anything? I don't talk to my brother. I haven't talked to him in months. Do you think I'd be stupid enough to tell him I was working with you? Or that I set up a deal with Sully?"

"Regardless, nobody can know about this. And trust me when I say, I know how your kind is when it comes to keeping secrets. Why do you think skells like yourself make such great snitches? 'Cause you can't keep your damn mouths shut."

Brayden didn't need, or want, to make any effort to defend himself against the allegations. Partly because it was futile to argue anything against a man like White, and partly because he knew the Narcotics boss was right. "All right. I'll be there. No worries. I want this over as much as you."

The playground was occupied mostly by families, couples pushing their young children in swings. The fire hydrant was no longer spraying water out into the street. Temps had dropped into the low eighties, markedly cooler than the previous couple days. Therefore, no need for the makeshift fountain.

Brayden sat on a bench and smoked a cigarette. He looked out on the families playing with their children. He visited this playground and others like it during his youth, but his memory of those times seemed far away and faded, like a dream with bits and pieces missing.

Some of the parents eyed him warily and moved away, taking their children to the far side of the playscape. He ignored their disgust and took a drag. He wondered how many of these kids would end up like him. No parent gave in to such thoughts. These moms and dads obviously assumed it would never happen to their child. No parent ever does. His never did. Weird to think of going from such a simple life to such a complicated, desperate one. A life, not unlike the ones he sat watching, laughing and giggling carefree in the park. His upbringing had left him unprepared for the ravages of drugs.

Brayden typically didn't allow himself time for this kind of introspection; he found it of little benefit to ask why. To pity himself over the twists of fate and series of bad decisions that had brought him to this phase of his life. Easier to move forward without looking back. Maybe it was the potential hazards of the impending deal with Sully. Or the fact he was now indebted to the manically dangerous Lincoln White. But sitting there on the warped wood of the bench, smoking a cigarette and waiting for White to show up, he gave in to the depressing circumstances of his current lifestyle. The dependency on a drug he hated. The destructive wake it left, driving a deep and formidable rift between him and his family. Brayden Kelly sat silently, hating himself more now than he had at any other time in his adult life.

The black Lincoln Town Car pulled up to the curb. The heavily tinted windows remained closed. Brayden could barely make out the driver's silhouette, but he knew it was White. No honk. No announcement of his arrival. The vehicle just idled quietly, exhaust seeping out from the muffler.

Brayden stood, squashing the cigarette underfoot as he approached. He looked around once, scanning for watching eyes out of habit, and then climbed in the backseat. The boxy sedan pulled away as the door was closing.

The front passenger seat wasn't occupied by Brooks, White's bulldog of a partner, but instead by the man he'd met earlier in the day at the Stop and Shop parking lot. During that meet the man hadn't spoken, and White didn't bother to make any introductions. Brayden felt a bit of panic at not knowing this man, but he fought to regulate it. He didn't like any unknowns this late in the game. It was an unnerving addition to an already complicated set of events. But he assumed the man must have a stake in the game to be accompanying White. He tried putting his mind at ease, thinking, or hoping, that if the deal went as planned tonight, then he'd be free of his debt to White. And he'd remove any chance of being Whitewashed.

They drove away in silence, which made the short trip seem longer. White pulled the Town Car into the Codman Yard service road off Gallivan Boulevard, the same spot they had used to stage the first buy into Tommy Sullivan.

Once they parked, the new man turned to face him. He looked to be about White's age. Experience lined his face. The man had kinder eyes than his counterpart, but he was shrouded in the same intensity, surrounded by the strange need or desire to influence and intimidate. During his encounters with law enforcement, Brayden had become quite familiar with men like this. Although his brother worked within the same circle, he never saw these qualities in him. He often wondered how some cops, like Michael, had managed to rise above it all. To steer clear of the badge's powerful influence.

"My name's Sharp. White's brought me in to support this deal you've set up. And trust me when I say this, I'm a guy you want in your corner."

Brayden didn't say anything. He didn't feel the man's words were an invitation to interact. He also assumed White had filled him in on all the necessary background leading up to this two-kilo deal.

"Listen and listen carefully. This is probably the most important thing you've ever done in your life. You've got to play this by the numbers and do everything we tell you to do. To deviate or freestyle, however minor, could result in a very bad end."

Brayden swallowed hard and played with the near-empty

box of Newports in his front pocket. He desperately wanted to pull out a cigarette but knew it wouldn't fly with these two.

White leaned into view. "My friend here is being polite. Let me break it down for your simple mind. Screw this up and you'll most likely end up dead."

He wasn't sure if the implied threat was meant to be a warning not to cross Walsh or White himself. On careful consideration, he decided it was probably equally applicable to both. Bad men with an equally high propensity for violence bookended him on this venture. A displeasing prospect by all accounts.

Sharp handed Brayden a tattered backpack with one broken shoulder strap. "Here's the money. It's thirty large. All marked and serial numbers recorded. So don't, even for a second, think about dipping your fingers in the cookie jar. You got me?"

"Nice bag." Brayden took the money bag and nodded.

"Figured it would fit your current state of affairs. You'd look a bit out of place carrying a briefcase."

Brayden eyed the tattered JanSport backpack. It wasn't lost on him he was holding thirty thousand dollars. His heart pounded and he battled against the whirlwind of thoughts as he imagined what he could do with that kind of money. Then he pictured White and what he would do to him if he acted upon such fantasy. The subsequent mental imagery was disquieting and dispelled any additional musings.

"That busted-ass junkie satchel is also rigged with a transponder. Leave it with them when you make the exchange. It will help us track the money after it's out of hand." Sharp tapped the bottom of the bag.

White smiled. "Basically, if they kill you and take the money, it will be a lot easier to recover it."

"But we're obviously hoping something like that doesn't happen. This is going to be a simple exchange," Sharp interjected. "We're going to have eyes on you the whole time. Trust me when I say this, you're in good hands. I know your brother well, and if I was able to clue him in on what we're doing with you, he'd vouch for me."

"Enough about having Saint Michael vouch for us," White snarled. "We don't need his glowing endorsement. You're in this too deep and you're doing this thing regardless."

"We're good after this, right? My debt settled and we can go our separate ways." Brayden injected as much confidence as he could muster in the face of these two imposing men.

"We'll see." White was momentarily lost in thought. "Yes. You do this thing for me and we'll consider your debt to society paid. Until, of course, you need my help again."

"No James Bond hidden cameras tonight? I thought you guys said you needed the video footage for these cases to fly at court."

"Not tonight. I can't have you any more nervous than you'd normally be. Plus, like Sharp said, we're going to have eyes on this the whole time."

"I guess now all we have to do is just wait," Brayden offered.

26

He watched from around the corner and waited until she was alone. She was cautious by nature and looked at every passing car. Vigilance was part of her trade, a survival mechanism she and many like her used to stay safe on the streets of Dorchester. Chloe Dobek had been working corners like this for years, long before Kelly's time on the job. She'd always been good to him in the past with regards to forwarding information. These exchanges were never free. Nothing on the street ever was. A quid pro quo etiquette existed, but it benefited both in different ways.

She'd provide information and Kelly looked the other way on any certain number of her minor transgressions. He'd bailed her out of plenty of jams. Mostly drug, prostitution, and larceny cases. His interaction with the long-time prostitute occurred with exponentially more frequency during his years in BPD's Narcotics Unit. Through their many encounters, Kelly learned Chloe was, at her core, a good person. It just took a bit to chip away at her hardened exterior.

The streets swallowed some people up whole, and when they were spat back out, they were never completely the same.

Over time Kelly had learned the woman's backstory, the horrible abuse and violence she'd faced in the early years of her adolescence ultimately shaping her into the person she was today. Those awful beginnings pushed her into the life, hooking to survive. Kelly had tried numerous times to get her back on her feet, but addiction and circumstance had made it a difficult path. No matter how long she'd been able to right her ship, she eventually always returned to the corner.

His efforts to save her had ingratiated him to her. And on one particular occasion, Kelly had forever solidified an unbreakable bond with the street walker when he stopped her pimp from beating her into oblivion. Kelly ultimately arrested the man, but not without his own struggle. The deranged peddler of women turned his aggression on Kelly, a mistake fraught with painful consequences. Kelly used it as an opportunity to school the man in the finer points of violence. Needless to say, the pimp made a visit to the emergency room before arriving at jail. Although he remained her handler, he never laid another hand on Chloe after that day.

Chloe got back on her feet after the incident with the pimp and, for a time, was doing well. She even spent a short period of time in a halfway house and worked at getting herself clean and sober. But history has a tendency to repeat itself, and before long she was back.

Kelly never quite gave up on her, and every time he passed her on the street, he would stop and check on her. These little visits were not great for her clientele, but she never turned away. He usually came bearing gifts in the form of a cup of coffee or a sandwich, some offering or gesture to show that he still cared.

At this point in the woman's life, Chloe, now in her late forties, was a dinosaur by prostitute standards. Her gaunt face and ravaged body were weathered well beyond her years, making her look closer to sixty. Kelly watched her lean up against a signpost as a faded green older model Ford pickup drove away after she finished whatever service the man had paid for.

Kelly pulled up in his Caprice, slowly bringing himself to a stop near the curb. He rolled down the window, leaned over the passenger seat, and asked, "Can I give you a lift?"

Chloe looked inside and smiled. "As I live and breathe, if it isn't Michael Kelly, the Saint of Dorchester." She peered down the street. "You know you kill my business every time you pay me a visit. The Johns can smell police a mile away."

Kelly chuckled. He'd been received by her the same way for years, but deep down he knew she liked when he stopped by. It was an excuse to take a forced break from the street life. "How you been holding up?"

"Best I can. These guys aren't looking for the old reliable ride as much as they are for the newer models that are out and about. But I hold my own, best I can."

"Yeah? Tell that to the guy in the Ford pickup."

Chloe leaned in the window. "I hope you're not here on business. I'd hate for you or your buddies to be picking off my one customer of the night. Not great for my bottom line, ya know."

"Not at all. I don't do the street bust thing anymore. They've got me in Homicide now."

"Homicide? Look at you, Mikey, movin' on up."

"I guess it's a matter of perspective. Anyway, it's just me this evening. And I'm here on a personal matter."

"Michael Kelly, coming to see me for a personal favor? This I gotta hear." Without further invitation, Chloe opened the door and slipped inside.

Kelly didn't have the natural turn-off or disgust some felt at having a used-up prostitute in the seat next to them. Maybe because he'd been around it so much during his time in

Narcotics. Or maybe because he watched his brother crash and burn on the streets, knowing well enough he wasn't much better off than her in his current condition. In some ways, Brayden might actually have been in a worse position.

He pulled away from the curb and drove off, knowing the longer he sat there, the more exposed she'd be. In the dog-eat-dog world of people caught in the street hustle, being seen riding with a cop was as good as being dead. Kelly drove around until he found a deserted lot and parked. Chloe licked her cracked lips and gave him a coy smile. "Please tell me I finally get to take you for your first ride on the Chloe Express."

Kelly laughed at her attempted prostitute humor. "Afraid not, Chloe. Just need a little bit of information."

"Your loss. Remember the offer is always on the table. I'll even give you the police discount." Then she dropped the act. "Anything for you. If I can help, I will."

"It's Brayden." Kelly was serious now, putting all joking aside. "Have you seen him lately?"

"I see him around every once in a while. You see a lot of people out here. But he doesn't talk to me. Maybe he doesn't remember how I helped you catch the guy who mugged your mom a few years back?"

"I'm sure he does. I think he's more ashamed of his current circumstances than anything else."

"I can see that. He's out here chasing the dragon. He didn't look too good last time I saw him. The sickness seems to have a hell of a grip on him." Chloe turned and looked out the window. "He's not the same kid I remember. The street did a lot of damage to him. Look at me. I'm not the woman I once was, nowhere near."

"You're holding up, though. Better than most." He watched the measured compliment work its magic. "Tell me about Brayden. When's the last time you saw him? I'm worried he's mixed up in something bad. I've hit all his old haunts, but I can't find him anywhere."

"Last time I saw him was yesterday. He was hustling somebody on the corner, trying to get a couple of bucks. I tried to flag him over, but he ignored me. I was going to spot him a ten. Split my previous few minutes of work with him so he could get straight. He chose not to come my way and accept my offering. He was gone a couple minutes later."

"When was that?"

"I don't know. I'd say early. Before lunch at least."

"Did you see where he went? Or maybe who he was with?"

"He was flying solo from what I could tell. And I didn't see where he went."

Kelly rubbed his tired eyes in frustration.

"I know he's your brother. And I know the type of man you are. Look what you've done for me over the years. Or at least tried to do. But Brayden's got some big hurdles to climb and I'm not sure he's ready to accept your help. How many times did you try and get me to listen? And your brother looks to be in a bad place. I'm gonna be honest with you, that dragon he's chasing seems to be getting the better of him. I've seen people like him, at that point in their life, and if something doesn't happen to snap him out of it ... Well, I usually stop seeing them altogether round here. You understand?"

"Why do you think I'm out here chasing my tail? I'm terrified he's on the downward spiral to a bad bottom. He's stopped talking to me. We had a little falling out a few months back and we really haven't talked since." Kelly lowered his voice to a mumble. "Maybe he hates me. I don't know."

"Probably not. He probably hates himself. He sees in you everything he never became." Chloe took a stick of gum from her purse and began chewing loudly. "I've pretty much written off every person in my life who knew me before this. I just couldn't stand to see the judgment in their eyes anymore. It's actually why I've always liked you, Mike. You never looked at me that way. Never looked down on me like I was beneath you. You're one of the only people to treat me like a human being." She waited for Kelly to look at her before continuing. "Do you know how rare that is out here? To not be seen for what I do for a living, but who I am? And I want to thank you for that."

Kelly silently accepted the compliment.

"Because of that, if there's ever any way I can help you, don't hesitate to ask."

"Thanks, Chloe. How about you take the rest of the night off?"

"Why would I do that? You know a girl's got to eat." She smacked her lips loudly around the gum.

"Would a hundred cover you for the night? Maybe you can take a break, get a good meal?" Kelly slipped her five twenties to thank her for the information, which, in the bigger scheme of things, wasn't much more than he had when she first got in the car. But it was enough to know that she'd be keeping her eye out for Brayden. He knew she'd call if she saw anything or caught any word. Kelly knew the benefits of always staying in touch with the street. Of keeping its pulse. As an investigator, you never knew when you would need its help.

He pulled back around the block as Chloe stuffed the hundred dollars into the small front pocket of her jeans without protest, tucking it neatly out of sight from anybody who may have been looking to collect. A protective force of habit. Satisfied the money was safe, she exited the vehicle.

She closed the door behind her, turned, and blew Kelly a kiss. "You know I'll keep my eyes and ears open. If I see him, I'll send him your way."

"Thanks again, Chloe. You know it goes both ways? If there's anything I can do for you, you know how to reach me."

"I do."

Kelly drove off and headed to his next spot, hoping to find more information on where his brother was hiding out. He needed to get ahead of whatever Brayden had gotten himself into before it was too late.

27

Brayden stood a short distance away from the Lincoln. He found the separation, however slight, worked to ease his frazzled nerves. His phone beeped with an accompanying vibration. He examined the incoming message and then put it away.

He looked at the two men eyeing him eagerly in the front seat of the waiting car. Taking his last drag, he called over to them, "I just got the text."

Brayden flicked his cigarette off into the distance. The embers trailed like a shooting star in the rapidly darkening sky as day gave way to night. He blew out the last bit of smoke through his nostrils before sliding into the back seat of the vehicle. "It's a go. Lower Mills over by those fancy apartments. Not sure why they'd pick such an uppity part of town. But this isn't my call."

White looked at him. "Makes pretty good sense to me. Close enough they're staying in the Dot but far enough away from today's shooting. It's an area of the neighborhood less likely for patrol units to be cruising around. At least for tonight. Most of the supervisors will be having units stay close to Dot Center for fear that something else is going to happen. If something else breaks loose, like a retaliation, everybody will want to be closest to the action." White paused pensively. "Actually, it's a really smart move. Maybe I should take a note from this guy's play-book." Then he laughed to himself. "Although, I pretty much wrote the handbook on these kinds of situations."

Brayden looked out the window as they pulled away. The drive wasn't far; nothing was within the six-square-mile boundary defining Dorchester. But White took his time, using back streets to avoid taking a direct path to the Lower Mills area, the southernmost point of Dorchester before the city abutted the quiet town of Milton.

The plan was simple. Brayden was to be dropped near the bus stop on Dorchester Avenue opposite Adirondack Place. White and Sharp would release him a block away from the bus stop, at a time that synced with an actual route schedule. It would give Brayden the cover story he'd taken public transport. He would then walk the several remaining blocks to the Baker Chocolate Factory Apartments, where the exchange was to be made. The walk, White figured, would help work up a little bit of sweat, adding believability to the ruse. Dropping him any closer risked potential exposure.

Brayden was confident in White's ability to foresee potential missteps. It was his job. And according to the Narcotics boss's self-proclaimed mastery, he'd written the book on this kind of stuff, even saying he wouldn't put it past Walsh to go so far as to check the bus's arrival times. It was better to assume their vigilance rather than to hope for their incompetence. Guys like Walsh didn't survive unscathed as long as they had without taking extra precautions every step of the way. Walsh's overcautiousness was a way of life that had, over the years, kept him from the confines of prison walls and helped him dodge doing any serious time.

White pulled the Town Car to a stop in front of a pizza shop.

Their position kept them within eyesight of the bus stop. They waited briefly until a large bus rolled up. In less than a minute it had dumped several passengers and retrieved new ones. The bus moved on, merging into light traffic. Brayden stepped out from the car as the bus moved past, leaving him in the spiraled smog wake. The diesel fuel added to the taste and texture of the city air, mixing with the smell of freshly baked pizza.

White cracked the window slightly and looked out at him. No twisted smile this time, just a seriousness in his eyes, deadly and cold, as he stared deep into Brayden's soul. "Remember what's at stake here. Try not to screw this up."

Brayden couldn't think of a witty response. His normal casual repartee was gone, sucked from him as the intensity of the moment took hold. And he knew, without White's unnecessary comment, everything that was at stake tonight.

Sharp shifted slightly in the seat, leaning into view. He offered him one last word of encouragement. "Listen, I know you're scared, but these people are like sharks. They'll smell your fear like blood in the water and they'll cancel a deal like this in a heartbeat if they sense anything is out of the ordinary. You know this guy Sullivan. You grew up with him. Be yourself around him. Do whatever it is you did the other day when you went off half-cocked and brokered this damn thing. Go out there and close the damn deal and make things right. Then maybe you can get this monkey off your back and get your shit straightened out."

Brayden turned away and began his walk. The air was cooler than the previous couple nights but still carried some of the heavy mugginess. A breeze kicked up between two buildings, and he paused for just a moment to let it flutter his shirt and pass over his sweat-soaked skin before continuing the journey.

He walked until he arrived at the building's red brick exterior. Brayden remembered when his father had brought him down to look at this building as a child. A factory, historically significant in the world of chocolate making, was abandoned in the mid-1960s when the company relocated to Dover, Delaware. It remained in a state of disrepair for nearly fifteen years, until the Boston Redevelopment Authority drew up plans for a revitalization of the area. And the historic building was now home to high-end apartments and the sprawl of shops that sprouted up around it.

Brayden remembered his father making him smell the outside of the red brick façade and telling him if he sniffed hard enough, he would catch a whiff of chocolate. Brayden placated him, never telling his father he couldn't smell it. All he remembered was the smell of brick and mortar. Passing the building now, he was tempted to give it another try. But the burden he carried drove him forward with no time for such diversions.

He was told to meet in the building's back parking lot. As he made his way there, Brayden suddenly felt out of place among the other pedestrian traffic, something he didn't typically feel in Dorchester, but in this area, converted and renovated, he didn't feel like he belonged. The affluent had taken root here. Its surroundings felt foreign. Nothing like the area he was from. Same neighborhood, different feel. And his discomfort bothered him.

He tried and failed to ignore the sideways glances of the wary passersby. His filthy, sweat-soaked shirt and pants were definitely out of place. He stopped and, using the reflection in a toy store window, took a moment and tried to fix his hair. Brayden slicked the greasy curled ends back, tucking them behind his ears in the hopes of trying to look a little less like what he was...a desperate junkie.

In that moment of self-loathing, he thought about the $30,000 in neatly organized stacks tucked inside the one-strapped backpack slung over his shoulder. The weight of the money was heavier in his mind than in reality. He began to think about all the possibilities cash like that could give a guy like him. But as soon as the thought entered his mind so did Lincoln White's face. Being Whitewashed trumped everything else. No amount of money would be worth crossing that man and guaranteeing a death sentence.

He stopped at the corner where the building wrapped around to the back. Brayden looked left and right, his instinctual survival mechanism once again kicking in. Although he was working with the cops and knew they were watching him right now, he still, out of habit, feared their reprisal. He scanned his surroundings—the crowd, the buildings, the cars—but couldn't identify one person who he'd deem a potential match to an undercover police officer's profile, something he'd grown quite savvy at doing over the years. Giving up his futile effort, he moved toward the back lot.

Amidst the rows of parked vehicles, a black Tahoe was running in the back end of the lot next to a large dumpster, exhaust rolling up from its rear. The vehicle was in a darkened section of the lot not adequately illuminated by the streetlights. The tall buildings surrounding the SUV cast an additional layer of darkness over it. Brayden couldn't see through the tinted windows, but he assumed Sullivan was most likely behind the wheel. Even so, he waited for the signal. No need to mistakenly approach the wrong car.

In the darkness, a quick flash of the high beams notified Brayden he was looking at the right vehicle.

Brayden made his way toward the Chevy, his heart pumping faster with each step. He felt a fluttering sensation radiating from the pit of his stomach. He realized it had been several hours since he last used. He'd been warned to be clean when this deal went down, but now he worried his sickness would add to his fear and make him seem all that more vulnerable to them. Just like Sharp warned, Sullivan or anybody else from Walsh's crew would be able to smell blood in the water and taste his fear. He just hoped it wasn't so obvious that he compromised everything he'd worked so hard for.

He crossed the lot quickly, maybe quicker than he should, but he wanted this thing over and done with. Now, more than anything, he wanted to rid himself of the money sack. He wanted to give it to them and let the cops deal with the rest. And then, hopefully, he would be able to take Sharp's advice and get his shit together once and for all.

He stood in front of the SUV's grill. The driver's side window came down halfway. Nobody was visible, but he heard Tommy Sullivan's familiar voice call out, "You gonna stand there like an idiot, or what? Get in the back, dipshit."

Brayden did as he was told and stepped around to the passenger side. He pulled open the back door and climbed inside. Sullivan was in the driver's seat, as he'd predicted. A man he'd never seen before sat in the front passenger seat. Beside him, with a gun pointed in his direction, was somebody he hadn't anticipated seeing—his brother's best friend, Bobby McDonough.

Bobby's eyes went wide at the sight of Brayden. He immediately lowered the gun and tucked it into the front of his pants. With fury in his eyes, he mouthed, "What the hell are you doing here, Brayden?"

Brayden, just as shocked at seeing Bobby, had no answer. He knew Bobby was one of Walsh's most trusted enforcers. He probably oversaw many deals like the one about to take place. Still, it never even dawned on Brayden that he'd be here. Bad enough White and Sharp were involved. Now with Bobby here, Brayden knew it was only a matter of time until Michael found out. Great! Now he'd never hear the end of this.

The man in the front passenger seat turned around. Though

he didn't know him, Brayden could tell he was not a man to be messed with. He held an air of intensity, not unlike White. "Let me see your damn money. It better all be there."

Brayden, still clutching one good strap of the backpack, unshouldered it and warily held on to it a bit longer as he tried to evaluate the situation and the man in front of him. He wanted to give him the bag, but he'd never seen him before. And in the world of drugs and money, knowing somebody was an important thing. Sometimes it was the only thing.

Sullivan turned, his big frame rubbing against the leather upholstery of the seat with a squeak. "He's not going to ask twice, Brayden. He's the guy who gets things done around here. Don't make a bad first impression. This is Fitzy. And trust me when I say this, you don't want to cross him."

Brayden handed over the bag, pushing it through the gap between the two seats and laying it down on the center console.

Fitzy snatched the bag, then pulled the zipper apart at the top and reached inside. Holding a stack of banded cash, he began thumbing through the bills. It was common practice among drug buyers to try and short dealers by throwing a couple twenties or hundreds on the outside of a bunch of ones, or worse, a bunch of cut newspaper. Tricks like that had been done often enough that it became common to check. More advanced criminal networks worried about the potential snares in making a deal like this. Transponders or die markers, the same safety measures employed by banks, were also used by cops. Smart criminals were now aware even the simplest crackhead could be made privy to some of that technology if they were working with the police. Law enforcement officials had tried and failed to snag Walsh. So, it made sense his guys were tasked with taking extra care to check everything before agreeing to any terms of a deal.

Then Bobby leaned in and said, "Gotta do it, man. Gotta run

your pockets to make sure you're not wired." His weapon now tucked in his waistband, Bobby's hands were free to begin searching Brayden. He ran them along the crotch, legs, and pockets, searching every possible place a weapon or recording equipment could be stashed. Not finding anything, he looked down at Brayden's feet. "Kick 'em off. Your shoes. Give them to me."

"You sure you want to do that?" Brayden asked. "Shit, Bobby, you know me. I mean is all this really necessary?"

Fitzy stopped playing with the stacks of money and looked up at him. "Is there a reason you don't want to take off your shoes?"

Brayden looked down at the worn-out Converses on his feet. "Yeah. They stink."

Bobby's mouth crept up into a barely perceptible smile as he extended his hand. Brayden kicked them off one at a time and handed them to him without any further resistance. The odor was bad enough for Bobby's nose to curl. Brayden was embarrassed, but also grateful his brother's lifelong friend didn't razz him about it.

He wasn't nervous about Bobby's shakedown. He'd made a mistake during his first time working with White by bringing his kit. He didn't do that this time. And the cops didn't give him any recording equipment to wear. So, he wasn't fearful they would find anything on him. He was grateful White hadn't made him wear a wire. Watching Bobby's thoroughness, he doubted he would have missed it.

He was only concerned about the transponder thing Sharp had mentioned. He didn't know where it was or how it was hidden. Brayden hadn't even bothered to look inside the bag for fear the temptation would be too great. Now, his nerves were increasing with each passing second as he watched the man in the front passenger seat rifling through the bag. He worried that whatever the hell was in there, this man would find it.

After having his pockets flipped, his shoes removed, and the entire bag examined, all three men turned and faced him, but it was Fitzy who spoke.

"All right. Looks like everything here is on the up and up. Money looks right." Fitzy leveled an intense glare at him. "I'm saying it looks right. I'm not saying it is. I'm not using a counter. If I get back and find out there's a twenty-dollar bill missing from this $30K, I'm coming for you. And trust me on that, you don't ever want me coming for you."

Brayden swallowed hard. He had never counted the money. Never thought to verify the count. He didn't even know how long it would've taken him to count that kind of money. He assumed Sharp or White, or both, would've counted it a bunch of times before handing it his way. But in that split second of self-doubt, he was overwhelmed with panic. He wanted to run. Break out of the car, run away, and never look back. *Bad enough when it was just White making the threats. Now I've got this lunatic breathing down my neck.*

Brayden was a quick study of people. He had to be if he wanted to survive on the street. His summation of the new guy, Fitzy, wasn't a positive one. He seemed just as crazy as White, if not more so. No veiled threats here. And in the short time he'd spent with the man, Brayden decided he didn't like him one bit. He swallowed his fear and, with as much courage as he could muster, said, "It's all there. Every last dollar. You won't be needing to look for me after this is over."

Fitzy turned and nodded at Sullivan, who reached under his seat and pulled out a small duffle. He set it on the center console and opened it. Inside were two small packages resembling shrunken loaves of bread wrapped in yellow envelope paper. Brayden did not reach for the bag or its contents. He waited until Sullivan zipped it closed and then tossed it on his lap.

Brayden reached for the door handle.

"You don't want to test it first?" Fitzy asked.

"I don't think my guy wants me cutting open a brick and testing the product. Plus, isn't this shit like super pure? I don't want to test something that isn't cut and stepped on at least twice, if not three times. I don't think my body could handle it."

They looked at him for a moment. Everybody seemed to be waiting for Fitzy's response. No one seemed to be breathing. Brayden certainly wasn't.

"Fair enough. We don't need you dying on us. Bad for business," Fitzy said nonchalantly.

"So, I can go now? We're good, right?"

"We're done here," Fitzy said.

Brayden pulled on the door handle and was beginning to step out when Bobby grabbed his arm and squeezed hard. In a terse whisper, he said, "I don't ever want to see you around here again. Whatever you think you're doing—it ends here. Tonight. You got me? If I do, I swear to God—"

Brayden pulled his arm free and stepped out of the car, shutting the door behind him, effectively cutting Bobby's righteous sermon short. The front passenger door opened, and Fitzy stepped out.

Fitzy eyed him as if sizing him up. He couldn't get a read on the man. Brayden squared himself and adjusted the bag strap in his hand. The weight of the two keys had a different feel than the money, but each tugged at him—just in different ways. Now he thought of the dope, and how long he'd be able to keep himself straight with the contents in his grasp.

Fitzy interrupted his train of thought. "You did good in there, kid. You came through with some big cash on short notice. A lot of guys talk about making these kinds of deals, but you did it. You might be a guy I want to talk to again sometime. Maybe we can work something out in the future."

Brayden wanted to be free, but he also didn't want to offend the man standing before him. He could tell the consequences of such a rejection would be extremely undesirable. "Sure. Okay. Whatever you say."

"It looks like you know Bobby pretty well. So, I figure I'll be able to get in touch with you through him when I need to."

Brayden thought of the whispered threat Bobby just leveled on him. He seriously doubted Bobby would want to help, but this guy Fitzy seemed to evoke a powerful presence. Brayden imagined he could be quite persuasive should the need arise. "Bobby and I go way back. He can find me."

"Gotta check to make sure everything comes out all right in the end. The money's got to be spot-on. And no heat. But if it squares up, you'll definitely be hearing from me again. We could make some money together."

"Sure thing. Money's good."

Brayden stepped aside and prepared to move out.

"Hey, it looks like you could use this." Fitzy held out his hand.

Brayden looked down and saw the familiar packaging. Fitzy slapped the bag inside Brayden's hand and gripped it in a forced handshake. A street handoff.

"I gotta keep my people straight."

My people? Now I'm tied to this maniac too? Brayden wondered if he'd ever catch a break.

"Consider it like a party favor. Just a little something to tide you over until those bricks in that bag get all cut up. It's good stuff. Trust me." Fitzy winked. "You'll be thanking me later. It'll put you on your ass."

Brayden didn't look down at the bag in his hand. He knew by feel alone what it contained. He felt a wave of excitement for the first time since this day began. The deal was over, the money was handed off, and he'd be able to give White the goods. And now he had a parting gift to wash away all his troubles.

He thought about doing what Sharp said and getting himself cleaned up. But the bag in his hand whispered its sweet reprieve from the sickness swallowing him. It called to Brayden in a language only those in his condition could understand.

He'd worry about getting clean tomorrow. Tonight, he was going to get himself good and high.

Brayden walked away. Before he left the lot, he stuffed the bag in the front slot of his underwear. White hadn't searched him before he set out for this deal like they had the other night, and he doubted they'd check him when he delivered the two kilos of dope. Why would they bother? Not like he could hide a brick of heroin up his ass. And since neither one of those keys were cut open or exposed, they would never suspect him of skimming. Besides, they didn't seem like the kind of guys who liked rummaging through a guy's crotch looking for a bag of dope. Those dirty jobs were left to their minions. So, in Brayden's world, he was having a winning start to the end of his night.

He walked back out toward Adams Street and began making the trek uphill to Dorchester Avenue and the bus stop where they'd dropped him off.

Brayden was seated in the backseat of the Lincoln again, though this time he was in a better position. The exchange with Sullivan was completed, and tucked in the front slot of his underwear was his truest escape, the single bag of dope. He just needed to finish his debrief with White and Sharp before he could partake.

Brayden handed over the small duffle bag containing the two keys of heroin. "Went as well as could be expected."

White took the bag and unzipped it, examining the contents. "Any problems?"

"No. But Sullivan brought two other guys with him. Bobby McDonough and some guy I'd never met before named Fitzy. He seemed to be in charge."

"We couldn't get a good look at him. It was dark. The lights in that section of the parking lot didn't provide much in the way of visibility." White shrugged. "I think we'll still be able to make this case work."

"Wait a minute. All that talk about watching over me was what? Some load of bullshit? Something you say to people just to make them feel better?"

"We were close by. Just couldn't get a good visual on the deal," Sharp said. "But you're saying Fitzpatrick was in charge of this?"

"Yeah. Well, they called him Fitzy. But it sounds like you know him by his full name."

"He's definitely on our radar. You're telling me you met with him face to face?"

"Like I said, he's the guy in charge. You didn't see him when he stepped out of the vehicle with me?"

"No. Too dark," White said defensively.

"Well, he did." Brayden was agitated. He pulled a cigarette from the box in his pocket and placed it in his mouth. He knew he couldn't smoke in the car, but having it in his mouth gave him a modicum of satisfaction. "If you'd been paying attention, you could've had your photo opportunity."

"What did Fitzy say to you while outside the car?" Sharp asked.

"He told me I did a good job in setting this deal up. And wanted to consider me for future ventures."

"Fitzpatrick said he wants to do more with you?" White asked, cocking his head.

"I guess so. He was impressed I was able to get the money together so quickly." Brayden saw the wheels turning in White's mind and became immediately concerned his big mouth had bought him an extended servitude. "I'm done. You said I do this thing and I'm out."

"You've got some kind of luck, kid." White's crooked smile appeared. "To be honest, not quite sure I'd call it luck, but whatever it is, looks like you're not off the hook yet."

"But I thought we were good?" Brayden whimpered.

"We are. Well, we were. Not my call if Fitzpatrick wants to bring you in. We've got an opportunity we need to explore here. One we really can't afford to pass on." White put his hands up as if to say it was out of his control. "In for a penny, in for a pound, I think the saying goes."

"You're a real piece of shit. You know that?"

"Don't press your luck with me." White's face contorted with anger. "It could end badly for you."

"Anything else you need to tell me about the exchange?" Sharp asked lightly, redirecting the conversation.

"No. Everything else went pretty smooth." Brayden tongue-toggled the unlit cigarette dangling from his lips. "Except for the fact that it now looks like I'm working for you guys indefinitely."

"Time will tell on that. But for tonight, I think you've earned yourself a little rest and relaxation." White dipped into an envelope on the armrest and pulled out three hundred in cash, then handed the bills back to Brayden. "Don't spend it all in one place."

Brayden tried to hide his eagerness as he took the money. He had hoped this payout would've been his severance pay.

"A little extra in there. Not our normal pay rate, but this

wasn't our normal buy operation. Don't kill yourself with it."
White put the envelope away.

Brandon stuffed the cash in his pocket. He thought about
the bag tucked neatly away in the lining of his underwear. "I
don't plan to."

He'd be fixed up shortly and now had an additional chunk
of change to spend. For the first time in recent memory, Brayden
felt as though he was holding a winning hand. A feeling almost
as good as getting high. Almost.

28

Brayden stepped out onto the sidewalk and stood under the streetlight while watching the black Town Car disappear up Dorchester Avenue. Although he knew he looked the same as he did when he first walked this quaint section of town, having cash in his pocket made him feel better about himself around the well-to-dos. And with this newfound confidence, he decided to linger around the Lower Mills area a little bit before heading back up to the neighborhood he knew best. He already had his drugs. He didn't need to score. And he now had money to walk into any one of these fancy restaurants and grab himself a bite to eat or drink. But that's not what he wanted.

He needed to get himself straight. To kick the sickness hanging over his head like a dark cloud. Brayden realized before he could do that, he needed to acquire a new kit. Even in this affluent part of town he only needed to walk for a few minutes before he saw somebody he recognized. It wasn't that he recognized the person by name. What he recognized was the addiction.

Brayden walked up to the man in dirt-covered clothing panhandling at the corner of Adams and Washington. For a split second, he felt sorry for the man and actually thought about slipping the guy one of his hard-earned twenty-dollar bills, but greed got the best of him. Instead he fished around in his pocket and pulled out a five.

Brayden got close to the man and spoke in a low voice. "Hey, man, you got a clean needle I can bum?"

The man looked up at him. His eyes were jaundiced and bloodshot, signs his body's functions were failing. "What'd you say?"

"C'mon, man. I know you heard me. I need to get right."

"Yeah, I guess I could hook you up. I got a few. Some cleaner than the others. I've got one I haven't used yet—still in the packaging, but it's gonna cost you."

Something in Brayden took pity on the man. Maybe it was the knowledge that he wasn't far from reaching the man's condition. He replaced the five he'd palmed and exchanged it with a twenty.

Brayden handed it to the vagrant, whose eyes widened as he examined the cash and saw its value. "Maybe you can get yourself straight with that."

"I'm gonna. Damn right." The man, who only seconds before looked to be on his last leg, was transformed by the newfound wealth bestowed by his junkie benefactor. He stood and handed Brayden the clean needle.

The two men separated and walked in opposite directions. The panhandler headed up Dot Avenue as Brayden headed down Adams. Opposite directions but each seeking the same end. To get high.

Brayden retraced the same path he'd taken earlier during the meet with Sullivan. He paused at the red brick building and again thought of his father. This time the memory of smelling the walls only carried a deep sadness. Brayden thought of how disappointed his dad would be if he were alive to see the current state of his life.

He moved further down the way to another favorite spot his dad would take him, the small bridge connecting Dorchester's Lower Mills to the northern tip of the Town of Milton that overlooked the rushing water of the Neponset River. The fast-moving waterway gurgled noisily, drowning out the sound of passing traffic.

Brayden leaned against the green metal railing skirting the sidewalk's edge and looked down at the white froth of the water. The temperature was cooler here, and he took a moment to enjoy the accompanying breeze carried by the river below. He felt a bit of the froth spray up from beneath him. The droplets tickled his skin and dampened his pants in a most refreshing sort of way, washing away the tension and stress from earlier. The water spray reminded him he was in desperate need of a shower. He planned to use some of the money to get a hotel room and get cleaned up after his fix.

Most of the traffic was now confined to vehicles. The pedestrians had begun their migration indoors as shops around the Lower Mills began to close up. The few people passing by paid little to no attention to him as he sat on a low guard rail set a foot back from the curb, his back to the motorists.

He was invisible again. And after several minutes without any foot traffic, he finagled the needle out of his pocket. Using a cap from a bottle of water he'd purchased on the walk down, he began prepping the load. Even in the dark, he noticed the powder was a little whiter than normal. Heroin typically looked like cocoa powder, but this was much brighter. Brayden assumed this must've been what Fitzy meant when he said it was good stuff.

He tore the bag in half, making it easier to access the powder inside. Brayden then set about gingerly tapping the edge of the bag on the lip of the plastic cap. The dope fell from the bag like fresh powdered snow.

He poured a tiny bit of water into the cap and then flicked his lighter. Brayden passed the flame underneath the cap, heating the water and dissolving the powder. His slurry complete, he loaded the needle, pulling back the plunger and drawing in the warm mixture. Brayden then took one last cursory scan of the area, verifying his surroundings were clear of potential onlookers. He didn't need or want somebody sneaking up on him and messing up his high.

Satisfied the coast was clear, he pushed the needle deep into his vein. He felt the rush as the heated fluid coursed through his body, warming him from the inside. The opiates rushing through his veins had a dizzying effect, and Brayden slid off the railing to the sidewalk below. Momentarily incapacitated from the injection, he was unable to gain motor function, and thus, the needle still hung from the injection point in his arm. He wanted to pull it out but couldn't.

The water seemed to grow louder. The cars zooming by caused him to shake. Everything around him was moving faster as he was slowing down. Panic set in as his heart began beating uncontrollably, thumping in his ears, drumming madly until he could hear nothing else. His skin was on fire and he felt as though he was burning up from the inside.

He looked around desperately, trying to find the bag, as if examining the residual powder would provide some answer to his rapidly declining condition. He'd had bad loads before, but this was different, and he knew it. All motor function ceased, and his body slumped forward. His head smacked hard into the warm concrete of the sidewalk. The light from a passing motorist flickered and quickly dissipated into darkness, his visual acuity gone.

His breathing became labored as his cheek pressed against

the concrete. He could taste blood but was incapable of determining the source. Brayden willed himself to move as convulsions began to rock his body. It was like somebody was pounding the walk with a jackhammer.

The thumping in his head continued. A rhythmic booming in his ears. He eyed the needle still protruding from his arm. He willed himself to move but his body resisted all commands, and his attempts to gain control of his limbs amounted to nothing more than a feeble wriggling motion.

The sidewalk's rough surface tore at his clothes and elbows as he worked to move himself inch by slow inch. Traffic moving past, the horns and exhaust fumes, added to the disorienting feeling. Each smell and sound became muddled in his brain, swirling into one crazy hodgepodge of overwhelming sensory overload.

He desperately wanted to get to his phone and call for help. The first and only person who came to mind was his brother. With his world crashing down around him, he wanted nothing more than to speak to Michael.

With an incredible concentrated effort, he managed to slip the phone out. Then, with his finger on the call button, everything went black.

Kelly had looped the block for what seemed like the millionth time. Exhaustion was starting to give way to hallucination. Over the last hour he'd done a double take on every homeless person or junkie he passed. His phone vibrated and snapped him from his haze. He answered a number he didn't recognize.

"Mike, is this you?" The voice was gruff but lined with concern.

"Yeah," Kelly answered. "Who's this?"

"This is Sergeant Connolly from the Eleven."

"Hey, what's up, Denny. Sorry, didn't recognize the number."

"My cell died. I had to borrow one of the rookies' phones."

"Been a long time, Sarge. What's up?"

There was a pause. The older, salty member of the BPD's Patrol Division cleared his throat. "Not sure there's an easy way to break it to you. It's your brother."

Kelly let his frustration out with a grunt. "Did he get himself jammed up again? I've been looking for him for the last few hours, driving around the neighborhood and hitting up some old contacts here in the Eleven. Couple of people seen him here and there, but I can't put him down. If you got him and you're holding him, then keep him there. Don't let him go. I need to talk to him. It's important."

"That's the thing. I've got him, but it's not like you think."

Kelly had always known this day might come. He'd fought like hell to make sure it didn't, but sometimes what you wanted and what you could control were two totally different things. "What happened? Is he dead?"

"No. Close, but no."

"Shot? Stabbed?"

"No, he OD'd."

"Where'd you find him?"

"Down here at the Lower Mills. He was unconscious and unresponsive when the first units arrived. They had to hit him with four or five blasts of Narcan just to get him to where his basic functions were kicking back in. He's in bad shape, Mike. Worst I've seen in a while. I've got him on the bus now. Ambulance is heading to Carney's ER."

"Make sure somebody rides with him or at least is at the hospital to ensure he stays. I can't have him ghostin' on me again."

"I will, but I don't think that's going to be a problem. He's in a bad way. I'm going to be straight with you. I'm not sure he's going to make it." Connolly groaned. "I'm seeing this crap every day. You know how crazy it's gotten lately. People are dropping like flies. When we have to hit somebody as many times with the Narcan as we did with Brayden, it's like a fifty/fifty crapshoot at best on whether or not he's going to pull through."

Kelly ignored the pessimistic outlook. "Tell whoever's standing by with Brayden to relay this message when he comes to: his brother is on the way. And whatever they do, don't let him leave."

"Will do, Mikey. And I'm sorry to be the bearer of bad news."

"Not your fault. I appreciate you reaching out."

"I would've called sooner, but your brother didn't have any ID. It wasn't until one of my guys recognized him that I made the connection. Plus, there was a bit of a delay on the dispatch end. Milton got the call first. Personally, I think they pushed his ass back across the line into the Dot. Didn't matter, once we realized it was your brother, we would've taken it anyway. But we've got him from here on out and we're going to take good care of him for ya, Mike. He's your brother, and that means he's our brother too."

"Thanks. That's good to hear. And right now, it means more than you know." Kelly hung up the phone and immediately dialed the first person who popped into his head.

29

Her legs still pulsed as Barnes used the steps outside her brown-stone building to stretch her tight calves. Her nightly run around the Charles River was completed. As much therapy as it was exercise.

She ran the seven-mile loop from her one-bedroom apartment on Gainsborough Street, through the crowded sidewalks, until she found her rhythm on the trail that shadowed Storrow Drive over the Harvard Bridge, then around MIT and returning back along Memorial. She moved at a smooth seven-minute and thirty-second pace. Nowhere near the pace of her college years, but strong enough to get in a good burn while taking in the sights of the city she loved. Running was a fun way to people-watch, and one of Barnes's favorite pastimes, aside from solving crimes.

She'd qualified for the Boston Marathon for the last ten years. Her finish times improved as she learned to navigate the course. She no longer feared Heartbreak Hill's steady ninety-one-foot incline. Over time she'd learned the hill's devastation on runners had little to do with its elevation and everything to do with its placement in the race, appearing at the twenty-mile mark. After her first bout with the race's legendary hill, Barnes learned a hard lesson about proper preparation. She adapted her training to include more interval hills and adjusted her technique, shortening her stride, leaning in, and attacking. This technique enabled her to maintain pace while others fell apart. And became a sort of personal mantra she now extended beyond the athletic arena. *Only by knowing your enemy can you train to defeat them.*

Running had always been a part of her life, but years ago it almost cost her everything. In 2013, she'd crossed the finish line in three hours forty-nine minutes. Her best time to date. Ten minutes later, while a volunteer was placing a shiny silver heating blanket over her shoulders on the back side of the runners' corral, the first explosion went off. Barnes's left thigh was struck by some of the blast fragments.

She controlled the bleeding in her leg by tearing a strip off the aluminum-coated blanket and cinching it down around her quadricep. Barnes didn't allow herself time to focus on the pain or the exhaustion from having just trekked 26.2 hard-earned miles. Instead, she went to work triaging victims in the surrounding area. Three died at the site of the bombing and multiple others were wounded. Once medics flooded the scene and took over rendering aid to the wounded, Barnes left to join the swarm of BPD officers in the frantic search for the bombers.

Exhausted and depleted, Barnes tapped into a reserve of strength she didn't know existed. The roads were already packed from race watchers and road closures from the 26.2-mile course. And with the explosion, they were a proverbial parking lot. Barnes decided to head to One Schroeder Plaza, Boston Police Headquarters, on foot, adding one and a half miles to her race-day total. Even with the shrapnel injury and the lactic acid built up in her thighs, she was still able to make the trek to headquarters in under fifteen minutes.

Once there, amidst the frenzy of activity, she immediately went to her locker and grabbed her sidearm and raid vest. She threw on some spare clothes over her race day attire and set out to join the manhunt.

Legs still quivering from her four hours of physical exertion along the racecourse, Barnes joined up with a group of detectives rushing out of the building. She didn't sleep over the next day and a half. Miraculously, she ended up with the takedown team the following night in Watertown.

Barnes distinctly remembered staring over the front sight of her Glock at the coward bomber as he lay tucked in, hiding under a boat. She watched as members swarmed the wounded terrorist. Bearing witness as he was taken into custody remained one of her most memorable life experiences to date.

That race bib was now in a frame above her living room mantel and served as a constant reminder as to why she did the job. On that day, she'd seen the worst humanity had to offer, but she also witnessed the strength and resiliency of the people of Boston. Especially among her brother and sister officers sworn to protect it.

Barnes climbed the three flights of stairs to her apartment. She entered and passed the living room where the glass-encased race bib rested. She quickly shed her damp clothes from tonight's run and tossed them atop her wicker hamper. She turned the shower on and stepped in just as her cell, sitting on the sink counter, began to ring. She pulled back the curtain and looked out to see the incoming caller was Kelly. She reached out, drying her hand on a hanging towel, and then swiped to answer, tapping the speaker icon.

"Hey, Mike, just stepped into the shower. What's up? You ever find Brayden?" she asked over the running water.

"I just did." His voice was uncharacteristically vacant. "That's why I'm calling."

"Where's he at? I can meet you."

"The ER at Carney."

Barnes turned the water off. "At the ER? What happened?"

"Connolly just called me. Patrol found him OD'd in the Lower Mills near the Milton line."

"I'm out the door in less than five. See you there."

"Thanks." Kelly ended the call.

Barnes turned the water back on and did a quick cool-water rinse to rid the sweat from her body. She then began rapidly drying herself as she moved into the bedroom. Not giving much effort to the toweling process, she threw on some clothes over her damp skin and headed out. She'd kept her promise and was moving toward the stairwell in under three minutes.

She raced out of her brownstone, her mind on both Kelly brothers. Her memory of the relationship she and Brayden once shared. And the one she currently shared with his older brother, Michael. Each uniquely different but endearing her to the Kellys in a way she didn't quite comprehend.

Kelly paced by the nurses' station. From his patrol days he was used to the hustle and bustle of emergency rooms. But standing here now, waiting for the authorization from the medical staff, was making him frantic with anticipation. The sliding doors to the ER opened and admitted a gurney carrying a loud drunken man in a blood-soaked T-shirt.

A doctor exited Room 3, ignoring the screaming rant of the intoxicated new addition to the floor. He walked directly to Kelly with a solemn expression, and Kelly's heart sank.

"It's okay to see him now," the doctor said.

Kelly regained his mental footing. "From the look on your face, I thought you were going to tell me he'd died."

The doctor took off his glasses and absently wiped at the lenses with the bottom edge of his lab coat. "It's been a busy night." He looked over at the bloody drunk. "And from the looks of things, it's not going to let up anytime soon."

Kelly nodded. "It's been a hell of a week for us too."

The doctor gestured to the room. "He's stable now. It was really touch-and-go for a couple of minutes when he first arrived. We're going to want him to stay for a couple of days. My recommendation is to try and convince him to voluntarily join our inpatient treatment option, so he gets cleaned up."

"I'll try to get it through his thick skull. But he's as stubborn as they come. How much did he use to cause the OD?"

"It's not how much but more a matter of what."

Barnes had been standing silently by as the two men discussed Brayden's condition. She cleared her throat, drawing their attention. "Not sure I'm tracking. We're talking about heroin, right?" she asked.

"His labs are showing it was Carfentanil. Not sure how much you know about it, but in simplest terms it's a synthetic opioid one hundred times more potent than heroin."

Kelly shook his head and fought the urge to punch something. "I know what it is. Don't see too much of that on the street. You're telling me somebody gave my brother a hot shot?"

"I'm not saying anything. All I can go by is the medical evidence, and it appears whoever gave him the drugs should be held responsible. Whether your brother knew what he was getting is something you'll have to discuss with him."

"I will." Kelly stuck out his hand and shook the doctor's. "And thanks, doc, for takin' care of my kid brother."

The doctor walked away and Kelly looked to Barnes, who seemed equally surprised at the information.

"Who would want to hurt Brayden? I mean I've heard of dealers using hot shots to rid themselves of a snitch, but it doesn't make sense to me."

Kelly rubbed his head in frustration. "I've got a couple names rattling around in my brain who might be wanting to shut Brayden up. Or maybe he managed to piss off the wrong people. Worse if we find out those wrong people are cops."

"Are you saying you think White or Sharp was behind this?"

Kelly shrugged and rubbed the base of his neck. "I'm not saying anything. Don't want to jump to conclusions. But one thing is certain, they're the last two people I saw my brother with. So, before this night is through, I'm getting some answers —one way or another."

"How about we start in there?" Barnes pointed to the private patient bay where Brayden was lying.

Kelly opened the door to Brayden's temporary room. He knew with the constant flow of new patients, the hospital staff would soon move him to another wing for follow-up care. The room was abuzz with softly beeping machines and the rhythmic pulsing of the various vital monitoring systems being used to keep track of his brother's recovery. An IV drip hung beside his bed and slowly fed him electrolytes to speed his recovery.

Brayden looked terrible. Kelly was saddened at the sight of him. He couldn't remember a time when he'd seen him so far gone. Kelly had become quite adroit at compartmentalizing the trauma he witnessed while working as a cop. He learned, through experience, how to tuck away those pieces of innate emotional response at seeing the horrors of the street. But staring down at his brother, he was left incapable of distancing himself from the pain of it. Barnes must've noticed his change in disposition because she placed her hand on his shoulder and gave a slight squeeze.

Brayden turned in his bed. His eyes went from Kelly to Barnes. He stared at Barnes just a little bit longer than his older brother, seeming more shocked at her presence than his brother's. He said nothing to either and rolled his eyes back toward the small television suspended in the corner of the room playing *Wheel of Fortune*.

"How are you holding up?" Kelly asked.

Brayden mumbled, "Been better."

"I can see that." Kelly was at a loss for words, and he struggled his way through the painfully awkward small talk, seeking anything to fill the void. "I spoke with the doc. Said you're going to be okay. They want to keep you for a couple days and make sure you don't relapse."

Brayden grunted.

"He offered to enroll you in one of their inpatient treatment programs. But it's voluntary."

Brayden turned his head toward Kelly. "Let me guess, you told him you'd do your best to convince me?"

Kelly decided there was no point in lying. Brayden would see right through it anyway. He had an uncanny way of reading people. Kelly always thought his younger brother would've made a great cop. But instead, he chose a much different path. "Yes. It's not a bad gig. Do a couple weeks. Get cleaned up, eat some crappy hospital food, and watch some television while your body kicks that crap out of your system."

"I don't need any long-term care. I'll be fine."

"No. You won't! Not if you keep going the way you are. You won't make it." Kelly watched his brother, searching his face for some sign he'd take the advice. He saw none. Only a vacant stare. "Did the doctor tell you what you shot into your veins?"

Brayden was silent.

"Carfentanil." He watched as his brother's blank expression changed to one of wide-eyed astonishment. "That's right. Whoever gave you that shot wanted you dead. Or at least close to it." Kelly sat on the corner of his brother's bed and rested a hand on Brayden's blanket-covered ankle. "So, how about it? Cut the macho crap and let me help you."

"How can you help me?"

"For starters, you're going to do the in-patient treatment. If not for me, for Ma. And Embry. My daughter doesn't need to see her favorite uncle dead before she turns ten."

"Favorite uncle? I'm her only one."

Kelly squeezed his brother's ankle a bit tighter. "That's beside the point."

Brayden kicked his leg free. "Get off me."

"And I need to know what the hell are you doing with White?"

Brayden's eyes widened at the mention of White's name. "You knew about that? How? He told me he wasn't going to tell you. Stupid to think I could trust a cop. Especially an asshole like White," he hissed.

"He didn't. They haven't told me anything. But don't worry, that's something he and I will work out in the very near future." Kelly paused and worked to regain his quickly diminishing composure. "So, let me hear it from you. What are you doing with White and Sharp? They are way too dangerous for you to be playing in their world. You've got street smarts. You, of all people, should've known better."

"I do know better. I'm not stupid! I got jammed up, Mike. You probably wouldn't understand. You've never been in my position. I was in a bad spot and played the hand I was dealt."

"Jammed up? How? By who?"

Brayden rolled his eyes. "White. Who do you think? You know it's not like the son of a bitch gave me a whole lot of options. Fairness is not in the man's vocabulary. The stories about him are true. That Whitewash bullshit is for real. You know, you worked with him." Brayden twisted the medical bracelet on his wrist. "He's not the kind of guy to cut a break. Shoot, he's not like you, Mike. You treated your snitches right. I hear talk on the street. You've got a good reputation. As good as a cop can get on the street. But White—well, that guy operates at a totally different level. And he's not a guy you can say no to. Not without dire consequences."

"Why didn't you come to me, Brayden? I'm your brother, for Christ's sake."

"I knew you were going to say something like that. I just knew you were gonna give me a lecture on what I was doing wrong. I've heard it all before," Brayden said through gritted teeth. "I guess I just didn't want to hear it again."

"You're right. I've been hard on you. Pushing you to get better, when I knew all along the only way you'd find your way out was if it came from within. For what it's worth, I'm sorry." Kelly knew Brayden was right. The "you're-screwing-your-life-up" lecture he'd given him time and time again over the years was tired and redundant. Most often the big brother coaching sessions led to fights, both verbal and physical. Sometimes it seemed to work. Other times not so much.

There were glimpses of sobriety following Brayden's rock-bottom moments. These lasted as long as months and as short as days, but they were a nice break in the cycle. Those periods without the in-and-out appearances, the stealing from their mother, and everything else that went hand in hand with addiction. Glimmers of the old Brayden would return, only to shift back at an unforeseen moment of weakness and it would begin all over again. Clean one day and sick the next. It was a vicious loop, and he'd become tired of it.

"I get it. I'm a screw-up. I let you down. I let Ma down. Not much else really to say about the matter. Maybe it would've been better for everyone if I'd remained flatlined on the bridge."

"You shut your mouth, Brayden Kelly. You being dead isn't better for anyone. I should have been able to give good counseling without sounding like a preachy lecturer." It was true, but he still wished his brother had come to him after running into White. The fact that he felt like he couldn't bothered Kelly to the core. He made a silent vow that from this day forth he would do a better job of looking out for his younger brother in ways he had failed to do in the past. "You're done working with White."

"That's not your call. This thing is bigger than you realize."

"If White had anything to do with that hot shot, I'm going to shut him down."

Brayden jerked his arm, tugging the IV tubing and jarring the stand holding the bag. "You can't take on a guy like Lincoln White! What are you going to do? Arrest a cop? You'd be killing your career. Throwing everything away for what? Me? I'm not worth it."

"Yes, you are." Kelly slapped the badge concealed inside his shirt. "You mean more to me than this badge."

Brayden's expression softened. "And I don't even know how I could help you, even if I wanted to. White doesn't tell me what he's doing. I'm not in on the bigger picture. Just a pawn in his game."

"Start by telling me what kind of work he had you doing. About the meeting you had with him and Sharp. Let me in on what you know and I can figure out where to go from there."

"White's goons caught me with a couple bags of dope. White offered me a deal. Work for him and any potential charges would disappear." Brayden shook his head in disbelief. "Hell, he even let me keep the dope he caught me with. I figured, shit— easy enough—do a simple buy or two for them and I'd be off the hook."

"Nothing with White is simple."

"It's my fault," Brayden muttered.

"Your fault? How so?"

"They had me do a cold buy into Sully. You remember Tommy Sullivan. Anyway, during the small talk with Sully I got the bright idea of trying to set something up a little bigger. Figured if I set up a deal big enough to pay my debt to White tenfold, it'd be enough to keep them Narcs off my ass and let me go about my business. I don't want to wait for the rest of my damn life for my debt to be paid to White. You know him, Mike. He has a tendency of bleeding people dry. Getting every last bit of work out of 'em. Basically, he'd turn some junkie like me into an indentured servant—a slave to his will until he chews me up and spits me out. I just didn't want it. So, I brokered the deal."

"What kind of a deal did you make with Sully?"

"Couple kilos."

"You arranged a kilo-level deal?" Kelly asked, equal parts stunned and amazed.

"Don't look so shocked." Brayden added his best attempt at his trademark cocky smile. "Hey, what can I say, I'm a good talker."

Kelly looked at his brother with a sense of bewilderment. A lack of sound judgment notwithstanding, he had been able to do what few others in his position could have. He was equally impressed Brayden's wisecracking sense of self couldn't be squashed, even in the confines of a hospital bed and under the current circumstances. Seeing it now, hearing his voice, the way he still carried himself after just coming back from death's doorstep, he had a newfound appreciation for his brother's strength.

"Okay, so your fast-talking helped you broker a deal for two keys of dope. And did the deal go down yet?"

"It did. Earlier tonight."

"If everything went smoothly, I can't imagine White still holding a weak possession charge over your head. That should have made you right with them."

"It did and it didn't. The deal went down, but the flipside is now Walsh's guy wants me to start working another deal." Brayden bit his fingernail, a nervous habit he took to when he was unable to smoke. "There was a guy at the meet who said he wanted to keep me on retainer for future work."

"Who?"

"Some guy I'd never seen before. Not that I know all of the guys in Conner Walsh's employ. But I'm familiar with most. They called him Fitzy." Brayden shrugged. "Like I said, I've never met him before, but Bobby was there. He could probably tell you more about him."

Kelly sat still upon hearing Bobby's name. The fact that Bobby was with Brayden just before he overdosed sent a wave of red across his face. "Let me get this straight. Did you just say Bobby was there? With you? When the deal went down?"

"Whoa, whoa, whoa, Mike! I don't need you going off half-cocked and getting all hot about it. No need to go grabbing Bobby by the collar and shaking him down. This was on me. All of it. You know better than most what Bobby does for a living. He just happened to be there."

"Bobby's with you. And a short time later you end up ODing after the fact. Tell me how that happened." Kelly's voice started to rise, bordering on yelling.

"It wasn't Bobby fault. I don't think Bobby even knew about it," Brayden backpedaled. "It was the guy Fitzy. He got out of the car when we were done. Told me I did good and handed me the bag. Told me to get straight. I figured it was some type of parting gift for a job well done."

Kelly's blood was boiling. He stood and began pacing at the foot of the bed while Barnes watched anxiously.

"I see that look in your eye, Mike. That 'I'm gonna kick everybody's ass' kind of look. I'm telling you the truth; Bobby didn't have nothing to do with me ODing." His eyes followed Kelly. "Like I said, it was the guy Fitzy who handed me the stuff. I'm being freakin' honest with you, Mikey. I was sick. Between the prospect of free dope and the money that I got from working with White, it seemed like it was turning out to be a pretty good night. I haven't had one of those in a very long time."

Kelly drew a deep breath and exhaled very slowly. "Yeah, pretty good night indeed. Was the plan always to hit the ER for your after-party?"

Brayden sighed and casually offered, "Shit happens."

"No, Brayden! This wasn't a shit-happens kind of night. Fitzy, whoever that is, gave you a hot shot. You know what that is? It's an intentional lethal dose." Kelly didn't give his brother time to answer the rhetorical question. "How many of your acquaintances have died in the last year? You, of all people, should know better."

"Mike, look at me. Look where I've ended up. Look at my track record the last couple years. I'm zeroed out, man." Brayden's head slumped like a turtle retreating into its shell.

"Doesn't matter where you're at in life. You're my brother. And I'm going to set this right." Kelly stopped pacing and stood at the foot of the bed. "I need you to help me figure out who this Fitzy guy is so I can arrange a little meet and greet."

"Here we go again, big brother to the rescue. You want to go beat up all the bad guys who hurt me. But guess what? I don't need you to. I can fight my own battles."

"Fight? Look at you, wrapped up in a hospital bed and pumped full of medicine. Did you know it took five canisters of Narcan to bring you back? Five!"

Brayden shrank down even further.

"If they hadn't found you when they did, there's a good chance you'd be on a slab at the morgue instead of that hospital bed. You barely made it out of this one alive. And so, yeah, I'm your big brother. And, yeah, I'm going to fight your fight. Because that's what brothers do."

"Well what if you weren't?" Brayden mumbled.

"What did you just say?" Kelly leaned over the end of the bed, bearing down over his brother's diminished frame.

"I said what if you weren't my brother?"

"Why would you ask such a stupid question?" Kelly was miffed. "I'm trying to figure things out. And you're wasting time posing hypotheticals."

"It's not a hypothetical." Brayden's tone held no trace of cockiness. "I asked because it's true. You aren't my brother."

Kelly pushed back from the edge of the bed and walked closer to Barnes, who was standing there quietly as the two men verbally sparred. "I don't know if you're delirious from the near-death experience or the meds they've got you on, but you're not making a bit of sense."

"Remember our last conversation? The one in Mom's kitchen a few months back?"

"Sure." Kelly remembered. His brother was drunk and mentioned something about a secret. A conversation his mother dismissed and ended without closure. And one that had been weighing on his mind ever since. But Brayden had taken to the street and he hadn't spoken to him since. He struggled with why his brother was bringing it up now.

"I don't know any simpler way to explain it to you. You're not my brother. Mom can fill in the blanks, but it's the truth."

Kelly felt suddenly woozy. As if the air in the room contained less oxygen than it had minutes before Brayden's preposterous declaration. "I don't understand what you're saying."

"We're not blood."

Kelly tried to process his brother's words, but they didn't make any sense. "How'd you find this out?"

"I was rummaging around in the attic, looking for some shit to pawn. Ya know how it is. I just needed to scrounge a few bucks to score a few bags." Brayden's eyes were downcast in shame. "I came across a shoebox. It had some old letters and whatnot. Long story short, there were things in those letters—about you. They were from your real mother."

Kelly pulled a nearby chair closer and crumpled into it. He heard the words his brother was saying, but more importantly, he absorbed the tone in which they were conveyed. Kelly had no doubt Brayden was telling the truth. His mind flashed back through time, trying to find a clue he'd missed in all these years. Under the weighty impact of the mental sucker punch his brother had delivered, Kelly couldn't allow himself to believe the life he'd known was shrouded in a lie.

"I'm sorry for the bad timing. Not sure there's ever a good time for something like this. I guess my near-death experience pushed this to the forefront for me." Brayden tried to push himself more upright. "It's a lot to take in. But I guess I just figured you deserved to know."

Kelly took several minutes to process what he'd learned. It reminded him of being in the boxing ring. Taking a staggering shot to the head. Those moments where the mind was confused but the body continued on, operating on autopilot. That's what he was on now—autopilot. Pops taught him the only way out of it was to focus on one thing until it became clear. And breathe deeply.

Kelly looked at a red button on the side of Brayden's bed. The icon centered on it was a blur. Kelly stared at it as the room around him continued to spin. With each breath in, the image began to clear, and the spinning slowed. Seconds passed that felt like hours, but Kelly now clearly saw the image embedded in the center of the red button, a white bell. With his focus restored, he realized he needed to push forward and not give in to the overwhelming concussive force of Brayden's revelation.

Kelly stood back up. "Listen, Brayden, as far as you and I are concerned, we're brothers. We always will be, regardless of where we started. Nothing you say is going to change that. And I'm never going to let anything happen to you again."

"I'm sorry to drop the bomb on you about the whole you being adopted thing."

"No, you're not," Kelly said. "You've been dying to tell me. Probably since you found out."

Brayden laughed. "I can't lie. It did make me feel a whole lot better about myself when I realized I wasn't genetically linked to your ugly ass. I always felt like a failure next to you, but now I can just, you know, blame it on bad genes."

Kelly wanted to laugh at his brother's jest. Although he wasn't in a place to engage him, he appreciated the effort nonetheless. "Let's put this conversation aside for now. It sounds like I need to have a very long chat with Ma. But currently we've got more pressing issues to deal with." Kelly paused momentarily to gauge his brother's willingness before continuing. At this point, he wasn't sure if the announcement about his adoption was meant as a diversionary tactic. "Brayden, you're the only one who can help us. We've got somebody going around killing people and making it look like a turf war. But I think there's more to it. We believe someone's making a move on Conner Walsh. And I need to understand the why, or at least the who, so I can put an end to it before more people die."

"I don't know how I can help you. It's not like I can reach out and call this Fitzy guy."

"Why don't you start by describing Fitzy? I'd normally run the name by Sharp, but apparently that seems to be off the table for now."

Brayden was pensive for a moment. "Not much to him, really. He's in his thirties, clean-cut guy, kinda square jaw. I mean, shit, you'd think he was a cop if I didn't know any better."

Kelly and Barnes perked up. "What'd you just say?" Kelly asked. "What makes you say that—the cop thing?"

Brayden's shoulders scrunched up into a shrug. "I don't know. It's just something in the way he looks at you. All you cops do it. This look of superiority and power. Big-timers like Walsh have it too, but those guys always have a bit of paranoia added in. Cops don't."

Barnes gave a soft chuckle. "That's an interesting summation. The only difference between cops and mobsters is paranoia."

"Hey, it's true." Brayden smiled. "Hell, I can usually smell you guys a mile away. And he had that kind of stink." He stopped rambling and looked up at them. "I know. Stupid, right?"

Kelly eyed Barnes and could tell she was thinking the same thing. And then Kelly remembered the meet with Sharp, how O'Malley had met with them after Brayden left. Kelly leaned closer to Barnes and whispered in her ear, "Do you think you could get me a picture?"

She mouthed, "Of O'Malley?"

Kelly nodded. Even under the circumstances, he didn't want to unnecessarily risk exposing a potential undercover officer to his drug-addicted brother. But the situation dictated a deviation from the normal protocols.

"Give me a second," she whispered. "I can access the database from my phone." She stepped outside for a second and fiddled with her cell phone. When she returned a moment later, she held up the phone so Kelly could see. "It's an old one. I'd guess just after the academy graduation. It's from the ID database. The picture dates back at least ten years."

Kelly shrugged. "Better than nothing." The image showed Patrick O'Malley wearing his dress blues and eight-point hat, the formal wear of the Uniformed Division of the Boston Police Department. "We show him this and we've crossed a line."

Barnes sighed. "At this point, it feels like the only way to get to the truth. Whatever that means."

Kelly brought the phone over to his brother. "You ever seen this guy before?"

Brayden looked at the picture. His eyes went wide, and he shoved back onto his elbows, scooting himself up into a seated position. He looked at the picture and then back at Kelly. "That's him. That's Fitzy. That's the guy who gave me the bag. Holy shit! You're telling me he's a frickin' cop?"

Kelly felt conflicted. He'd just exposed an undercover to his brother. He hoped for all concerned, the loyalty between brothers was strong enough for Brayden to hold that information tight.

"Brayden, you've got to do a better job of keeping this secret than you did about my adoption. This is the kind of dirt that gets people killed if exposed. And I'm not just talking about this guy, but anybody who knows about it. You know as well as I do, the people running this show are as dangerous as they come, Walsh and White alike."

Brayden was silent and he rocked slightly in the bed.

"I think it's best you take the doctor up on his rehab offer. Safer for you in here than out there. Agreed?"

Brayden nodded slowly. "Agreed."

"Let me do what I can to get this thing sorted out. Keep yourself invisible for the time being while we do that. Understood?"

"Okay." Brayden lay back into the bed, suddenly looking exhausted. "Mike, you be careful out there. Something's really off with that guy. He's a scary dude."

"You came back from the dead tonight." Kelly put a hand on his brother's shoulder. "I think I can manage. Remember, we're Kellys. And we're tougher than the average person." He'd said similar things in the past, but in light of the information about his birth, he felt the impact of *we're Kellys* was somewhat diluted.

"Thanks for looking out, Mikey."

"Don't thank me. It's what brothers do."

Brayden reached up with his opposite hand and gripped the one Kelly had placed on his shoulder. "And Mike, do you think you can keep this between us? No need to tell Ma about me being in the hospital."

Kelly smiled. "Too late."

Brayden released his grip and his head drooped. "Great."

"At least she can stop worrying. She now knows where you are. And it's a hell of a lot better than being dead."

"We'll see if that stands true after she reads me the riot act."

"Don't worry. I'm sure Ma will be in here to beat your ass sooner rather than later." Kelly squeezed his brother's shoulder tight. "You take care of yourself. I'll be back to check on you."

Brayden looked up. "Watch your back out there. These people don't care if you're a cop or not. They're dangerous."

"So am I. Plus, I've got Kris here to watch my back."

Kelly and Barnes walked out of the ER.

The former Golden Gloves boxer turned Boston homicide detective was filled with a focused rage he hadn't felt in a very long time.

31

Kelly and Barnes sat in his Caprice in the Carney ER parking lot. He slid out his cellphone as another ambulance pulled up. This time the passenger was an elderly female. As she was hustled inside, Kelly dialed the number.

"Mike?" Bobby McDonough sounded confused.

"Hey, Bobby, you'll never guess where I just walked out of," Kelly said, making no attempt to mask the sarcasm in his voice.

"Not really in the mood for games tonight. I couldn't tell ya."

"The ER."

"Everything okay?" Bobby asked sincerely, immediately dropping the attitude.

"Nobody goes to an emergency room because everything's okay. That's not the way it works. They're called emergency rooms for a reason."

"Jeez! Bite my head off, why don't you. I haven't talked to you in forever. Well, that is unless you want to count our little conversation this afternoon when I was in cuffs. Thank you, by the way, for not taking those damn things off. My wrists are still sore." Bobby huffed.

"Well, they're off now, aren't they? But don't think for a second I wouldn't gladly put them back on."

"Mike, seriously, what's gotten into you? You're all fired up."

"It's Brayden." Silence from the other end. Kelly could hear his friend breathing, but no words followed. So Kelly decided to fill the dead air. "I know you were there. Tonight. At the deal."

"Mike, look, I—"

"I'm going to ask a question, and for your sake, you better give me the right answer." Kelly exhaled slowly, working to contain his anger. "Did you know about the bag of dope Fitzy handed my brother?"

"What bag of dope?"

"You didn't see Fitzy get out of the car and hand Brayden something?"

"He got out, sure. I saw that. But I didn't see anything else. Figured it was Fitzy just being Fitzy. Ya know? Adding an extra threat for good measure. He's a bit of a prick when it comes to that sort of thing."

"He added something all right, it just happened to be a hot shot. He hit him off with a bag of Carfentanil."

"Shit. Is Brayden okay?" Bobby asked with genuine concern.

"He is now. After five doses of Narcan. And some extra effort by the ER staff here at Carney."

"Mike, I was going to call you about Brayden being there today. I really was. As soon as this shooting stuff settled down, I was going to let you know about Brayden getting mixed up in the drug side of things. Figured maybe you could talk some sense into him. Or knock it into him."

"So, you're telling me you didn't know Brayden had set the deal?"

"I didn't. Walsh caught wind that Sullivan was trying to do a deal on his own. Instead of shutting it down, he sent me there to supervise. When I saw it was Brayden, I actually grabbed him and told him to cut the crap and that I better not see him again pullin' some shit like this. Swear to God, I didn't know."

"Where do we go from here?"

"I guess that's up to you. Depends on whether you believe me or not."

Kelly thought for a moment. The two men had been friends for as long as Kelly could remember. And one thing always remained true. They never lied to each other. They held back— their conflicting lifestyles dictated it at times. But they never lied.

"Things are a bit crazy around here, Mike. Walsh is trying to sort this mess out before it spirals completely out of control." Bobby sounded exhausted.

"Maybe I can help in that regard."

"You? Help Conner Walsh? Why on God's green earth would you do that?"

"I'll tell you one thing, it's definitely not out of the kindness of my heart."

"What's your angle?"

"Your crew is in the middle of something bad. And I don't think it has to do with the Corner Boys. Somebody's making moves. And I don't think the threat's coming from outside. Do you understand what I'm getting at?"

"I do, and I've got an idea of who you might be talking about."

"If we're thinking about the same individual, then I think I can help. But to do that, I need you to set a meet for me."

"A meet? With who? Nobody from this crew is going to be caught dead talking to a cop. I'm pretty sure Walsh would put two in my skull if he knew you and I were having this conversation now."

"I want to meet with Fitzy. And don't worry about Walsh. I

won't tell him if you don't." Kelly chuckled softly at the joke, one they'd used too many times to count.

"Seriously, Mike. How am I going to set a meet with somebody he doesn't know? Everybody's on high alert around here. He'd never bite."

"He's not going to be meeting with me. Set the meet with you. I'll be your plus one for the evening."

"Sometimes I wonder who takes more risks in our friendship and who asks more of the other."

"I didn't tell you to join Walsh's gang. In fact, I tried to stop you. Numerous times. And many times, in the past, I've bailed you out."

"Okay. Forget I said anything."

"I would never ask you to do anything that could put you in harm's way, but people are dying, Bobby. More will surely follow if I can't stop the person responsible."

"Tell me what you're thinking, and I'll let you know what I can do."

"Let me guess—your problem is with Fitzy. Walsh doesn't trust him. It's the real reason Walsh asked you to chaperone the deal. He could care less if Sully pulled in some extra money. He'd either take his cut or beat him within an inch of his life for breaking some mob code. Walsh had you tag along to keep watch on Fitzy. Tell me I'm wrong."

"You're not. Fitzy's been getting big balls lately, standing up to Walsh in front of the crew. Things are delicate right now, to say the least."

"I think Fitzy knew Brayden is my brother. I think it's the reason he gave him the dope." Kelly rubbed his temples. Speaking the words aloud was almost enough to make him sick.

"Why would somebody intentionally target a cop's brother? That's like committing suicide. It'd be open season on that person, if it was figured out."

"Maybe he thought it would derail me from my investigation. Dead family members have a tendency to do that. I don't know the why. I just know he did it. And I'm not going to rest until he and I discuss that matter face to face." Kelly paused long enough to take a sip from a lukewarm bottle of water resting in the center console cup holder. "And that's where you come into play."

"How do you know it wasn't Sullivan? Maybe it was his idea?"

"Let's not waste time beating around the bush. You already said it. Walsh is concerned about Fitzy. Brayden said it was Fitzy who handed him the bag. Plus, Sullivan would never dare. He knows I would knock his teeth down his throat. That big idiot's been afraid of me since middle school."

"That's definitely a true statement." Bobby stammered for a split second as he asked, "You believe me that I didn't know about any hot shot, right?"

"I know you well enough to know when you're telling the truth. So, yeah, we're good on that front," Kelly said. Barnes was sitting beside him in the passenger seat, patiently listening to one side of the conversation. "I need to know. Can you do this thing for me?"

"How long do I have to think about it?"

"Here and now. I need this done. Tonight, if possible."

"You're asking a lot of me, Mike. If he catches a hint this is a setup, I'm a dead man."

"I understand what's at stake. I wouldn't have asked if I had an alternative. Right now, I trust you more than most of the people I work with, minus Barnes and a handful of others."

"Not sure that's comforting to hear there's dissension in your ranks too."

"Let's work together to settle things back down and get the

world spinning in the right direction. Find Fitzy for me. Bring him into the open."

"Are you going to tell me what you know about him? Besides the Brayden thing, it seems like you're going about this in a very delicate fashion. Why not just snatch him up yourself? If Brayden's given you a statement, can't you just arrest him on that? Or at least detain him for questioning?"

Kelly knew his friend was too smart not to question his motives. "Not sure I can. All I can say is it's complicated."

"Let me get this straight. You're asking me to set this guy up but you're not willing to tell me what it's all about?"

"We made a promise to never lie to each other. I'll never break that. And with that in mind, I can't tell you some things. Maybe someday. Just not right now."

"I'll need to make something up to get him to meet me."

"Why don't you tell him you got another deal lined up. Or tell him you've got his cut from the deal and want to offload his payout. I really don't care what you tell him, but set it up. You're the criminal, Bobby. Seems like coming up with some ruse shouldn't be too much of a complication."

Bobby cleared his throat. "Okay. I'll come up with something. Give me a bit and I'll get back to you."

"I owe you."

"Seems like if I remember correctly, you said that to me when I helped you find that rapist you were looking for. And if I recall, from our last go-round in Pops's back lot, we haven't completely resolved that issue yet."

"We'll circle back to that some other time when this is all said and done. For now, I need this favor."

"Fair enough. I'll reach out to Fitzy and get this lined up. You got a plan once I do?"

"I will. Simple is always the best. Just get him pinned down and I'll take care of the rest."

"Consider it done. But Mike, you don't blink around this guy. You got me? He's a special kind of crazy."

"I'll be fine."

"I'm not sure how he's gonna react once he realizes I'm bringing a cop to a meet."

"Just promise me, if this thing breaks bad, you make sure to get the hell out of there." Kelly took a serious tone. "You and I— we're family. And from what I learned from Brayden tonight, you might be as close to blood as he and I."

"What's that supposed to mean?"

"That's definitely something for another time."

"I'll call you back in a few when it's set. Be ready to go at a moment's notice. Fitzy usually likes to stay close to Dot Center. So, if I were a betting man, it'll be somewhere around there."

"I don't know how this thing is going to go down. And I don't want to put you in a position you don't want to be in. One that's going to possibly compromise you to your boss."

"Mike, I get it, all right. You're looking out for me. But Fitzy is dangerous. After the stunt he pulled with Walsh today, I'd probably be looking at a promotion if the guy ends up takin' a bullet."

"This isn't a hit, Bobby. I just need to get some answers, and I think he's the only guy who can set the record straight." Kelly was tempted to tell his friend the truth about the links to the convenience store shootings but decided against it. "I'll be standing by whenever you're ready."

"I hope this goes the way you want."

"Me too. And Bobby, for what it's worth, thanks."

Kelly hung up the phone and looked at Barnes.

She looked back at him in surprise. "Are you really planning on going head to head with O'Malley? Knowing that he's the puppet under White and Sharp?"

"I can't force you to come with me on this. We're getting into some gray area here. And believe me when I say it, I won't judge you if you want to step back from it."

Barnes's face contorted. Her green eyes narrowed. "I can't believe you just said that. What kind of partner would I be if I left you when you needed me most?"

"I just know it's not a normal request. Even if this meeting goes smoothly and is uneventful, we're still probably going to be screwed for exposing a UC in the field. I'm not sure what that could mean for your job."

"This job means nothing to me if we're going to turn a blind eye. And if tracking a killer ruffles some feathers along the way, then so be it."

"Hell of a start to your first week in Homicide."

Barnes offered a half-smile. "With any luck we'll both still be in the unit come next week." Her smile dissolved. "I am worried about you in all of this. My concern is that after seeing Brayden laid up in there, you're coming at this whole thing from a very personal angle. And you know as well as anybody, this job can't be personal."

"You're right. I'd be lying if I told you it wasn't, but that bastard gave my brother enough drugs to kill a damn horse. And I don't think it was by accident." He squeezed the steering wheel to release some of the tension building up inside him. "I'm starting to question how much White and Sharp know about this too. Guys like that are control freaks. Seems strange they'd let O'Malley run wild like this without their knowledge."

"You can't take on everyone, Mike. Fighting the good fight means knowing when you're up against an unbeatable opponent."

"That's the thing, Kris. I'm undefeated." He gave her a wink to soften the cockiness of his comment. "And I plan to keep it that way."

"One thing's for certain, you are as stubborn as the day is

long." Barnes reached over and touched his arm just above the wrist. "I guess I just don't want to see anything happen to you," she said, her voice softer than normal.

Kelly looked at the emerald green of her eyes. Without thinking, he drew her close. Leaning across the Caprice's center console, he did something he never thought he would do. He kissed Kristen Barnes.

The kiss lasted for only a brief second, and Kelly wasn't sure what to make of his decision. He waited for a response. Something. Anything. This was the first woman he'd kissed since his wife left him. Although it felt good to feel her warm lips against his, and she hadn't been repulsed enough to pull away, she still hadn't spoken. With each passing second, the silence between them grew more awkward.

"Well, that was completely unexpected."

Kelly ran the gambit of possible retorts and came up empty. All he could muster was a sheepish, "Sorry."

"No. Don't be. It's just—we work together now. Not sure how something like this plays out in the field."

"Me neither. And I really don't know what came over me." Kelly felt his cheeks warm. He strangely welcomed the feeling. It was such a departure from the stress and anger of the day. "I'm not an alarmist by any means. But I really don't know how this meet with O'Malley is going to play out tonight. And after my brother's unforeseen disclosure about my life, I guess everything feels a little out of whack."

"And that kiss somehow helped?"

"Yes. It did. I also don't want to leave things undone or unsaid. And I've felt, ever since the last time we partnered up, that there was something more to us. I hope I wasn't wrong."

"Your timing couldn't be worse."

"Why? You have a boyfriend?"

"No, you dipshit. We're in the middle of a triple homicide

investigation. On the verge of possibly disrupting and exposing a long-time deep cover operation into the biggest crime organization in Boston's history. And this is the time you choose to show an interest in me?"

"When you put it that way—"

"If you and I survive the next couple of hours and maybe days, how about we try this again under a more appropriate setting."

Kelly's redness subsided and his nerves settled. "What? My department-issued Caprice isn't romantic enough for you?"

They both laughed as the phone resting between them on the center console vibrated. Kelly clicked on the incoming text message. The address for the meet appeared. It was close to where they were located. And it was set for thirty minutes from now.

As they read the message, their faces shifted from the frivolity of the previous minutes to serious. The distraction of the kiss was now gone, and they had to focus on developing a plan of action. It wasn't every day a mob enforcer arranged a meet between two cops. And Kelly needed to factor in a wide range of possibilities.

32

Kelly watched Bobby McDonough standing outside the building's dimly lit exterior. He'd been waiting for almost seven minutes. Five minutes past the agreed-upon meet time. Kelly figured if O'Malley was smart, he would've gotten on location earlier and set up nearby with a good vantage point. A smart cop would take extra precautions.

Bobby stood by without showing any outward sign of worry. Criminals were not typically known for their punctuality. So, being a few minutes late wouldn't put up any major red flags. Bobby worked for the mob, which meant he didn't punch a nine-to-five time card. And therefore, meeting times and schedules were less likely to be closely adhered to.

The building at the corner of Gibson and Sturtevant looked abandoned. Junk cars littered the narrow street on both sides. The building had been painted white at some point in time, but it had long ago begun to peel and crack, revealing the muted gray of the primer undercoating. The space had once belonged to a private ambulance company and had rollup bay doors along the Gibson Street side. Kelly had no idea what Walsh used the place for now. There was no company sign or logo anywhere on the exterior of the structure. Kelly assumed the mob kingpin had properties scattered throughout the city similar to this. Secured locales where meetings, like this one, could take place in relative obscurity.

Bobby was waiting by the blue door on Sturtevant. Kelly had released Barnes a block and a half away on Park Street. She was making her way in on foot and would stage, as best she could, toward the back side of the building. Kelly was further on Sturtevant, parked behind a rusted-out Durango. The bulky vehicle provided ample concealment. Kelly had arrived ten minutes after receiving Bobby's message and twenty minutes before the scheduled meet time. He wanted to ensure his position long before O'Malley arrived.

The only movement since Kelly took up his post was Bobby's arrival. The waiting game had begun. He watched Bobby carefully, worried he'd put his best friend in harm's way. He couldn't fathom the guilt if something happened to him. Especially if it happened due to something he'd orchestrated.

A few minutes later, headlights flooded the Gibson Street side of the building. A dark sedan rolled to a stop near the corner, the light washing over Bobby. The engine and lights cut off, casting the corner back into darkness. A man stepped out, and even in the dim setting, Kelly could easily make out the features of Patrick O'Malley, or, as Bobby knew him, Billy Fitzpatrick, AKA Fitzy.

Kelly watched as the two men shook hands. Even at a distance the exchange appeared to be a bit awkward, a forced sign of respect. Bobby said there'd been tension in the ranks. Fitzpatrick was likely guarded. Maybe worried Walsh had sent one of his top enforcers to end whatever squabble he'd had with the man.

The fact that O'Malley even showed shocked Kelly. If Kelly had judged the man right, which he hoped he had, he likely would have been too afraid to tell anyone else about the meeting, maybe even White or Sharp.

The two men exchanged a bit of small talk and then dipped inside the building, disappearing from view as the blue door closed behind them. Issues could easily be handled within the building's walls and, if Kelly ventured a guess, probably had been. Any evidence would be cleaned up with relative ease and security. The location made the place relatively invisible to unforeseen witnesses. Plus, the building was set back several blocks from any residential area, decreasing the likelihood of accidental exposure. These were all good reasons for O'Malley to pick this spot. And all bad reasons for Bobby.

Bobby told Kelly the door would be left unlocked once they were inside. He said he'd make sure of it. There were no windows, making it easy for anyone to approach unseen. Bobby had also given him a basic layout, describing it as a simple design. Most of the bottom floor was still just drywall and concrete floors. No work had been done since Walsh acquired the building, and possibly never would be. One door, minus the old ambulance bay doors. One way in and one way out. Basically, it was an isolated box, set into the backdrop of Boston's Dorchester. Close enough to the Savin Hill Gang's home turf. And so, by all accounts, it was the perfect meet spot.

Kelly waited for one very long minute after the door closed and then exited his vehicle. He walked over, keeping his weapon in the small hip holster covered by the shirt he had untucked over it. No need to display badge or gun here. This was not an on-the-books meeting, and not one he hoped would fall under the scrutiny of a police investigation. This was to be a simple Q&A.

Kelly closed the distance quickly. He scanned O'Malley's car. Empty. Then he stopped for a brief moment outside the blue door and listened intently. It was difficult to make out the conversation through the heavy steel door, but he could still hear its tone.

Fitzy was agitated and did little to belie his suspicion. Before things got too hostile, Kelly decided to make his entrance.

He twisted the knob and pulled the door open, then stepped inside. The room wasn't much brighter than it had been outside. A single light bulb hung from its wire in the center of the room, lighting the interior well enough for him to see the men's facial expressions.

As Kelly entered the room, O'Malley's back was to the door and he spun to face the newcomer. His sharp eyes made contact with Kelly's. Surprise quickly gave way to anger, and then the man turned his attention back to Bobby. "You're working with the cops?"

Bobby, quick on the uptake, replied, "How do you know he's a cop?"

O'Malley glared at McDonough. He was caught off guard by the redirect, unprepared for the retort.

"I asked you a simple question. How'd you know he was a cop?" Bobby waited for a split second before continuing. "But seeing from the dumb look on your face and the fact you can't think quick enough on your feet, I'm pretty sure I can take a wild guess at the answer."

"You don't know shit!" O'Malley moved his hands toward the small of his back. In a flash they reappeared, holding a gun. "Don't you frigging do it, Bobby! Don't you reach! Everybody be cool!"

"You need to put that down!" Kelly commanded.

O'Malley turned his attention to Kelly, the gun now pointed at his face. Kelly's hand was near his waist, his fingertips grazing the bottom of his shirt near the holster. He hadn't expected O'Malley to react this way. Or to escalate things this quickly.

"Don't you reach for it, Mike. Swear to God, I'll put you down if you do."

"What the hell happened to you?" Kelly asked.

Bobby, using the distraction, immediately went for the revolver he had tucked in his front waistband. He brought it up quickly, aiming it at O'Malley. "Put the gun down, you crazy son of a bitch!"

O'Malley kept his own weapon level at Kelly's forehead. Admittedly, Kelly had been in only a few other situations where a weapon was pointed at him. And in those moments of life and death, he had come out victorious. But now, under this unique set of circumstances, he was clearly at a disadvantage. His gun was still holstered, and in the world of action versus reaction, he understood there was no way he'd be able to draw and fire in time, if the need dictated. Right now, his sole focus was on slowing things down. He was silently angry at himself for not predicting how rapidly this meeting could have escalated out of control.

Kelly raised his hands slowly and took one step forward. If nothing else, he wanted to close the distance between him and O'Malley. If circumstances presented an opportunity, he might be able to parry the shot or at least deflect the weapon to a less vital point of aim before discharge. At this point, everything was a crapshoot.

Bobby's gun was still pointed at O'Malley, who turned his gaze, but not his gun, and looked out of the corner of his eyes at both men, keeping each in his peripheral vision. "I'm gonna kill him if you don't drop your gun!"

"You can't win this thing. You're not walking out of here alive," Bobby said with a calm, steady voice.

Kelly had never asked his friend the specifics of what he did for Walsh. But watching him now, displaying such a high level of control under such dire circumstances, he realized he'd been in situations like this in the past. Bobby held the revolver steady.

O'Malley, on the other hand, was coming unraveled. His eyes jittered and his body had a minute tremble. "Don't think for a second I won't shoot him dead."

"What the hell happened to you, O'Malley?" Kelly asked.

Hearing his real name, O'Malley spun and focused his attention solely on Kelly.

Bobby heard the name and quickly surmised the situation. "Holy shit! You dirty bastard! You? You're the one who's working for the cops? We knew there was a mole. Never figured you for a snitch."

"He's not working with the cops. He is one," Kelly said, looking at Bobby for his reaction.

"What? Fitzy? No way! I've seen him do stuff. Bad things. No cop, not even an undercover, could get away with the shit I've seen."

"Shut up, Bobby! You shut your damn mouth!" O'Malley's eyes were wide enough for Kelly to see the whites around his pupils on all sides. He was unhinged.

"Like giving a cop's brother a hot shot?" Kelly asked, unable to hide the anger from his voice.

Now O'Malley's eyes ping-ponged between the two men rapidly.

"You knew he was my brother," Kelly hissed. "You knew that and you gave him the Carfentanil."

O'Malley smiled, wild-eyed, like he was possessed. The sight made Kelly wonder if the man was high on cocaine. Regardless, he was clearly out of control. The gun in O'Malley's hand trembled.

Kelly figured it was better to keep the man engaged and mentally off balance in the hopes he'd find a window of opportunity to turn the tables. "What was your plan? Or have you slipped so deep into your role as a bad guy you don't even know anymore?"

"As soon as I found out you got the case and not Anderson, I realized I had to get you off my back. I knew you would be coming for me. Those idiots, Sharp and White, told me they exposed my name to you."

"Not exactly. They did give up the fact a UC was working inside Walsh's crew. But they didn't give up your name. Hell, I didn't know it was you until I followed Sharp and White for their meet."

O'Malley shook his head. "Doesn't matter now. I remembered you from back in the day. You always were a stubborn prick. What'd they call you? Saint Mike? And now look where all your righteousness has got you."

"You think killing me is going to fix what you've done? You went rogue. You're a mess. Nobody's going to protect you now. I came here for answers. It was supposed to be a conversation. Never even planned to tell Bobby about you. Who you really are. But you decided to pull the gun! So, put it down and we all walk out of here."

O'Malley's smile broadened. "You think you understand what's really going on here? You think you have any clue as to what is happening? You don't! Sad thing is you're probably going to die here today not knowing why."

"You're not going to kill me. You're a cop. I'm a cop." Kelly was trying to convince himself as much as O'Malley.

O'Malley laughed. "That's a good one. I haven't felt like a cop for a very long time. Actually, your death is going to make things so much better for me. At least you won't be up my ass anymore. Which is a good thing. I was hoping your brother's death would've had that effect. But a bullet to the head works just as well. You can join your former partner Danny Rourke as another one of Boston's unsolved murdered cops."

"There's no way Sharp is backing your play. White's an asshole. A big one. But even so, I can't see them turning a blind eye to what you're doing here."

"That's the problem with you, Mike. You can't see the big picture. And the truth of the matter is, neither can they."

Kelly recalled his conversation with Sharp in his office. He'd said the same thing. "Whatever it is—whatever you've cooked up—it's going to end here. Tonight."

"Still the optimist. You're definitely a glass-half-full kinda guy. I can see that. Let me break it down for you. Bobby here's going to lower his gun. Because he knows, deep down, I can get my shot off first. He also doesn't want to piss off the man who is about to take over Walsh's crew. It would be a really bad move for him career-wise."

"What are you talking about?" Bobby asked.

"I'll fill you in later, unless you still think killing me is such a good idea?" O'Malley waited a brief second. "Good. Now lower your gun."

Bobby hesitated for a split second and then brought his gun down. Kelly watched his best friend give up the only leverage in his fight for survival. His stomach turned.

Kelly looked at Bobby. His friend's head was bowed slightly, avoiding any direct eye contact.

"They're going to solve this crime. Trust me. All the pieces will be neatly laid out. But they won't come for me. You know who's going to get blamed, who's going to take the fall for killing the hard-charging Michael Kelly—Saint Mike?" O'Malley paused, but only long enough to take a breath. "Conner friggin' Walsh! So, in effect, your death with bring an end to the most notorious gangster's reign. And with it, usher in a new era."

Kelly furrowed his brow. "And how are you going to pull that rabbit out of your hat?"

"Because I'm holding his gun." O'Malley kept it aimed at

Kelly's forehead but canted it slightly. "I think you'll recognize it. Went missing a few years back from evidence. But it's magically resurfaced. Maybe you heard?" O'Malley's overly sarcastic tone bit at Kelly's ears.

Bobby looked at O'Malley. "No way you're going to be able to pull this off."

"You'd be surprised what I can do. I'd like you by my side for the second phase of this thing. You're a trusted right-hand man. It'd also be nice to have somebody who knew my secret. One person that I didn't have to lie to."

"But you're a cop," Bobby said.

"I am. The Boston Police are going to control the Savin Hill Gang from within. We'll run everything."

Bobby laughed. "You're out of your damn mind. Why in the world would the BPD do that? Work with the mob?"

"We would be the mob. The old way of playing cops and robbers doesn't work. It really never has. It's just like legalizing marijuana. Now the government can regulate it and even turn a profit. This is the future of policing. Where cops regulate crime from the inside." O'Malley shrugged. "Sounds crazy, right? I guarantee you that violent crime drops to an all-time low within one year of me taking over. Boston will soon be labeled the safest big city in America. Maybe the world."

Kelly smirked. "You're doing this for the betterment of society? My ass."

"Me? God no. I'm doing it for the power. The people who came up with this wild idea, they're in it for all the altruistic reasons. But you can't run a gang without a guy like me or Walsh at the helm."

"And where do I fit in?" Bobby asked. "How long until I become a liability to you for what I know?"

"Don't look a gift horse in the mouth, Bobby. I need a guy like you. A solid guy who can get things done. Hell, you set me up tonight. And that's not an easy thing to pull off." O'Malley eyed Bobby. "So, how about it? Ready to usher in the new era of the Savin Hill Gang?"

"Just like that? I'm part of your conspiracy to overthrow Walsh?" Bobby asked.

"You've got one chance to prove your loyalty to me." O'Malley thrust his chin in Kelly's direction. "Kill him. Here and now. And you're in."

Bobby turned and faced Kelly. "I'm sorry, Mike."

O'Malley lowered the gun off Kelly's face, but still pointed it in his general direction as he took one step to the side. Bobby stood next to him so that the two men were almost shoulder to shoulder.

He raised his pistol and pointed it at Kelly. "Do you want to see it coming or face away?"

Kelly looked at Bobby, and then over to O'Malley.

"I think I'd rather see it coming." Kelly fought the tremor of adrenalin in his extremities.

Bobby raised his revolver. He steadied his gun hand, bringing his left up to support. It was, by all accounts, a good shooter's stance as he widened his feet slightly beyond shoulder-width. He aimed, cocking his head slightly to the left and looking at Kelly down the short barrel. And then Bobby winked.

Kelly dove for the ground as Bobby shoved hard to the left with his shoulder, butting into O'Malley's right arm. The blow interrupted the point of aim and sent the undercover cop sideways.

O'Malley staggered and turned to Bobby.

Kelly fished for his sidearm as he hit the ground. Then he heard a loud bang.

Seconds passed like minutes while his brain worked to process what he'd heard. He looked up to see Bobby standing over Patrick O'Malley's collapsed body, blood leaking out from the underside of the undercover cop's head.

Kelly jumped to his feet and scrambled over to his friend.

Bobby stood still, staring down at the body on the ground, his finger still on the trigger. A tendril of smoke seeped out of the snub-nosed barrel.

"Bobby, it's me. Take your finger off the trigger," Kelly said reassuringly.

His lifelong friend shook his head clear and did as he was instructed. He then lowered the weapon and looked over at Kelly. "He was going to kill you. I knew it. I saw it in his eyes. No doubt in my mind he was going to shoot you if I didn't step in."

Kelly put his arm on his friend's shoulder. "I know. I know." He exhaled and felt a wave of exhaustion crash over him. "I never saw that coming. I mean, sure, I thought he'd be angry. I thought there'd be a confrontation. I was actually hoping for maybe a fist fight. But I didn't think he was going to flip the switch like that." Kelly leveled a gaze at his friend. "Thank you."

Bobby shook his head. "It's a weird thing to thank somebody for. Killing a person doesn't usually warrant it. And it wasn't just anybody. It was a damn cop."

"You heard him. He hasn't been a cop for a long time. Badge or otherwise. In the truest sense, I don't know if he ever was. The uniform doesn't make you a cop. It's what you do with it that matters."

"Either way. Good cop. Bad cop. He's a dead cop, and I'm the one holding the gun."

"Not necessarily. I think there's a way we can all win here."

"Mike, we're in an abandoned building where I just shot an undercover police officer in front of another cop. You tell me how this plays out that I don't spend the rest of my life in prison."

"We weren't here," Kelly said calmly.

"Huh?"

"I'll call it in anonymously and then wait for my boss to call me to the scene."

"And then what?"

"And then I'll give O'Malley the treatment he had planned for me. I'll work the case, but I guarantee it will be unsolved. Because we've got no witnesses, no cameras, and no murder weapon." Kelly looked down at the gun in Bobby's hand.

"Are you sure about this?"

"Less than a minute ago, I was a dead man. So, yes, I'm sure. Any other way we try to do this thing is a guaranteed death sentence. For both of us."

The door swung wide and both men jumped.

Kristen Barnes came in, gun pointed ahead of her. She froze as she caught sight of O'Malley's body.

"What happened?" she cried out as the door closed behind her.

"I'll explain later. Right now, we need to get out of here."

With Barnes now in the loop, Bobby looked more worried than he had moments ago. "There are two people I trust in this world above all others," Kelly said. "One is you, Bobby. And Kris is the other."

Bobby stuffed the revolver back into his waistband.

"Time for us to go," Kelly said.

The three retreated out the door. Kelly stopped to wipe the doorknob clean. The street was still deserted.

"Bobby, make sure that revolver doesn't ever come back. It can't resurface. Understood?" Bobby nodded, then ran off into the night.

Kelly and Barnes drove out the one-way on Sturtevant to Park Street. Five minutes later, when they were far enough away from the scene, he placed the call.

33

Kelly and Barnes sat in the Caprice and waited. He'd placed the anonymous call into dispatch from a blocked number over fifteen minutes ago. The call was simple enough. He muffled his voice with a napkin placed over the phone and relayed to the dispatcher that he was walking his dog on Gibson Street when he heard what sounded like a single gunshot coming from inside one of the buildings near the intersection with Sturtevant. They asked if he saw anything else and Kelly ended the call. Now the waiting game had begun.

They listened to the police radio in their unmarked. Patrol units had flooded the area. After the recent violent crime wave, members of district C-11 would be on high alert.

A supervisor had just radioed for all units to physically inspect the interior of all the buildings in a one-block radius from where the caller had reported the shot fired. It was only a matter of time now before they found the body. The blue door had been intentionally left unlocked for this very reason. No need to delay the inevitable. And Kelly wanted to get this monkey off his back as soon as possible.

"Got an unlocked door. Corner of Sturtevant and Gibson," a patrolman announced over the radio. "Making entry."

It was quiet. Kelly envisioned the patrolman entering and clearing the room, checking the body for signs of life before vacating back to the street.

"We've got a man down. Single gunshot wound to the head. No signs of life."

"The clock has started." Kelly looked at Barnes, who still seemed to be deep in thought. She hadn't said much since leaving O'Malley's body.

"How do you know we'll be the ones to get the call?"

"I don't. They could call in anyone. But I figured it'll match the pattern of crime we've been tracking the past couple days. Based on the affiliation with Walsh and the area, we'll most likely get tapped."

Barnes exhaled a long, slow breath. "It's scary."

"Listen. I understand. I'm asking above and beyond. I can drop you at home. You were never here."

"It's not that."

"What then?"

"When I heard the gunshot, I came running. I was terrified, moving purely out of fear."

Kelly gave her a look. "You've been in high-stress critical incidents before. What was different this time?"

"You."

"Me?"

"I kept thinking you'd been shot. When I entered, it took my brain a second to process. When I saw O'Malley on the ground, I thought it was you."

Kelly was silent.

"That's why I reacted the way I did when you kissed me. I care about you, Mike. Always have. Even when I was dating Brayden for that short spell years back."

"I—I didn't know."

"It's just ... our job is dangerous at times. And I don't know what I'd do if something happened to you."

Kelly searched for words to provide some peace. To make their circumstances seem normal. But he couldn't come up with anything.

His phone vibrated. Kelly was grateful for the interruption. Barnes also looked pleased to change the subject. It was Sutherland.

"Hey, boss. It's late. Never good when you call late. What do you got?"

"They got a body at Gibson and Sturtevant. Single gunshot wound to the head. Could be related to the others."

"Anything else?" Kelly tried to remain casual. Just another body.

"One of the sergeants recognized the vic. Patrick O'Malley."

"Why does that name ring a bell?" Kelly feigned confusion.

"He's one of us."

"O'Malley. That's right. I haven't seen him in years. Thought he quit. Or moved. Or something."

"Apparently, he's been working undercover for several years, infiltrating Walsh's crew. There are going to be a lot of eyes on this one. So, play it by the numbers."

"Undercover? Thought we didn't do those kinds of things anymore. Too dangerous and all."

"Neither did I. That is, until a few minutes ago, when I got the call from Sharp. O'Malley was one of his guys."

"Okay. We're still working the scene, right?"

"For now. But I can already tell this is going to be a political shitshow. Get your ass down there quick as possible."

Sutherland hung up. Kelly looked over at Barnes, who was staring at him in awe. "What?"

"For a saint, you're a hell of a liar."

He tried to smile but came up short. "Get ready, because you're up next."

As if on cue, Barnes's phone began to ring. She answered, "Hey, Sarge. I already got the heads up from Kelly. He's picking me up shortly. We'll be on our way in." She hung up, the call over before it started.

Kelly put the car in drive. "Ready?"

"As much as I'll ever be."

34

Kelly parked the Caprice on Gibson a half block from the corner. He and Barnes got out and approached a young patrolman working the line. "Detectives Kelly and Barnes. Homicide." His badge hung visibly. In a big department where the ranks were constantly being filled with new faces, it was becoming more common for him to run into cops he didn't know.

The young officer nodded and they slipped under the tape. Several uniformed personnel hovered near the blue door. It was closed.

Sergeant Connolly approached. "Hey, Mike, how's your brother doing?"

"Good. He's in recovery." Kelly shook the sergeant's hand. "Thanks again for looking out. I owe you one."

"Aw, think nothin' of it." Connolly looked at Kelly and Barnes with their crime scene bags in hand. "You caught this one too? They ever give you a day off?"

"Not lately. Maybe if everybody would stop killing everybody else for a minute, I might get to put my feet up."

"Fat chance." He looked toward the door. "You know who's face down in a pool of his own blood in there?"

"I do. Sutherland briefed me. Who knew we even had deep cover guys anymore?"

"That's what I said. Half these guys never even heard of Donnie Brasco. I mean—shit—what are they teaching 'em these days."

"We best get started before the brass circus arrives," Kelly said, softly dismissing the veteran sergeant.

"Some of the guests of honor are already here."

"Who?" Kelly looked at the closed blue door, his mind racing as he tried to picture who could've beaten him to the call.

"Sharp's in there. So's White."

Kelly tried to stay calm. He wanted to scream. He wanted to yell at the good sergeant for letting two non-Homicide personnel into a crime scene after it had been cleared and before the first official walk-through. But he didn't. Instead, he maintained a casual looseness and rolled his eyes. "What can you do? Oh well, best we get started."

Kelly turned and walked over to the door. The same blue door he'd walked through earlier, this time under totally different circumstances. And everything he did from this point forward would mean the difference for the rest of his life. He intentionally gripped the doorknob with ungloved hands. He wanted to contaminate that piece of the scene and would document it as a mistake later in his report. He didn't want to risk explaining why his DNA popped up.

"I expect better from you," a voice said from behind him.

Kelly turned to see the familiar face of senior crime scene technician Raymond Charles. "Oh shit. I wasn't thinking." Kelly looked down at his ungloved hand. "It's been a long couple days."

"Make sure you note it in your initial report," Charles said in a fatherly tone.

"Of course."

Kelly began to pull open the door when Charles put a hand on his wrist and stopped him. "Mike, I need to talk to you about something."

Charles was uncharacteristically soft-spoken. "Sure, Ray. What's up?"

Charles looked around nervously. "It's something that's going to have to wait until we're in private."

"Okay. Let's run this scene and then we can regroup back at the office."

The crime scene tech let go of Kelly's wrist, but the worry didn't leave his face.

Kelly released the doorknob and retrieved a pair of latex gloves from his pocket. Donning them, he opened the door.

Inside, Sharp and White stood near Patrick O'Malley's body. They both looked up as Kelly and his crime scene entourage entered.

"Not sure why you two are on my scene," Kelly said sternly. "You see the body near your feet? That makes this my jurisdiction. My case. And being that, I need you both to leave. Immediately."

"Not going to happen, tough guy," White said in his normal sardonic manner.

"Excuse me?" Kelly accepted the challenge, stepping forward into the invisible boxing ring he saw in his head.

"Mike, we're running the show on this one." Sharp inserted himself into the conversation, firm but less confrontational than his counterpart. "I know it's a homicide, but O'Malley's my guy. OC is taking it. White and his guys are going to assist."

"That's not how it works," Barnes offered.

"I think you'll find, in this case, it is," Sharp said.

Kelly stood dumbfounded.

"Don't worry, we'll be sure to keep you in the loop," White snarked.

Kelly looked at the man. He remembered his glass jaw and thought hard about reminding the head of Narcotics about his right cross. Barnes must've read the hatred and anger spewing from his tense body language because she put a gentle hand on his shoulder and whispered, "He's not worth it."

Feeling her touch and hearing her voice had a calming effect. Not completely soothed, but enough so that he didn't send White's teeth down his throat.

"Charles can stick around and help process. But, Kelly—you and Barnes can go," Sharp said matter-of-factly.

Kelly began to turn away when he noticed the gun on the floor near O'Malley's right hand. It wasn't the 9mm semi-automatic O'Malley had pointed in his face. The gun—Walsh's gun—had been replaced by a sub-compact Glock 23. Somebody had switched it out. Kelly eyed both men standing near the body, and then he saw the slight bulge in the small of Sharp's back. Nobody would notice unless they were really looking. And Kelly was really looking.

He knew there was no way he could confront them, not without exposing that he had been in the room with O'Malley. That meant the one piece of physical evidence linking O'Malley to the Talbott Street convenience store murder was gone. Sharp either knew about the murder or was taking the 9mm Ruger, with links to a Walsh case, with them when they cleared the scene.

Kelly said nothing. He turned and walked out the door.

As Kelly and Barnes headed back toward their car, Sergeant Connolly called out, "Hey, Mike, go get the son of a bitch who did this to one of our own."

One of our own? Connolly was a good cop. And a good man. He'd spit if he knew the truth about the dead man in that room.

Kelly, at a loss for words, merely got in his car and drove away. He was suddenly exhausted, wanting nothing more than to sleep. Maybe he'd wake up and it would all turn out to be a bad dream.

35

Kelly had dropped Barnes off at her car, still parked in the lot at Carney Hospital, before heading home. There was no real traffic and the drive only took him a matter of minutes.

He tried to slip in as quietly as he could. It was late. He was tired and wanted nothing more than to shower off the horribleness of the past several hours and then sleep for days.

He was worried that the creaky door would wake his mother, but he saw, to his dismay, that she was still awake, bingeing old *Jeopardy* episodes. He was confident his mother had already seen most, if not all, of them at one time or another. Her torrid love affair with host Alex Trebek continued.

She turned as he entered. "Well, I haven't seen you in a while. I was starting to worry. I do wish you'd call when you're going to be gone for this long, Michael."

Kelly had heard this same spiel numerous times since moving back in with his mother after the divorce. He was used to her concern and offered no response. He walked into the living room and gave his mother a kiss on the forehead. "Ma, it's late. You should be sleeping. Only way that hip is going to heal properly is with rest."

"I am resting. You see I've got my feet up in the chair. Now don't you fuss over me. I'm just fine. But you look like you haven't slept since I last saw you."

"I don't think I have." Kelly turned and started to make his way to the stairwell.

His foot hit the first step when his mother said, "I spoke with Brayden tonight. Went to see him at the hospital."

Kelly had been so wrapped up he'd forgotten to check back in on Brayden. "How's he holding up?"

"Good as can be expected. I think he's agreed to spend some extra time there. Maybe he can get better once and for all."

"I hope so too. He's got a tough road ahead of him. But he's a Kelly. And we're as tough as they come."

Kelly stood there with one foot on the first step and his hand on the railing, preparing to ascend the single flight to the second floor.

"He told me about your conversation."

He froze, knowing what she was referring to had nothing to do with Brayden's overdose. Every thread of his life was unraveling around him. His faith in the job. The truth about his family. All of it.

"It's been a really rough night. I don't know if I'm up for talking about this right now, Ma. I don't know if I'm ready to hear what you have to say."

"Now, Michael Kelly, you get your Irish ass over here and you sit down. Tired or not. Good day or bad. You're going to have a listen to your mother. Because what I have to say matters. Whether you are ready or not to hear it—it's time you did. This has been a long time coming."

Kelly knew better than to ever cross his mother when she cursed. And so, like an admonished schoolboy, he turned and walked back into the living room. He took up a seat next to his mother, and she muted the TV. In the background, somebody had won some fantastic amount of prize money and was jumping up and down hysterically.

"So, what is it? What's my story?"

"First off, let me tell you that I've loved you since the day you came into this house, and nothing I'm going to tell you now will change that. You are my firstborn and you always will be. But I think it's fair you know where things started. Maybe in some weird twist of fate, it'll give you a sense of peace."

Kelly was uncharacteristically anxious. "I guess I'm as ready as I'll ever be. And you're right. This night's as good as any."

His mother took a deep breath and then reached out, taking his hand. "When we first came here from Ireland, we had nothing. Now I know you've heard me tell it a thousand times before. But you're going to hear it again. Your father worked his tail off at the docks until he raised enough money to open the package store. And here I am, still running the same store today. God rest his soul." She paused to make the sign of the cross.

"But there's something else I never told you. We struggled to have a family. I mean, can you imagine an Irish family without kids? We were childless. And I prayed on it. But nothing came. I'd assumed my womb was barren. I didn't know what to do with myself. And then one day, I came upon a situation. A girl, terrified and scared. I saw that she was with child. And I felt for her. She was standing on the corner outside of our store, crying uncontrollably. She was inconsolable at first. I don't think she even knew I was there. I took her inside the store, and I sat her down in the back by the cooler and propped her feet up. I gave her some water and let her cry herself dry. I think she cried for an hour straight before even uttering her first word. When she did speak—her voice was that of an angel." Kelly's mother pressed her free hand over her heart and closed her eyes momentarily.

"She told me her story and I quickly learned why she was so

upset. She'd been a nun in a local convent not far from here. She was a young girl in her early twenties. And then, as nowadays, young girls had urges. Even nuns. And to spare you those details, she found herself in a situation. And being with child in the early eighties was bad enough if you were a single mother, but can you imagine what her life would have been like after leaving a convent?"

Kelly processed his mother's words without interrupting.

"Michael, you were born to a nun. It couldn't get more biblical than that, unless it had been an Immaculate Conception. Of course, this was not the case. And this was a story of Dorchester, so it was with humbler beginnings."

She paused and looked at him. A little light in the back of her greenish-blue irises sparkled.

"This next part might be a little hard to swallow."

"Harder than 'your mother was a nun?'"

"Yes." She exhaled slowly. "I don't know if telling you right now is the right thing to do, but its burden has been on my shoulders for far too long."

Kelly huffed. "Nothing you tell me right now is going to do anything more to me than what's already been done. I can take it. Whatever it is."

She patted his hand. "I truly believe fate brought your mother to my storefront that day. She was desperate, Michael. And you know better than most that desperate people do dangerous things. She was on her last leg. I heard it in her voice, and I saw it in her eyes. I don't think she would have made it another night on her own. I found a note in her pocket. She had made preparations to end what she believed to be an unforgiveable mistake."

"A mistake?" Kelly muttered.

"Please let me finish. It's important you understand who your parents are."

"You keep saying 'parents,' but I'm only hearing about my mother. What about my father?"

Her eyes watered. "As I said, she was in a bad way. I couldn't let her leave the store. I ended up closing it down for the day. And I just sat with her and listened. She grew up not too far from where I did, just outside of Doolin. Can you imagine the sense of kindred spirit we felt? Michael, she was a lovely girl, beautiful both inside and out."

She paused to dab her eyes with a tissue. "It's the way things were back then in big Irish families. The oldest males were put into the priesthood and the youngest daughters were sent off to a convent. She was the youngest in her family of seven. And so, her path was written. Although, as paths go, she took a slight detour. Being in the United States, she took an opportunity to see a little bit of it for herself. And one night, being a young girl of the cloth or not, she found herself in the company of a man who, to use her phrase, 'set her world on fire.' She told me he was something to behold. So, love was born in a pub in South Boston. And as things happen, their one night together resulted in a pregnancy."

"I guess that rules out the whole Immaculate Conception thing."

She chuckled a little bit at his jest. "I'm all over the place with this story, but I just don't know how to tell you all the things I need to say. I knew this day would come, but now that it's here, I'm rambling like a loon."

"There's no wrong way, Ma. Say what's in your heart. Tell me what you need to say. Get it off your chest and let me deal with it. I'm a grown man."

"After she found out she was with child, your mother left the convent. She turned to your father for help—for a chance at a new life. It turns out your father wasn't what she thought him to be. After learning who he was, she became terrified of him.

When I found her on that day, in front of the store, she was living on the streets. Desperate and ready to take her own life. And had she, it would've, in turn, taken yours. I couldn't allow it. I had never met you. But I wanted a baby so badly. And on that day, in the back of the store, I made a deal with her. A deal that I'm breaking today by telling you this."

His mother cleared her throat and took a sip from the beer can resting on the nearby end table. "I let her live with us. Here in this house. She stayed upstairs in the room we now use for Embry. I'll show you the few things I kept from that time. Mind you, there's not much. So don't get your hopes up. But she stayed with me for the last four months of the pregnancy. After you were born and she was released from the hospital, she left and, sadly, never returned. At one point during her stay, she told me she had plans of going back home, but I seriously doubt that her family would ever take her in. Not after she left the convent in such a way. She did speak about starting over. She wanted to buy a one-way ticket to Australia. My hope is she made it there."

"What was her name?" Kelly asked softly, not sure if the inquiry would hurt his mother.

"Cara McCarthy."

"And my father? You keep mentioning him without saying his name. Do you know who he was?"

She was quiet and looked at the TV, taking temporary refuge in the timeless face of her favorite host. Then, she turned back to him. "Who he is doesn't make you who you are. You need to understand me on that account. Michael Kelly, you are a good son, and you're a good man. I love you. Your father loved you. And your brother, as messed up as he is right now, he loves you too."

"Ma, say what it is you don't know how to say."

"Your father is not a good man. From what I can tell, he never has been. Worse, he's dangerous."

"Who is my father?"

A tear rolled down her cheek, something he hadn't seen happen since the day his father died. By all accounts, she was a tough woman capable of tucking all the sadness deep inside, but once the first tear fell, a second trailed it.

"Your father is Conner Walsh."

A hushed silence followed. Kelly heard his mother's words. He heard the name she uttered, but some part of him needed to hear it again. He wasn't quite sure what he was expecting, but hearing the name of Boston's most notorious Irish mobster come out of his mother's mouth was surreal. He considered confirming that his mind hadn't played some fanciful trick in his state of exhaustion. "Did I hear you correctly? Did you just say Conner Walsh?"

"I'm sorry, my son, but if it's any consolation you bear no resemblance. Not in looks or spirit."

"I don't know what to do with this information, Ma. I don't know how to use it."

"Don't. Just hold on to it. Hold on to the memory of your mother."

After hearing the true story of his birth, Kelly felt no sense of disconnect from the woman sitting next to him. If anything, he felt closer to her now. She had chosen him. Of all the people in the world, she had somehow found him. He was not angry she had held this secret for so long. He wasn't angry that she chose now to release it. Every experience in his life up to this moment had been steered and guided by this woman's hand. Regardless of who his biological parents were, this woman holding onto his arm was his mother.

Kelly leaned in and kissed her head, just like he always did before going to bed. "I'm not going anywhere. I know this was a hard thing for you to tell me, but it doesn't change anything. You're my mother. And Brayden will always be my brother.

Maybe someday I'll have a sit-down with Walsh." Kelly gave her a gentle smile and wink. "More likely, I'll either put cuffs on him or a bullet in his head."

His mother made a sound he'd never heard before—a soft whimper—as tears began to flow. It was as if a dam that had been holding back years of pain was finally released. The conflict of keeping such a secret from her eldest son was now unleashed in a river that poured from his mother's eyes.

Kelly took a knee in front of his mother. Instead of his normal nighttime departure routine, he pulled her close and let her sob on his shoulder until she was done. It was the least he could do for the woman who'd loved him through all of his ups and downs.

Her tearful outburst subsided, and Kelly released his mother. "I love you, Ma. Now it's time for both of us to get some sleep."

36

The phone vibrated across the end table rhythmically. Kelly woke disoriented and answered.

"Mike?" the distinct voice on the other end asked.

"I must've overslept. What's up, Bobby? Everything okay?" Kelly asked groggily.

"I'm sorry. I couldn't sleep. I'm losing my mind. I don't know how I'm going to get away with what happened last night. Thinking hard about making a run for the border."

Kelly cleared his throat. "Trust me. Nobody's going to be coming for you."

"How do you know?"

"Because they're already covering it up."

"Covering it up? How? I don't understand."

Kelly was now sitting up. He took a sip of the water on his nightstand. "The gun he was going to kill me with, the one that disappeared from evidence years ago. I left it there on purpose, hoping to tie these shootings to O'Malley, at least the one on Talbott. Was also planning on reopening the case against Walsh with it."

"Yeah. Okay. What about it?"

"They took it. Swapped it out."

"What's that mean? Who took it?"

"Doesn't matter who. It just matters that it happened. I know they're going to do everything in their power to spin this thing to make O'Malley a hero."

"Why does that mean I'm safe?" Bobby sounded desperate. On the ragged edge.

"There's no evidence to tie you to the scene. No witnesses. No cameras. Nobody besides me and Barnes know about the meeting, right?"

Bobby was silent.

"Who else knows?" Kelly asked, reading his friend's silence.

Bobby let out a loud sigh. "Walsh."

"Walsh? Why would you tell him?"

"He'd find out. I don't know how, but that guy always knows. Figured it was best if I went to him first."

"The fact that you're calling me now means he didn't kill you. What'd you tell him? Did you tell him about me?"

"Yes."

Kelly thought for a moment. "I need to speak with Walsh."

"You asked me that a while back. Remember? Right after you busted the side of my face."

"I remember. And I'm asking again now."

"He won't meet with a cop."

"He will now. Especially after what you told him about last night." Kelly paused and thought about his late-night conversation with his mother. "He and I have a few things we need to catch up on."

Bobby gave a frustrated groan. "I don't know about this."

"What's the worst that can happen?"

"Real funny. Especially after what happened last night."

Bobby sighed. "Tell you what, he goes to St. Peter's every Sunday."

"Conner Walsh goes to church?"

"I guess he's got lots of sins to confess. Doesn't go regular hours, though. He goes after the 9:00 a.m. service and spends a little time by himself before the Portuguese service begins."

Kelly looked at the time. It was a few minutes past eight. "Tell him I'll be stopping by today. Maybe he'll feel like confessing to me." Kelly chuckled at his own joke.

"I'll tell him. Doesn't mean you'll get in."

"You're not going to be there?"

"Can't. There's something I got to do."

Kelly's phone alerted to another incoming call and he looked at it. "Bobby, I've got another call coming in. Got to take it. Be in touch. And don't worry, I've got your back on this."

Kelly ended the call with Bobby and switched over to the incoming. "Good morning, Ray. I'm starting to wonder if you ever sleep."

"We need to talk." The senior crime scene tech cleared his throat. "Somewhere I can meet you?"

"I've got to follow up with something around ten. I'm free until then. Can I buy you a cup? How about the Dunkin' on Mt. Vernon Street?"

"I know it. Be there in thirty, if that works for you?"

"It works. See you then."

The Dunkin' Donuts at the corner of Mt. Vernon and Dorchester Avenue was more like a hybrid convenience store. But it was close enough to St. Peter's Catholic Church for Kelly to be able to introduce himself to Walsh after meeting with Charles.

He waited in his car for the older crime scene guru to show. A few minutes later he saw the man pull up.

Kelly met him at the door. "Mornin', Ray. You look like hell warmed over."

He grumbled under his breath. "Good to know I look better than I feel."

"I think you're due for an extra-large cup today."

"You definitely owe me. And after what I'm about to tell, you're probably gonna want to trade the coffee for something harder."

"I am all ears." Kelly's eyebrows rose.

"Not out in the open. Let's grab a cup and head to my car."

A few minutes later, Kelly was seated in the passenger seat of Ray's Buick Regal. Ray took a long swig from his cup and Kelly followed suit, removing the lid first. He hated to drink coffee through a plastic covering. He liked the coffee to hit his lips as the steam warmed his face. "I'm ready whenever you are, Ray."

"I know Mainelli told you about the shell casings coming back to the missing gun."

"He did."

"I did the comparisons on the round found in that investigator's shoulder to the one in the dead clerk, Josh Daniels. It all matched. Same gun. Same one used in the Walsh murder trial that went south."

"Doesn't matter anymore. The gun's gone. No way to tie it to our shooter."

Charles took a sip from his cup and eyed Kelly warily. "And how do you know that?"

"I just do. It's a dead end. Trust me on that."

"Okay." Charles set the cup in the holder and turned to reach for something behind him on the back seat. A manila file folder. "I've got something I need to show you."

"Is this about the shooting from last night on Gibson?" Kelly was suddenly concerned for this master of evidence's need for a private venue.

"No. It's about the Muriel Burke murder."

Kelly breathed an imperceptible sigh of relief. He'd almost forgotten about Burke in the chaotic chase of the last twenty-four hours. "I assume you found something important. But why go to all this trouble of telling me like this?"

"I ran the swabs. I know the autopsy hasn't been scheduled yet, so I wanted to get as much evidence processed as I could with what we had."

"You're killing me, Ray. Just tell me."

"I've got a positive match. Looks as though you were right about her being a fighter. She got a piece of our doer."

"He's in the system? You said positive match."

"Not in the criminal database, though."

"I don't understand. If he's not in the crim—"

"Police." Charles handed Kelly the file. "You're going to need to see this for yourself."

Kelly opened the folder and looked down at the photograph. He'd seen the same photo yesterday when Barnes had pulled it up on her phone. The man who'd killed Muriel Burke, witness to the Tyson's Market shooting, was Patrick O'Malley.

He'd figured out the store shootings. He assumed it was part of some destabilization plan. Although Kelly doubted he'd ever be given access to the specific details. And he imagined shredders were working overtime right now.

"Nothing?" Charles asked.

Kelly looked over and realized the man was on the edge of his seat, waiting for some reaction to the news.

"I'd actually figured O'Malley for the store shootings. Without the gun, it'd be a theoretical conjecture destroyed at the supervisory level. Never figured him capable of this. I assumed it was a clean-up job by one of Walsh's guys."

"O'Malley strangled that woman to death." Charles drowned himself in his large cup of dark roast coffee.

"How many people know about this?"

"Sutherland. And now you." Charles eyed him carefully. "What are you going to do with it?"

"I'm going to submit my findings. All points of my investigation lead to O'Malley. Whatever he set out to do when he first went undercover changed him." Kelly thought of Muriel Burke's body and the brute force used to take her life. "Strangulation is a personal method to go about murdering somebody. I'm guessing if I dug deep enough a lot more skeletons would fall out of O'Malley's closet."

"I don't know if that's the best course of action."

"We've got evidence. Right here!" Kelly held up the file for effect. "He doesn't get a pass because he's dead. Or a cop."

"I didn't say he gets a pass. But if you go after him, they'll bury you so deep you'll never see the light of day again."

"Three bodies go unspoken for. Three permanent red cards on my Murder Board." Kelly looked at the file again. "It's our job to speak for the dead. If I truly believe that, how can I turn my back on what I know."

"Because what you know—and what's in that file—is a guaranteed death sentence."

"So why'd you bring it to me? Why not keep it between you and Sutherland, and let it disappear into the void?"

"I figured there may come a time when you need a little leverage."

"Leverage?"

"You grabbed the handle last night at the crime scene. You did that ungloved."

Kelly shrugged. "I told you. I was tired. I made a mistake. It won't happen again."

"Hasn't happened before either. I've worked plenty of scenes with you. From the very first one, I saw how meticulous you approach each and every scene. As good as they come."

"What are you getting at, Ray?"

"Last night you weren't. You barehanded a doorknob on a building with one entrance pointing to a dead body. A boot rookie wouldn't have made that mistake. But you did."

Kelly didn't bother trying to refute the claim. Charles made the argument and made it well.

"I know you. At least, I hope I do. I fancy myself a good read of people—not just the dead. Whatever your reasons, I don't want to hear it. O'Malley was as bad as they come. What happened in that room dies with you."

Kelly thought about how to answer in a way that wouldn't incriminate himself.

"The scene's been processed. And if you're wondering— you're in the clear," Charles said.

"It's not what you think."

"Like I said, I'm treating it like Vegas. What happened in there stays in there." Charles finished his coffee. "I just wanted you to know you're in the clear. Just make sure you document the knob touch in your supplemental report."

"I will." Kelly closed the file folder.

"Keep that file in a safe place. Sutherland's a good guy, but he's looking for a way out on his disability rating and isn't going to ruffle any feathers. My guess is any link to O'Malley's DNA we found under Burke's nails will soon disappear as well—if it hasn't already."

"Why are you looking out for me?"

"Because you're one of the good ones. You still bleed blue."

"Thanks for looking out, Ray." Kelly tucked the folder under his arm and opened the door to leave.

"Where to now?"

"I've got a family thing to sort out," Kelly said as he shut the Buick's passenger door.

37

Kelly parked on the street. Traffic from the 9:00 a.m. Mass had let out twenty minutes prior. The final wave of parishioners, mostly elderly, made their way out. Kelly saw Walsh enter the main doors of the ornate church. Tommy Sullivan stood on the top step outside the door, acting as some kind of bouncer. The large man did his best to look the part. Kelly almost laughed out loud at the man's impression of a presidential secret service agent working a protective detail. He even wore dark sunglasses for the occasion.

Satisfied Walsh was settled inside and the last patrons were gone until the next Mass, Kelly made his way over to the church. He walked the concrete steps to where Sullivan stood guard.

"No visitors," the large man said.

Kelly lifted his T-shirt and exposed his badge. Not that he was there on official police business, but Sullivan wouldn't know that.

The big man folded his arms and smirked. "No visitors means no visitors. That goes for cops too."

"Oh, I'm sorry, Sully. I wasn't asking."

"Not happenin'. Turn around and head back to wherever it is you came from." Sullivan made a shooing motion.

"Your boss is expecting me."

"Mr. Walsh don't like visitors during his time here. It's one of his particularities."

Kelly tired of the man. "Hard way or easy way, Sully. Doesn't really matter to me. But one way or another, I'm walking through those doors."

"You ain't so tough. It was a lucky shot you got on me when we were kids. Try that shit now and I'll cave your skull in."

"I'll give you five seconds to step aside." Kelly began silently counting down.

Five ... four ... three ...

"You aren't going to—"

One.

Kelly stepped forward quickly. Sullivan raised a fist and swung down hard. Kelly anticipated the larger man would meet aggression with aggression and planned accordingly. He side-stepped as Sullivan's fist passed by.

The momentum carried the top-heavy man forward and down. The narrow steps played their part and he lost his footing. While he was off balance and out of control, Kelly countered.

He pivoted his body and swung a hard right hook, the devastation of the blow worsened by the downward movement of the big man's head. Kelly's front knuckles collided with the lower tip of Sullivan's nose, flattening it with a crunch.

The impact buckled the colossus, and he fell down the concrete steps to a walled landing below. He groaned loudly in a bunched heap.

Kelly stepped inside the church.

The center aisle's brown square tiles seemed to echo each

footstep he took. The rows of pews were empty. In the second row sat a solitary man. Conner Walsh.

The head of the Savin Hill Gang sat facing the altar. He didn't turn when Kelly entered and the doors banged shut behind him.

Kelly approached. And now, feet from the meeting he'd desperately sought, Kelly wondered what to say.

"I've been wondering when you'd come around?" Walsh spoke with the rasp of a lifetime chain smoker but the confidence of a Kennedy.

"You're a hard man to get a hold of."

"I see Sullivan didn't stop you."

"Couldn't is a better word. Might need to invest in some better bodyguards."

"Why? You lookin' for a change of employment?" Walsh turned to face him as Kelly stood in the aisle outside the pew. "Matter of fact, I just had a position open last night."

"I heard."

Walsh slid over and tapped the space on the wooden bench he'd just vacated. "Have a seat."

Kelly sat. He was now closer than he'd ever expected to get to the mob kingpin. He thought of all the violence this man had committed in his rise to power. Kelly dreamed of the day he'd slip the cuffs on him. But he knew today was not that day.

"Bobby told me you'd be coming."

Kelly nodded. "I'm willing to tell you something, but I need something from you in return."

"You first. Once I listen to what you have to say, I'll determine its value and then decide whether it equals to what you're asking of me."

Kelly thought of arguing the order of this arrangement but realized that would be pointless. "Your gun is out in the world again."

"What gun?"

"The gun you used to kill Terrance May."

"And why is that news worthy of an exchange?"

"Because the police have it. Well, one particular member has it."

"Why would the Boston PD have that weapon and not use it against me?"

"They did. It backfired. It was used in the two convenience store murders. They were coming at you from a lot of angles."

"And yet, here I sit." Walsh stared at Kelly. "Tell me, Detective Kelly, why would you come here to tell me this? You don't seem like the type of cop who would want to share such things with somebody like me."

"I don't like it. Not one bit. I'd much prefer to throw you in jail for the rest of your miserable life."

"But?"

"But it's not going to happen. At least not yet."

"Tell me what it is you want to know."

"Eight years ago, my partner, Danny Rourke, was murdered. His case remains open and the killer was never brought to justice. I think you can tell me who the killer is."

"All this for a dead partner? I'm impressed. Maybe you should come and work for me. That kind of loyalty is rare these days."

"So, how about it?"

"Let me think on it and get back to you." Walsh unwrapped a Tootsie Pop and stuffed it in his mouth. "Anything else I can do for you?"

"Do you remember a Cara McCarthy?"

Walsh smiled. "You've done good for yourself. Definitely beat the odds."

"You knew? When? How long have you known I'm your son?"

"I've always known. This is my neighborhood. I run everything around here. Nothing happens without me knowing." Walsh raised an eyebrow. "So, what now? You want a piece of the action? Become heir to the throne?"

"Fat chance. I just wanted you to know that I knew. And that knowing changes nothing. The first opportunity I have to put you away, I'll be standing behind you with the cuffs in hand."

Walsh laughed. "Many have tried, and all have failed."

The pew creaked as Kelly stood to leave.

"I'll be seeing you around, Detective."

"Count on it."

Kelly walked out of the church to see Sullivan sitting on the steps holding his nose.

"I think you broke it, asshole."

He ignored the man and walked away. In a matter of days, Kelly's life had been turned upside down, and he knew the journey to redemption was far from over. But he was a fighter. And as Pops always said, *fighting solves everything*.

38

Kelly stood outside the office door. He banged loudly and waited.

A minute passed before the door opened. Sharp stood before him. "I'm surprised to see you here."

"What I have to say needs to take place inside," Kelly said.

Sharp opened the door wider and stepped aside. The members of the Organized Crime Unit looked up from their cubicles as Kelly entered. "Need a moment alone with Detective Kelly," Sharp announced to the room.

Without question or comment the three detectives in the office got up and left. Sharp then ushered Kelly into his office.

Kelly sat as Sharp took his seat behind his desk. He didn't bounce a ball or put his feet up. No jovial playfulness was present in the man today. He leveled an intense stare at Kelly. "So, what is it we need to discuss. Because if you haven't noticed, there's a dead cop whose funeral is set for a day from now and I've got a lot to do before then."

"How much did you know?"

"That's a pretty wide-open question. Feel like narrowing it down a bit?"

"O'Malley gave my brother a dope bag loaded with Carfentanil. He effectively tried to kill him with a hot shot."

Sharp's face twisted and he shook his head slowly from side to side. "What are you talking about?"

"The deal you oversaw—the two kilos my brother set up—O'Malley handed Brayden the bag at the end of it."

"That's insane!" Sharp's typical confidence waned. "I would never authorize something like that."

"What about White?"

"Look, Mike, I know you two have a history, but Lincoln White would never try to take out your brother. That I can assure you."

Kelly exhaled slowly, trying to maintain his calm. "Your word with me isn't what it used to be."

"This thing has gotten way out of control."

"I think that might be the understatement of the century." Kelly watched the Organized Crime boss squirm. "O'Malley killed Muriel Burke."

Sharp slumped back in his seat. "I didn't lie to you when we sat in this office last time. Well, at least not totally."

"What do you mean?"

"I hadn't heard from O'Malley. He missed several check-ins and wasn't responding to my emergency meeting request. After you came here and started poking around, I was able to get him to meet with me."

Kelly listened carefully. He knew some of what Sharp was saying was true. At least the part about meeting with O'Malley after Kelly confronted him. "And what'd you discuss at your meeting with him?"

"I suggested we look at pulling him out."

"I don't believe you. I think you and White were pulling his strings all along."

"I really don't care what you believe. I know the truth."

Sharp grabbed his tennis ball, but instead of bouncing it off the wall he just squeezed it. "The convenience store plan was supposed to put the gun back in play. The gun that would bury Walsh. O'Malley got it out of evidence to prove his worth to the gang. And then we decided to put it to use when Walsh thought it was long gone."

"You authorized the murder of an innocent store clerk just to put a gun back on the street?"

"No. The convenience store was supposed to ramp up the turf war between the Corner Boys and Savin Hill. We needed Walsh's people to see him as weak if we'd ever be able to put O'Malley in as his replacement." Sharp rubbed at the back of his neck with his free hand while compressing the ball with the other. "O'Malley put a fake tattoo on his neck to make it seem like them. He wasn't supposed to kill the kid. Just wing him."

"What happened? Why'd O'Malley break from the plan?"

"Good question. Our last conversation didn't go well. His wife is dying. Maybe he was in too long. One thing's for certain, he was operating way outside the guidelines."

"And what now? You're just going to give him a pass because he was killed?"

Sharp sat forward. "I never should've asked this of him. The assignment was too much for him. Hell, probably would've been too much for anyone."

"What about Muriel Burke?" Kelly asked through clenched teeth.

"She and the clerks are a casualty of this, but there's no way this operation can be exposed. It would destroy this department and taint the name of any officer, past or present. If you try to expose this, they'll bury you. And I don't mean career-wise."

"Who do you mean by 'they?'" Kelly's head was spinning.

"Just be happy that you don't know. And the longer you keep

it that way, the better off you are. You're a good cop. I'd hate to see this get the better of you." Sharp hung his head. "In its purest form, the plan to overthrow Walsh and assume control of his crew seemed a work of genius. But I guess you can never really account for the human factor. Not that it matters, but if I had known O'Malley was responsible for Burke's death, I never would have let him out of my car the other day."

Kelly stood to leave.

Sharp remained head down and only managed to cast his eyes upward at him. "We need guys like you out there, Mike. For what it's worth, I'm sorry this thing broke bad."

"Save your apology for the three families who'll get no justice or closure."

Kelly walked out of the office. He moved down the hall and stopped in front of the door to Homicide, peering through the window to see Mainelli and Barnes talking near their cluster of cubicles. Instead of entering, he turned and walked down the hall toward the second-floor stairwell.

Kelly knew there was only one place he'd be able to clear his mind.

On his drive to Pops's gym, he thought about Ryan Murphy, the kid he'd found hiding behind the dumpster. He hoped the boy had taken him up on his offer.

He walked inside the gym's rear entrance. Kelly stopped in the doorway and set his bag down. He saw Pops in the far corner. A rope was extended between two posts separated ten feet apart. Kelly watched as Ryan Murphy was taught the finer points of bobbing and weaving. The first of many lessons the young boy would learn inside these walls.

Kelly watched the timid teen and saw himself in the boy. Both had come from rough beginnings. Michael Kelly had risen above it all. And standing here now, as he watched his mentor in action, Kelly knew Ryan had a fighter's chance at doing the same.

THE PENITENT ONE
A BOSTON CRIME THRILLER NOVEL

A Boston priest found murdered.
A city demanding answers.
A cop hellbent on justice.

Detective Michael Kelly faces the most demanding case of his career. To solve an unspeakable crime, Kelly must push the boundaries of his own personal safety to hunt this killer.

Nobody is safe from The Penitent One.

Get your copy today at BrianChristopherShea.com

JOIN THE READER LIST

Never miss a new release! Sign up to receive exclusive updates from author Brian Shea.

Join today at
BrianChristopherShea.com/Boston

Sign up and receive a free copy of
Unkillable: A Nick Lawrence Short Story.

YOU MIGHT ALSO ENJOY...

The Nick Lawrence Series

Kill List

Pursuit of Justice

Burning Truth

Targeted Violence

Murder 8

The Boston Crime Thriller Series

Murder Board

Bleeding Blue

The Penitent One

Never miss a new release! Sign up to receive exclusive updates from author Brian Shea.

BrianChristopherShea.com/Boston

Sign up and receive a free copy of
Unkillable: A Nick Lawrence Short Story

ABOUT THE AUTHOR

Brian Shea has spent most of his adult life in service to his country and local community. He honorably served as an officer in the U.S. Navy. In his civilian life, he reached the rank of Detective and accrued over eleven years of law enforcement experience between Texas and Connecticut. Somewhere in the mix he spent five years as a fifth-grade school teacher. Brian's myriad of life experience is woven into the tapestry of each character's design. He resides in New England and is blessed with an amazing wife and three beautiful daughters.

 facebook.com/BrianChristopherShea

twitter.com/BrianCShea

 instagram.com/BrianChristopherShea